PICTURE ROCK

CROSSWAY BOOKS BY STEPHEN BLY

BOOK THREE

THE SKINNERS OF GOLDFIELD

PICTURE ROCK

STEPHEN BLY

CROSSWAY BOOKS • WHEATON, ILLINOIS

A DIVISION OF GOOD NEWS PUBLISHERS

Bly

Picture Rock

Copyright © 2001 by Stephen Bly

Published by Crossway Books
    A division of Good News Publishers
    1300 Crescent Street
    Wheaton, Illinois 60187

Cover illustration: Paul Bachem
Cover design: Cindy Kiple

First printing, 2001

Printed in the United States of America

Library of Congress Cataloging-in-Publication Data
Bly, Stephen A., 1944-
    Picture rock / Stephen Bly.
      p.   cm. — (The Skinners of Goldfield ; bk. 3)
    ISBN 1-58134-254-3 (alk. paper)
    1. Gold mines and mining—Fiction. 2. Goldfield (Nev.)—Fiction.
3. Nevada—Fiction. I. Title.
PS3552.L93 P54 2001
813'.54—dc21   2001000056
                                      CIP

15	14	13	12	11	10	09	08	07	06	05	04	03	02	01
15	14	13	12	11	10	9	8	7	6	5	4	3	2	1

In memory of

Aunt Rose,
Aunt Myrtle,
and Aunt Dola

And [they] did all drink the same spiritual drink;

for they drank of that spiritual Rock

that followed them:

and that Rock was Christ.

1 CORINTHIANS 10:4 (KJV)

FOREWORD

October 13, 1973
Mr. Hayworth McGuire
Bunkhouse Books
146 Delta Avenue, Suite E
Stockton, CA 95206

Dear Mr. McGuire:

Enclosed are the galleys of "Picture Rock." Thank you so much for allowing me to review them. As you suggested, I've noted in the margin any clarifications.

You are quite right. Daddy was a remarkable man. Self-educated. Simple. Incredibly principled.

It is my humble opinion that history is not a story about events, but a journal about people—ordinary people who were placed in difficult situations. When they publicly fail, they become our villains. When they publicly succeed, they are our heroes.

And some, like Daddy, succeed in such obscurity. They are only heroes to the very few who know them well.

When the histories of Goldfield, Nevada, are finally written, there will be names like Tom Fisherman, Harry Stimler, William Marsh, Lucky Jack Gately, Al Myers, George Nixon, Tom Lockhart, Ace Wilkins, and, of course, George Wingfield. However, I am sure none will recall Orion Tower Skinner. Daddy wouldn't have wanted it any other way.

I remember when he led us unarmed into that violent, deadly scene with the striking miners and did what no man thought possible. In my mind I can still hear the sheriff shout, "Skinner, you are either a very brave man or a lunatic. Either way, I predict you will be dead by morning."

Looking back, I know there were many nights when neither

he nor Mama slept much. They would sit out on the balcony of that one-room apartment above the cafe and talk of the virtues of California and the vices of Goldfield.

She was always so worried about becoming a widow. She was a very strong-minded woman, self-sufficient and independent, in a day and age when such was a rarity. But she was terrified at the thought of losing her man.

We all grew up in Goldfield—not just because of the years we spent there, but due to the lessons we learned. None of us—not Rita Ann, nor Tommy-Blue, nor I, nor Punky—ever forgot walking those miners to safety. Daddy had pulled us aside and lectured, "Remember, there are worse things than dyin'. Standin' by while others needlessly kill each other is one of them."

It was in Goldfield that Daddy discovered he could defuse all the explosive confrontations . . . except one.

I wonder who at the present time are the men in our country who could do that? Perhaps the times are not tough enough for hidden heroes.

They certainly were in the late summer of 1906, in Goldfield, Nevada.

Corrie Lou (Skinner) Merced
Dinuba, California

P.S. Would it be possible to note somewhere the passing of Silas Paul (Punky) Skinner on January 26, 1973? Never in my saddest dreams did I think I would be the last of the Goldfield Skinners.

ONE

Goldfield, Nevada, August 12, 1906

Dola Mae Skinner inspected the woman straight in front of her. Something in the tired eyes caught her attention.

Not pathetic, but haunting.

Not hopeless, but used up. So worn . . . so exhausted. Dull eyes with dark circles and thin wisps of eyelashes, like used thread on a tattered sheet.

She reminds me of someone from my past. Perhaps a friend from childhood? A schoolmate? A neighbor girl? I know I've seen those eyes before. I imagine they were bright blue once.

Dola tried not to gape at the woman although she studied the beige dress with worn, slick brown velvet collar and cuffs.

It's as if she's been wearing that dress for months . . . years. I wonder if she even takes it off at night? Look at those wrinkles around her eyes. Oh my . . . she must be fifty if she's a day. Poor dear, she needs a little of Dr. Bull's Eye Elixir. No, I don't suppose even that would help. But perhaps a little lipstick—and rouge would brighten those sunken cheeks.

She's much too old to have been a schoolmate of mine. Perhaps she was in Orion's class. Or maybe she had a younger sister in Orion's class. That must be it—she's someone's older sister. But whose?

Bleached skin. Pale, thin, tightly drawn lips. The narrow, pointed chin. Honey, I don't think you've had a good meal in weeks.

Dola closed her eyes, and when she opened them, she locked her gaze on the woman's hands.

Well, look at that little gold band. I'm glad you're married, honey. There is probably some very plain man who is dearly in love with his very plain wife. I'm happy for you. But those hands. Oh, my . . . callused, rough . . . are those age spots on the back already? I presume you work at a laundry or maybe out in the fields. They make a cold cream for hands now. But that costs money, and if you had money, you'd certainly want a hot bath and a good meal.

Dola took in the sagging shoulders and thin chest.

Sweetheart, I would guess you married young, because there just isn't much left there to attract a man.

The woman tugged at an earlobe.

I suppose all ears are funny-looking. Earrings would help. You've probably never worn earrings. And that hair. Oh, dear . . . straight and stringy, mousy-brown, streaked with gray and parted in the middle. I don't suppose much can be done with that. But at least you could keep it in your combs—instead of letting strands shoot out in all directions, like cats dropped into the bathtub.

The woman grinned slightly.

Was that a dimple? Honey, that was almost a pleasant smile. When you were young, I bet those dimples teased the boys . . . at least the plain boys. And the teeth . . . well, I have to give you credit. You have the straightest, whitest teeth I've ever seen.

But you are plain.

Not much we can do about our looks. We were all created in God's image. Sometimes He likes wrapping that image in a simple, plain package—that's all. I don't suppose it matters what you look like, dear, as long as you're happy. You are happy, aren't you? How tragic it would be to look like that and be sad too.

Dola heard a scuffle behind her.

"Mama, Tommy-Blue said I have fat legs," Corrie sighed. "I don't have fat legs. They're just full of muscles. Besides, he shouldn't be lookin' at my legs, should he?"

"I didn't know fat was bad," Tommy-Blue protested. "I thought 'fat as a pig' was a compliment. It *is* a compliment, isn't it, Mama?"

Three-year-old Punky toddled to her side and clutched Dola's beige skirt. "My mama's purdy!"

Dola Skinner ran her fingers through his silky, curly dark hair.

Rita Ann strolled up to her mother.

Dola studied her oldest child. *She is almost as tall as me.*

Rita Ann stared straight ahead. "'In mine eye she is the sweetest lady that ever I looked on,'" she quoted.

"And modest too," Dola chided.

"Are you two going to stand there and stare in the mirror all mornin'?" Tommy-Blue griped. "Daddy's out front in the wagon waitin' for us!"

Dola stepped back from the huge dresser mirror, leading Punky by the hand. "Girls, get your hats. It's time for our Sunday picnic."

"Why do we have to wear hats, Mama?" Corrie whined.

"To keep the sun off your delicate skin."

Corrie licked her finger and rubbed something sticky off her arm. "My skin ain't all that delicate."

Rita Ann tugged the lace cuffs down on her purple gingham dress. "Well, mine is!" she insisted.

"Can we take a shovel? In case we find some pay dirt?" Tommy-Blue asked.

Dola released Punky's hand long enough to set the flat straw hat on her head and tie the yellow ribbon under her chin. *Tommy-Blue is right, Lord. I spent way too much time looking in the mirror. I ask Your forgiveness. I am exactly the way You made me. I won't try to second-guess that.*

"Carry me!" Punky demanded.

Dola lifted the three-year-old to her hip. A sharp pain hit low in her back. She gritted her teeth and waited for it to ease.

"Mama, can I bring my Shakespeare book?" Rita Ann begged.

"It's permanently attached to your hand," Corrie teased.

"It is not! I never take my Shakespeare to church."

Corrie brushed her palm across her nose and then wiped it on the skirt of her chocolate brown dress. "That's because Daddy said you couldn't."

Rita Ann clutched the big book with both arms. "And I mind my father, unlike some."

"And what is that supposed to mean?" Corrie shot back.

"You know perfectly well what that means."

"I do not!"

"Girls!" Dola called out as she shuffled toward the front door of their above-the-cafe apartment. "It's Sunday—a day of rest and worship. How about resting from arguing with each other?"

"It's too hot to argue much," Corrie conceded as she traipsed down the stairs.

"'Two women placed together makes cold weather,'" Rita Ann recited.

"Perhaps a little less Shakespeare would be nice today too," Dola commented. Each downward step reinforced the pain in her lower back. When she reached the swept wooden floor of the Newcomers' Cafe, she put the toddler down.

He ran to the open front door shouting, "Daddy-Daddy-Daddy-Daddy-Daddy!"

Columbia Street looked Sunday-afternoon-quiet when O. T. drove around the corner and parked in front of the Newcomers' Cafe. The only visible dust was stirred by the plodding feet of the two mules that pulled his wagon. The sky was desert clear and light blue, with a hue of alkali dust so fine most folks forgot it was there.

But a man's lungs never forgot, and O. T. loosened his black Sunday tie, unfastened the top button of his boiled white shirt, and then coughed. He peered inside the cafe at neat rows of tables with inverted wooden chairs stacked with Rita Ann's precision.

O. T. surveyed the spindly peach tree, freshly watered and yet yellow-leafed. It seemed to quake in the half-barrel in which it was planted.

That's the sickliest-lookin' fruit tree I ever seen. Course, it's the healthiest one in Goldfield. Lord, Dola Mae don't have many possessions in this world. She never asks for any. And You know I've never been able to afford much. But how she loves that little peach tree. It's her heart's delight, and I'm askin' that You help it to grow. May she have the glory of makin' a big ol' fresh peach pie from it.

O. T. stared at the vacant front door of the cafe for several seconds. He coughed again.

Lord, I've never known any woman on earth who was so peaceful and content with so little.

O. T. peered down at the frayed hems of his best duckings.

And it's a good thing.

A boy with brown bangs bouncing under his floppy-brimmed hat yelled, "Hi, Daddy! Boy, isn't this a great ore-findin' day? Can I bring the shovel? I'll bet we find a new claim. I can feel it in my bones!"

O. T. studied his ten-year-old son. *Lord, does a man use up all his energy when he's young? I don't think I ever had that kind of stamina. He's never tired, never melancholy, never bored. Every moment of every day is an adventure to Tommy-Blue. It's not the goal but the journey that excites that boy.*

"I get to sit by my daddy!" Corrie's voice rolled out of the cafe.

O. T. smiled. *No one else begs to sit by me. No one else calls me "my" daddy. No one else reduces all of life down to relationships. Nothin' matters to that girl but people. An inspiration . . . and a challenge.*

A thirteen-year-old with perfectly tied dark pigtails dangling under her straw hat emerged from the cafe, small nose turned up, chin high, shoulders square, and a big, heavy book pressed against her flat chest. "Does my hat look dumb?" she asked.

"You look as pretty as a poppy on a field of spring green," O. T. replied. Then he winked.

"'It is a wise father that knows his own child,'" she countered.

He laughed and coughed at the same time. "I take it that is not from *Taming of the Shrew?*"

"No, it's from the *Merchant of Venice*, act 2, scene 2," she explained.

"Daddy-Daddy-Daddy-Daddy-Daddy!"

"Punky! Where have you been?" O. T. called out. "Why, I haven't seen you for at least fifteen minutes!"

"Help me," Punky demanded with outstretched arms.

Tommy-Blue lifted the three-year-old into the back of the farm wagon.

Dola exited the cafe and closed the doors behind her. Her hat was fashionably tilted to one side, and a closed yellow parasol was tucked under her arm.

The beige dress fits well, shows off her trim waist.

She turned to examine the peach tree.

Always sort of majestic, she is. Holds her head up, shoulders back. There is a contented pride in that woman.

Dola glanced up and smiled at him.

Oh, Lord, that is the most disarmin' smile. The twinkle in her bright blue eyes, the dimpled grin, the beautiful complexion, and those teasing eyelashes. Lord, You did real good when You made that lady. There are women in this town who spend many dollars a month on cheek powder and eye creams and lipsticks and fancy curling irons and gold jewelry hangin' about their necks and ears, and they don't come close to my Dola Mae.

I haven't done a lot of smart things in my life, but marryin' that lady is the highlight of my wisdom and the thrill of my soul. Orion Tower Skinner, you are a lucky man . . . a mighty lucky man.

"Why, children," he blurted out, "who is this beautiful, charming lady with you?" He stood up and yanked off his hat. "Must be some visiting European princess." He bowed, sweeping his hat before him. "Welcome to my humble coach, Princess. May I offer you a ride?"

She blushed and took his hand as he reached down.

"It's just Mama," Corrie giggled.

"Oh, yes, of course," O. T. replied. "Sometimes her beauty blinds me."

Dola pulled herself up into the wagon. The children climbed in after her. As the wagon lurched out into the street, she scooted next to him and clutched his arm. O. T. glanced down under her hat. He could see tears rolling down her cheeks.

"What's the matter, darlin'?" he whispered. "Did I say something wrong?"

"No," she whispered back. "You said something right. You always know what I need to hear. You are a jewel, O. T. Skinner. A rare jewel, and I'm the luckiest woman on earth."

When they reached the top of Goldfield Summit, Tommy-Blue stood up and held on to his father's shoulder. "Look, Daddy, behind the White Mountains . . . there's the Sierra Nevadas! I can see all the way to California!"

"We can all see the mountains," Rita Ann reminded him.

"But I can see further than anyone," Tommy-Blue declared.

Eleven-year-old Corrie stood beside her brother, shoulder to shoulder. "Can you see the sun shimmer off that lake between those two mountain peaks?"

"Which mountain peaks?" he asked.

"Those two tallest ones," Corrie said.

Tommy-Blue pushed his hat back and scratched his ear. "Which ones are those?"

"I believe the tallest is Mt. Whitney," Rita Ann explained. "And the other Mt. Brewer. They were named for the geological survey team that mapped and recorded much of the data in California almost fifty years ago."

"Oh, those mountains," Tommy-Blue mumbled.

"Can you see the lake?" Corrie repeated.

"Sure," he murmured. "Anyone can see that lake. I can even see the big old redwood tree at the back of the lake. Can you see it?"

"The one with the lightning damage on top?" Corrie asked.

"Nah, the one at the back of the lake is bigger."

Corrie cupped her hands around her eyes. "The one by the volcano?"

"There are no active volcanoes in the southern Sierra Nevadas. Mt. Lassen in the southernmost part of the Cascades is the closest volcano," Rita Ann lectured.

"Well, I didn't say it was an *active* volcano," Corrie mumbled.

Rita Ann laced her fingers together in her lap. "Perhaps it's only a cinder cone."

"Yeah, it's a cinder cone made out of obsidian!" Corrie exclaimed.

"I can't see it," Tommy-Blue admitted.

"Neither can I," Rita Ann added.

Corrie pointed west. "It's right there behind the lake."

"Is it black obsidian or red obsidian?" Tommy-Blue demanded.

"It's . . ." Corrie chewed her tongue a moment. "It's clear obsidian."

"Clear? Rocks aren't clear."

"Quartz is clear! Lucky Jack Gately gave me a piece out of the Corrie Lou Mine, and it's as clear as Mama's crystal goblets. So there!" Corrie insisted.

"If it's clear, how can you see it?" Tommy-Blue challenged.

"Well . . . I—I can see the tree's reflection off it."

The wagon began to slow.

"Are we stopping, Daddy?" Rita Ann asked.

"I thought we'd give this old man a ride," O. T. explained.

"What old man?" Corrie asked.

"You three with eagle eyes overlooked the man under that big hat in the shade of the Joshua tree." O. T. pointed ahead.

"It's Fergus!" Corrie shouted. "Hi, Fergus! How have you been?

Did you find your cousin in Schurz? Did you ever get her house back for her? Did you go to San Francisco? Are you hungry? We're going to have a picnic supper. Would you like to come on a picnic?"

The old Paiute rubbed his wrinkled, leather-tough chin. "Does she ever stop talking?"

"Only when she sleeps," Dola replied.

"No, she doesn't! She mumbles all night long," Rita Ann complained.

Corrie dropped her round chin to her chest. "At least I don't snore."

"I do not snore!" Rita Ann asserted.

"I do," Tommy-Blue admitted. "But it never wakes me up."

"That is good," the old Indian said.

Punky sat up from his sleeping position on Dola's lap. "Fergus-Fergus-Fergus-Fergus!"

"You have a very friendly family," the stoic old man commented.

"We would be delighted to have you join us on a picnic," Dola offered.

Fergus studied the back of the wagon. "Do you have plenty of food?"

"Mama cooked two whole chickens!" Tommy-Blue announced.

"We have more than we can eat," Dola informed him. "Lucian and Omega LaPorte had to cancel out at the last minute."

"It was thoughtful of them to do so," Fergus said.

"But I get the chicken livers!" Corrie cried. "It's my turn."

"Well, I believe I will come anyway." Fergus very slowly climbed into the back of the wagon with the children.

"Corrie, move back and let Fergus sit with me and Mama," O. T. ordered.

"I would rather sit with the children," Fergus announced.

"What are you doin' out here on the south side of town?" O. T. asked.

The old Indian stared out across the bleak, bare desert. "Looking for a camel."

"There are no camels out here!" Tommy-Blue protested.

Fergus winked. "Now you tell me. I was told Tom Fisherman was out here, but I did not find him."

"Why do you want to see Tom Fisherman?" Tommy-Blue asked.

Fergus leaned against the weathered side board. "I heard he talked to my cousin recently."

"The cousin who had the house in Goldfield?" Rita Ann quizzed.

"Yes, she is the one. I have looked for her for months. I didn't find her in Schurz. Perhaps she went on a vacation. A long vacation." Fergus yanked off his black felt hat and straightened the eagle feather.

Tommy-Blue scooted over and sat down beside the Paiute. "What's your cousin's name?"

"Gerta Von Wagner," Fergus announced.

Corrie's hand flew to her mouth. "What?" she giggled.

"That is the reaction I get from most people."

Dola bounced Punky on her lap. "Well, it sounds very . . . eh, German," she said.

Fergus nodded and licked his lips. "It is."

"But—you are—she is—," Rita Ann stuttered.

"How do you know my cousin is not German?"

Rita Ann frowned. "I assumed she was Paiute, of course."

"She is. She worked for a childless widow lady named Gerta Von Wagner. The woman died and left my cousin some inheritance, and she thought it was too good a name to waste."

"So she goes by Gerta?" Dola quizzed.

"Yes. But I sometimes call her by her Paiute name," Fergus replied.

"What is that?" Corrie pressed.

"Tse-Ubat."

"What does that mean?" Tommy-Blue asked.

"Stinkbug."

"I think I'll call her Gerta," Rita Ann remarked.

"And Fisherman saw her?" O. T. probed.

"I met a man in Tonopah who said he knew Abieto, and Abieto said his brother talked to Fisherman's cousin, and the cousin said that his mother had seen Fisherman's mother only a couple of weeks ago, and she said she thought Tom had mentioned Tse-Ubat—but she couldn't remember for sure. He might have said he met Tse-Tsat."

"What does that mean?" Rita Ann asked.

Fergus closed his eyes. "Flat Stinkbug."

Standing behind O. T., Corrie pointed across the desert. "Look, there's an auto car parked over there!"

"It's our auto car!" Tommy-Blue declared. "Hud said he might have it runnin' again by today. Boy-oh-boy, would you look at that! He's a successful mechanic, you know."

"Yes," O. T. murmured, "he successfully stretched a two-week job into twelve months."

"It's much too far away from town to be our auto car. Hud said he was going to drive it only a few blocks to make sure the fuel tank didn't leak," Rita Ann interjected. "He said it wasn't safe to drive it out of town yet."

"It *is* our auto car," Tommy-Blue insisted. "Isn't it, Daddy?"

O. T. studied the horizon. "It sort of looks like it. . . . Yes, I believe you're right, son."

"There's Hud. . . . Look, he's waving at me!" Corrie exclaimed. "I like Hudson Frazier. Who's that with him behind the parasol? I can't see."

"It better be Haylee Cox, or he's in big, big trouble," Rita Ann said.

"I believe it is Miss Haylee," O. T. affirmed.

"What are they doin'?" Corrie quizzed.

"I imagine they are tryin' to get the auto car fixed," Dola explained.

O. T. slapped the lead line on Ada's rump, and the mules hastened their trot. "Maybe they were waitin' for help to come along."

"In the backseat?" Tommy-Blue pursued.

"It is very comfortable in the backseat," Fergus said.

Corrie jumped down out of the wagon and ran toward the auto car. "Hi, Hud! Hi, Haylee! What are you doin' out here? Did the auto car bust? What were you doin' in the backseat?"

Hudson Frazier rubbed his unshaven face as if to mash the blush out of it. "Howdy, Mr. Skinner . . . Mrs. Skinner. Say, you don't happen to have a can of that gasoline, do you?"

O. T. pushed his hat back. "Afraid I've never even seen a can of gasoline. Did you run out?"

"Yes, sir, I think I did. I put in three gallons, and I figured it would take us out to the Double Dunes and back. The gasoline tank held up fine. I think there must be a leak in the fuel line again."

"Hi, Haylee," Rita Ann called out as she stood up in the back of the wagon.

"Hi, Rita Ann." Haylee clutched the high collar of her dress. "I'm glad to see you."

"You are?"

The seventeen-year-old raised her thick, teasing eyebrows as she sauntered over to the wagon. "Yes, we were afraid we might be stuck out here all night."

"But it's only three miles back to the summit and another mile down from there. Shoot," Tommy-Blue added, "me and Danny Rokker could have walked that in an hour if we hadn't stopped and collected rock specimens."

Haylee whipped around toward Hud Frazier. "Four miles? You told me you thought it was twelve miles back to town!"

"Well, you know . . ." Hud stammered, "the desert has a way of spinnin' a man around. Don't it, Mr. Skinner?"

"I'll give you that one, Hud." O. T. studied the car. "Do you need a tow into town?"

"We could wait here until you brought us some gasoline," Frazier offered.

"Why on earth would you want to stay out in the desert heat?" Dola questioned.

"The auto is in the shade of them boulders," Hud pointed out.

Dola raised her eyebrows. "That was quite fortunate."

"Yes," Haylee added. "We almost coasted right over there. I only had to push it fifty feet or so."

O. T. studied the smooth cheeks and dancing eyes of Haylee Cox. "*You* pushed it?"

"I had to steer," Hud mumbled.

"Why don't you two climb in the wagon." O. T. motioned. "We're goin' on a picnic."

"What about the auto car?" Hud asked. "Ain't you afraid someone will steal it?"

"That would be a blessing," O. T. maintained. "Besides, it's not goin' anywhere. I mean, it's out of gasoline, isn't it?"

"Yes, sir, it is."

"Then we'll tow it into town on the way back. It won't be the first time Ada and Ida have towed that auto car."

"Haylee, you can sit back here with me," Rita Ann called down. "We can read my Shakespeare book together."

"This day ain't turnin' out like I figured," Hud mumbled as he helped Haylee climb into the wagon.

Dola glanced over at O. T. "No, I imagine it isn't," she offered.

"'Fortune brings in some boats that are not steer'd,'" Rita Ann declared.

"Where does it say that?" Haylee asked.

"In *Cymbeline*, act 4, scene 12," Rita Ann replied. "Sit over here, and I'll show you."

Haylee scooted in between Rita Ann and the side of the wagon.

"Boy, you was lucky we came along," Tommy-Blue announced

as Hudson Frazier slammed his head back against the picnic basket and pulled his hat down over his eyes.

O. T. drove the wagon past the boulders.

"I don't suppose it is time to eat yet," Fergus called out.

Dola scrutinized the thin old Paiute. "No, we're hoping to look at the Pear Blossom Mine and then stop at Frambuesa Springs to eat."

"What does Frambuesa mean, Daddy?" Corrie probed.

"It means raspberry," Rita Ann interjected.

"I didn't ask you. I asked my daddy!"

"If big sis says it means raspberry, then it means raspberry," O. T. said. *Lord, it ain't easy havin' kids smarter than I am.*

"There was an old prospector named Cletus Frambuesa," Fergus explained. "He got killed, and they named the springs after him."

"How did he die?" Corrie asked.

"I believe Indians ambushed him," the Paiute explained.

"Did they scalp him?" Tommy-Blue prodded.

"I don't remember. I was just a small boy."

Tommy-Blue's eyes grew wide. "You were there?"

"Why would I want to be in Mojave territory? My grandmother used to say that killin' Frambuesa was one of the few decent things the Mojave ever did. He was a very disagreeable man. He had a habit of shooting someone every time he got drunk."

"How often was that?" Tommy-Blue inquired.

"Almost every night, if the stories are to be believed," Fergus said.

"Look, Daddy," Corrie Lou called out. "There's a mule with a side saddle."

O. T. studied the animal on the eastern horizon. "It's a burro."

"Where's he goin'?"

O. T. glanced over his shoulder to the north. "Back to town, I reckon."

Corrie leaned her chin on O. T.'s shoulder. "Why?"

"Because that's where he lives. He's headed home."

"Who do you think he belongs to?" Corrie asked.

"That lady up there!" Tommy-Blue pointed to the top of the trail.

"That's Lupe," Dola called out.

"You can't tell from this distance," O. T. insisted.

Dola turned to the back of the wagon. "Girls, who is that lady up there?"

Rita Ann and Haylee glanced up. "That's Lupe!" they called out in unison.

"How can you tell that?"

"Because no one on earth walks like that except Lupe Martinez," Dola replied.

O. T. scratched his neck. "But all you can see is her . . . her backside."

"That's the only part of her that walks like that," Dola explained.

When the sound of creaking wagon wheels and the clomp of mule shoes reached the woman in the dark dress and black parasol, she turned around and raised her hand to her forehead.

"Lupe!" Corrie called out. "What are you doin' out here dressed like that? Mama says black ain't a good thing to wear on a hot day. Do you want to go on a picnic with us? It's goin' to be fun!"

The short, wide woman flashed a white-toothed grin. "Aye ye! This is an answer to my prayers!"

O. T. pulled his wagon up. "Was that your donkey?"

"Yes, I must have lamed him. I believe he was used to a lighter load."

O. T. stepped down and offered his hand to the young Mexican woman. "Where are you headed? Can we give you a lift?"

She climbed up and sat beside Dola. "To the Pear Blossom Mine."

"Why?" Tommy-Blue asked.

"To check on my father. He did not come home this morning."

"Perhaps he stopped somewhere before headin' home." O. T. climbed back up to the wagon seat.

"His shift is over at 8:00 A.M., and it is after lunch. None of the night crew from the Pear Blossom have come home," Martinez explained, flicking her thick coal-black hair over her shoulder. "I can't imagine why. He's worked night shift for two months and has always been home by 9:00 A.M. I am very worried."

"If there had been an explosion or cave-in, someone would have come to town for help," O. T. said. "I was over at the livery and didn't hear a thing."

"I suppose so," Lupe continued, "but the mine owner, Mr. Fleming, doesn't do the usual thing."

"Don't you know him, Orion?" Dola asked.

"Yep. Jakob Fleming's a strange one. He sends his assay samples in a double-locked iron box. No one but Fleming and Mr. Tolavitch have keys. The reports come back the same way."

"That's not strange—just cautious," Dola interjected.

"Did you ever see him?" Lupe asked.

"No," Dola replied.

Lupe put her finger on her flat brown nose and pushed it to one side. "His nose is turned sideways."

"What?" Rita Ann called out from the back of the wagon.

Lupe glanced over her shoulder. "He got it smashed when he was young, and it points toward his shoulder."

Corrie's eyes grew wide. "Really, Daddy? Does he look odd?"

O. T. shrugged. "Ain't none of us perfect, I reckon."

Perched on the southeast side of the Crispa Hills two miles south of Blackcap Mountain, the Pear Blossom Mine was shielded by a six-foot sheet-iron fence. Blowing sand had dulled the metal surface, and it looked like straight rock jutting out of the desert floor. There were no trees in sight. No grass. Nothing green. Just dry desert and a couple of distant Joshua trees.

The only sign at the gate read: "KEEP OUT: This means YOU! P. B. Mining and Milling Co. Violators will be shot on sight."

O. T. drove the wagon alongside the gate.

"My, this doesn't look very hospitable," Dola murmured.

"Why do we have to stop here?" Corrie whined.

"Because I asked Mr. Fleming if Tommy-Blue could come along sometime, and he said I should bring the whole family."

Dola glanced around the wagon. "Did he know we have ten in our family?"

"Is it time to eat yet?" Fergus pressed.

"Is this where your father works?" Rita Ann asked. "It looks so depressing."

"When you work underground, it don't matter what the surface looks like," O. T. said.

"How do we get their attention without incurring their wrath?" Dola asked.

"'Never anger made good guard for itself,'" Rita Ann recited.

"Who said that?" Haylee asked.

"Mecaenas to Octavius Caesar, concerning Antony in *Antony and Cleopatra*, act 4, scene 1," Rita Ann explained.

O. T. climbed down, strolled up to the warning sign, and opened it like a small cupboard door. He reached in and grabbed a sisal rope and tugged. The loud clang of a school bell caused those in the wagon to flinch.

"What are you doin', Daddy?" Tommy-Blue called out.

"Ringin' the doorbell," he replied.

A double-barreled shotgun was shoved out a small opening.

"Go away!" a deep voice threatened.

"I need to talk to Mr. Fleming," O. T. explained.

"He's got enough trouble. Go on down the road," the voice demanded.

"What kind of trouble?" Lupe Martinez called out from the wagon.

"Are you Mr. Porter?" O. T. asked.

"No."

"Gabe Landusky?"

"Nope."

"I thought I knew most of the bosses out here," O. T. continued. "Who are you?"

"Who are you?" came the reply.

"I'm O. T. Skinner. I work for Tolavitch's Assay Office and—"

"You deliverin' an assay?"

"No, Mr. Fleming invited me to bring my family out and look at the mine this afternoon."

· "He didn't tell me nothin' about company."

O. T. leaned his hand against the sheet-iron fencing. The sun-reflected heat caused him to immediately pull it back. "Could you ask him, please?"

"And ask about my father," Lupe shouted.

O. T. stepped a little closer. "Yes, Miss Martinez is concerned about her father, Redolfo Martinez. He's one of the night shift miners."

The shotgun barrel disappeared with a curse. The little door slammed shut.

"What did he say, Orion?" Dola called out.

"You don't want to know, Mama."

"Is he going to get Mr. Fleming?"

"That remains to be seen."

"What do we do now?" she pressed.

O. T. fingered the sweat off his eyebrows. "Wait, I reckon."

"We could eat," Fergus called out. "There is shade on the east side of the fence."

"I could dig for color!" Tommy-Blue shouted.

"We were better off back at the auto car than perched out here in the sun," Hud remarked.

O. T. examined his mules. "Just give it a minute," he said.

The sweat rolled down O. T.'s face and soaked the collar of his white shirt. After a long wait, he opened the little cupboard door. "Well, I'll be . . ."

"What is it, Daddy?" Corrie called out.

"They took away the bell rope."

"Perhaps we should go on," Dola suggested.

"Not until I find out about my father," Lupe insisted.

"Yes, yes. You're right," Dola agreed. "I forgot. Then perhaps we should eat here, Orion."

"Ain't much of a picnic site," O. T. said. "I was hopin' to treat you better."

"We'll make do," Dola said. "How about sittin' in the wagon shade right in front of the gates?" she suggested.

O. T. studied the bare, brown Mojave Desert dirt. "I suppose we'd be right in their way, wouldn't we?"

"I believe so."

"Let's do it then," he declared.

"Can I dig for pay dirt?" Tommy-Blue hollered.

O. T. rubbed sand out of the corners of his eyes. "I reckon you can after you help unload the goods."

Dola and the girls stretched a quilt across the dusty roadway. They began to seat themselves in the limited shade of the wagon, Dola's supper spread out before them.

Lupe Martinez paced in front of the locked sheet-iron gate shouting, "I demand to know what happened to my father!"

Tommy-Blue was digging a hole next to the tall fence.

"I believe that's all we have," Dola apologized. "I wasn't sure how many to prepare for. I'm certainly glad I cooked two chickens."

"It'll do, Mama." O. T. glanced over at the fence. "Tommy-Blue, come on, boy, it's time for a blessin'."

"This whole Pear Blossom Mine is a waste of time, I figure. Ain't no color out here," Tommy-Blue sighed.

"Your face is very red," Fergus pointed out.

"That ain't the color I'm lookin' for."

O. T. bowed his head. "Lord, we appreciate—"

"Hey, what do you think you're doin' out there?" a voice blasted from the little sign-door.

"—how You have amply supplied—"

"Daddy's prayin'," Corrie hollered, her head still bowed.

"—for our every need—"

"You cain't do that!" the man shouted.

"Ain't no law against prayin'," Tommy-Blue yelled back.

"'His worst fault is that he is given to prayer; he is something peevish that way,'" Rita Ann quoted.

"—and we give You thanks for this food—," O. T. continued.

"You cain't camp out there. This is private property," the man at the gate blustered.

"It's a county road," Hudson Frazier called back.

"—and ask Your blessin' upon it—"

"What's that Indian doin'?" the man demanded.

"He's eatin' a chicken leg," Corrie reported.

"Reverently," Fergus mumbled as he licked his thin, bony fingers.

"—and forgive this heathen for interruptin' our prayers."

"You all are goin' to have to move along! I've got a shotgun here, you know."

"Do you intend to shoot women and children?" Haylee called back.

"In Jesus' name—"

Lupe marched straight for the little window. "I demand to know the whereabouts of my father."

"Do you speak Mexican?" the man questioned.

"Do you?" she shot back.

"Nope."

Lupe Martinez broke into a litany of angry Spanish. Dola blushed even though she could understand none of it.

The sign-door slammed shut.

"Amen and amen." O. T. put his hat back on his head and studied the faces of those around him. "Well, Mama, I believe it's time to start eatin'."

Rita Ann stared at Fergus. "Some have already started."

"I could not help myself. The chicken was begging me," Fergus declared.

Dola passed out blue-enameled tin plates. "That was quite a disjointed prayer, Mr. Skinner."

"Kind of like prayin' at the cafe. Nobody but the Lord listenin'. Which is sort of the point of prayer, I reckon." He turned to Lupe, who still paced in front of the gate. "Come on, Lupe, have some lunch."

"I must find out about my father."

"I predict in two minutes or less Mr. Jakob Fleming will come right out here and see us," O. T. announced.

Lupe marched back to the others. "Why do you say that?"

"'Cause he'll smell Mama's chicken. No man can resist that."

O. T. didn't turn around when the iron gate swung open behind him.

"His nose ain't that funny-lookin'," Corrie giggled, her hand to her mouth.

Tommy-Blue's mouth dropped open. "It looks like a pig snout!" he gasped.

"A nice pig," Corrie corrected.

"Skinner, what in blazes are you doin' out here!" a man shouted.

Jakob Fleming stood six feet tall and stocky. His wide-brimmed, dark felt hat sagged almost to his shoulders. Thick white hair curled out from underneath. He was an imposing figure even without a nose that looked permanently pressed against a pane of window glass.

"Mr. Fleming, this is my wife, Dola, and my family and friends."

"Would you like some chicken, Mr. Fleming?" Dola offered.

"No, I wouldn't. What's this all about, Skinner?"

"Just a family picnic."

"In my front yard?"

"It don't look like a yard to me," Corrie protested.

"You invited me to stop by for a tour of your mine. I suppose this is not a good time," O. T. remarked.

Fleming pulled off his hat to wipe his brow. The white hair exploded in every direction. "Sorry, Skinner, I got trouble here today. No tours."

"What kind of trouble?" Lupe remarked.

"Who's she?"

"Her father is one of your miners who didn't come home this mornin'. She's lookin' for him," O. T. explained.

"He's one of those Mexican anarchists?" Fleming huffed.

"What's an anarchist, Daddy?" Corrie probed.

O. T. brushed alkali dust out of his mustache with his fingertips. "I reckon he means a miner who wants to join a union."

"We ain't Union," Tommy-Blue boasted. "We're Confederates!"

"What's goin' on, Mr. Fleming?" O. T. asked.

The big man studied all those sitting on the blanket. "Skinner, I need to talk to you in private. Could you step in here?"

O. T. stood. Dola shoved two fried chicken thighs into his hand and then nodded toward Jakob Fleming. O. T. meandered with the mine owner over to the partially open gate. "You had lunch yet, Mr. Fleming?"

"I've got a crisis on my hands. No time to eat."

O. T. shoved a piece of chicken toward Fleming. "Try some of Dola's chicken. She's a good cook."

Fleming let the shotgun hang to his side and took the chicken. When they stepped inside the fenced area, six carbine-carrying men strolled between the gate and the headworks of the Pear Blossom Mine.

"What's this all about, Mr. Fleming? I've never noticed armed guards here before."

"Skinner, there isn't anyone in Nevada I'd tell this to except you. With God as your witness, you've got to keep it to yourself."

O. T. licked his fingers and nodded.

"Last night I had a crew blastin' away in a lateral tunnel at 600 feet down. And do you know what they found?"

"No, sir, but I reckon I'm about to."

"They blasted into a cavern of picture rock."

"Pure gold?"

"I'm guessin' it will assay at 75 to 90 percent pure," Fleming declared. "It's as big as a barn and hangin' from the ceiling and walls like it was the U.S. Mint in Carson City."

"Congratulations. So that's why you need armed guards. But what about Mr. Martinez?"

"My crew boss didn't inform me until 6:00 A.M. By then the Mexican crew had worked that ore for three hours. You can imagine the consequences."

"I reckon I'm a little dull, Mr. Fleming."

"High-grading! Those Mexicans stuffed their clothes with my gold."

"You caught them with your gold?"

"That's just the point—they won't cooperate. By the time they came off shift, I had gone to town and hired these armed guards. I've got more coming from Virginia City tomorrow. But I wanted the Mexicans to go over to the shop and strip off their clothes so I could see how much they were stealing."

"And they refused?"

"Yes. They were quite hostile about it. That proves they're guilty. We're at an impasse." Jakob Fleming took a big bite of chicken. "I'm afraid there will be violence."

"You plannin' on holdin' them hostage until they agree to be searched?" O. T. picked chicken from his teeth with his fingernail.

"Precisely." Fleming rubbed his mouth on his dusty suit sleeve and took another bite. "Many of the big mines are goin' to a changing room."

"Well, I think you ought to give them a warnin' that it's comin' and give 'em a chance to quit if they don't like that procedure."

"I'm not letting them go until they return my picture rock!" Fleming stripped the bone clean with his teeth.

O. T. glanced over at the headworks. "But you don't know that they took anything."

Fleming tossed the bone near the fence and licked his fingers. "Of course they did. Wouldn't you if you were in their place?"

O. T. looked him squarely in the eye. "No, sir, I wouldn't."

"What am I goin' to do, Skinner? I can't have miners stealin' me blind." Fleming pulled a white handkerchief from his back pocket and wiped his hands.

"Could I go talk to them?"

"Do you speak Spanish?" Fleming pressed.

"No, sir, but Miss Martinez does. I could take her with me."

"You won't stir up trouble, will you?"

"Mr. Fleming, I reckon you already have all the trouble you need."

"What am I supposed to do while you talk to them?"

"There's more chicken out there," O. T. offered.

Fleming paused, then glanced out the front gate. "Yes, you're right," he murmured. "I'll wait for you out by the fried chicken."

TWO

Men with lever-action carbines surveyed each step O. T. Skinner and Lupe Martinez made toward the headworks building of the Pear Blossom Mine. Most wore last week's beards and last year's tattered suits.

Skinner's jaw was set as square as his broad shoulders while he studied their faces, their eyes, their hands, their weapons. *Where did Fleming find these men? On the bench in front of the Northern Saloon? They aren't gunmen. Not like Lucky Jack Gately or the Wilkins brothers. One's carrying an old '73 Winchester, but he's got .30-30 bullets in his belt. And one even has an old single-shot Sharps.*

"Skinner, what are you doin' out here?"

O. T. turned near the door to see the wild bangs of Pipestem Drusky flop across his eyes like a horsetail swatting flies. His arms were four inches longer than his white shirt and suit coat. His tie was tied in a square knot and dangled halfway down his unbuttoned vest.

O. T. tipped his hat. "Afternoon, Pipestem. You got yourself a new job?"

The man stepped close enough to Skinner that his unbathed body radiated heat as well as odor. "It ain't permanent. Jist day money. But it's good. Seven dollars a day."

O. T. scanned the other guards. "That's good. You'll probably want to take that money, get yourself all cleaned up, and buy a new suit of clothes."

Pipestem spat a wad of tobacco into the dirt yard. "Why would I want to do that?"

O. T. glanced at the woman under the black parasol. "Pipestem, do you know Lupe Martinez? She works for Dola Mae at the cafe."

Pipestem Drusky tipped his dirty brown felt hat. *"Buenas dias, señorita."*

"Buenas tardes," she replied, keeping her brown eyes focused on the closed door of the headworks building.

Drusky stepped closer. "Say, Skinner, do you know what's goin' on here?"

O. T. studied the man's wild, bloodshot eyes. "Pipestem, I was hopin' you could tell me. I'm just out for a Sunday ride. Why are you here?"

"I don't know nothin', Skinner." He rubbed his unshaven chin, the carbine dangling at his side. "Someone kicked me awake this mornin' and said they was paying seven dollars a day to stand around and guard some unarmed Mexicans. But I ain't seen no Mexicans except you, ma'am. They're all in that there buildin', I hear."

"Where were you when they woke you up?" O. T. asked.

"I had me a good time last night, and I was sleepin' it off on the bench in front of the Yukon Saloon."

Skinner glanced down at the gun. "I presume they armed you?"

"Ain't this somethin'?" He held up the carbine. "This is a Winchester '92, .25-20, and they gave me four .38-40 bullets. What am I supposed to do with them?"

O. T. glanced around the yard. The other guards stared back as if expecting him to attempt something. "Well, Pipestem, don't jam them in your gun."

"No, sir, that's a fact. I reckon I'm just supposed to stand here and look mean." This time when he spat tobacco, half of it dribbled on his chin. He wiped it on his soiled suit coat.

O. T. clamped his lips and looked away. *Pipestem Drusky couldn't look mean if you shot his dog. I don't believe I've ever seen such a sorry mob of mine guards in my life.*

"Say, what did them Mexicans do anyway?" Pipestem pressed. "I don't even know why they need to be guarded."

He didn't tell them about the picture rock, of course. These bummers would be harder to keep out of there than the Mexicans. "What did Mr. Fleming tell you?" O. T. quizzed.

"Told us nothin'. Except we was supposed to keep the Mexicans in this here buildin' until some regular guards arrive. We get the seven cash dollars no matter when we are relieved. I hope they come soon. It's hot out here, and I'm tired of standin' in the sun. And I'm gettin' mighty thirsty for somethin' juicier than water. What did them miners steal?"

Lupe Martinez had closed her parasol and carried it in front of her like a stagecoach shotgun. "They didn't steal anything," she snapped.

Drusky stuck his carbine barrel down his boot and scratched his leg. "Then where do you two think you're goin'?"

O. T. pointed to the headworks building door. "Mr. Fleming wanted us to talk to the miners."

Drusky pulled off his hat. He had a bald spot on top of his head not much bigger than a biscuit. "What are you talkin' to them fer?"

"Maybe there's a way to settle this so you don't have to hurt yourself with the wrong ammunition in your gun."

Drusky spoke in such a low voice that O. T. had to strain to hear the words. "I ain't goin' to get hurt, Skinner. I ain't shootin' nobody. Not even a Mexican. I just want the seven dollars—that's all. No matter what I look like, I ain't no gunslinger."

O. T. glanced at Lupe Martinez and caught the laughter in her eyes. He held the door open for her, and she sashayed through ahead of him. The sheet-iron building covered the massive headworks of the Pear Blossom. Huge electric pumps hammered in the background.

A small, thin man with short hair rushed over to greet them, shouting over the hum of foot-wide drive belts. Lupe and her father embraced, and O. T. listened to an avalanche of uninterrupted Spanish tumble down like a creek during spring runoff. When they finished, Lupe stepped back over by O. T. The Mexican miners huddled around them.

"What did your daddy say?" Skinner raised his voice to be heard. "How are they?"

"They are tired and hot, and they want to go home."

"Would you interpret if I visit with your father?"

"Certainly."

O. T. stepped in front of Lupe's father. "Mr. Martinez, I'm O. T. Skinner. Your daughter Lupe works for my wife at the Newcomers' Cafe."

He waited for Lupe to speak to her father and then interpret. "He says he knows all about the Wall Walker. And he is grateful for you and Mrs. Skinner giving me a job."

"Lupe, ask him what's going on here." O. T. pulled off his gray felt hat. "I want to hear their version of the story."

O. T. studied the tired eyes of the other dirty, sweaty men. Even with the six-foot-tall exhaust fans at the end of the building, there was little air movement. Sweat rolled off their dark brown faces. *It must be 120 degrees in here. It's nice and cool down in the shaft, but up here a man could have a heat stroke.*

Lupe held her father's rough, callused hand. "Daddy said that when they came off their shift this morning, they were lined up at gunpoint and told to strip off their clothes."

"Do they know why?"

Lupe nodded. "Because Mr. Fleming thinks they have stolen gold."

"I hear lots of mines have changin' rooms. I suppose it sort of goes with the job," Skinner replied.

Another man stepped up to add his opinion.

Lupe explained, "He said that when they were hired, they were told there would be no changing room and no one searching their lunch buckets."

O. T. glanced at the round tin lunch buckets stacked behind them. *I reckon Fleming didn't figure on a cavern full of picture rock.*

"They want to know what is going to happen to them and when they can go home," Lupe continued.

"Did they take any gold?"

"Mr. Pachaco says they have taken no more than to be expected."

Skinner raised his eyebrows. "Expected?"

"It is part of being a hard-rock miner. Like givin' a tip to a waitress at Fred Harvey's depot cafe."

"Is that why they refused to take off their clothes?"

She blushed. "No."

"Then why?" Skinner pressed.

Lupe lowered her eyes and stared at her feet. The twelve miners studied O. T. "Mr. Skinner, these are very poor, yet very proud men. Every penny they can save is sent back to family in Mexico. They keep next to nothing for themselves. Most of these men do not have any undergarments. They were much too embarrassed to strip down in front of the likes of those armed guards outside."

O. T. studied the eyes of the men one at a time. He smelled dirt, sweat, gear oil, and garlic. The dim electric bulbs that hung high above made the grime in the air glow. The sweaty faces glistened. Engines in the background continued to pound while they all waited for him to speak.

Lord, it's like they want me to figure this out. I don't know what to do. I don't know what I'd do if I was them.

O. T. wiped the sweat off his mustache, unfastened the top button on his shirt, and tugged off his black tie, tucking it in a suit coat pocket. "I think they ought to get out of this building before they melt," O. T. instructed. "Lupe, ask them if we turn our backs, are they willing to pile up the gold they took on that platform scale over there?"

"What?"

"I want to be able to walk out there and tell Mr. Fleming that they aren't carryin' one ounce of gold."

The miners huddled around Lupe Martinez as she gave them O. T.'s advice. Then she stepped over near O. T.

"They are not happy, but they said they would do that provided no one watched."

"You and me will go out and talk to Fleming while they unload their stash. Tell them we'll be right back."

The air outside was well over 100 degrees, but it had an almost fresh, cool feel as O. T. stepped back into the yard and led Lupe Martinez toward the front gate. Pipestem Drusky followed them.

As soon as O. T. and Lupe had entered the Pear Blossom, Dola latched onto the mine owner. "Mr. Fleming, have another piece of chicken!" she insisted.

"Thank you, Mrs. Skinner, don't mind if I do. Things have been so hectic I haven't eaten since last night."

"It is not good to miss a meal," Fergus piped up.

Chicken breast in hand, Fleming studied the old Paiute. "Are all of these your family, Mrs. Skinner?"

"Yes," Fergus blurted out with a grin. "I am her oldest son!"

Corrie burst out laughing. "Fergus is our friend! He's an Indian, you know."

"Mr. Fleming, I see you got guards at the mine. You must have some good ore down there. Does it shine in the lantern light? How much per ton do you think it will run? Are you chasin' a lead? Can you shovel it up and put it in sacks? I read once that at Cripple Creek they shoveled it straight into gunny sacks. Boy, I wish I could see somethin' like that." Tommy-Blue took a deep breath and then shoved a dill pickle into his mouth and puffed out his cheeks.

"Tommy-Blue is very interested in prospecting." Dola tore off a hunk of bread and handed it to the mine owner.

"I can see that," Fleming mumbled through a big bite of chicken.

With apricot jam smeared on his chin, Punky plodded over and sat in his mother's lap.

"And who is this healthy, young man?" Fleming asked.

The three-year-old's eyes widened. "I'm Punky, and my mama's purdy!"

"It's a little game he plays," Dola said, her face already flushed by the hot desert sun.

"You need not apologize for a child's devotion, Mrs. Skinner."

Dola wiped Punky's face with a damp rag. *And you, Mr. Fleming, did not confirm this young man's opinion.*

"Are you goin' to shoot the Mexicans?" Corrie blurted out.

"Corrie Lou!" Dola scolded.

"No, young lady. Just want to make sure our gold stays where it should. A lot of folks invested in this mine, and up to now they haven't earned their money back. I'm tryin' to make sure they do. We don't want to shoot anyone."

Hud Frazier peered in through the open front gate of the mine. "Then why did you hire armed guards?"

Fleming glanced back. "It's a rather ragged band—all we could get this morning on short notice. I've got a machinist makin' steel doors for the cavern. As soon as they're mounted and locked, it will only take a couple of reliable men to guard the entrance."

"I'm afraid I've never owned anything valuable enough to need to be locked up. A person can sleep better that way," Dola remarked. "Do you sleep well, Mr. Fleming? Your eyes look tired."

Fleming paced between the gate and the farm wagon. "Not half as tired as they're goin' to be. I won't sleep soundly until the gold is dug out of that cavern and safely at the smelter."

Rita Ann shoved her wire-framed glasses high on her upturned nose. "When Romeo went to buy poison at the drugstore, he said,

'There is thy gold, worse poison to men's souls, doing more murder in this loathsome world than these poor compounds that thou mayest not sell.'"

"Rita Ann likes Shakespeare," Tommy-Blue explained through a mouthful of cold, mashed sweet potato.

"And she likes boys!" Corrie snickered.

"I do not . . . well, not ALL boys!" Rita Ann corrected and glanced at Hudson Frazier.

"Mr. Fleming, I certainly hope your gold brings you happiness. Why on earth have gold if it doesn't bring joy to your life?" Then Dola pointed to the large basket. "You must try some cherry pie."

"My mama has a peach tree," Punky announced.

"Is the peach tree purdy?" Fleming asked.

"No!" Punky said. "Mama is purdy!"

"Enough of that. . . . Look, here come Orion and Lupe." Dola pointed toward the open gate.

Fleming pulled out a white handkerchief and wiped chicken grease off his fingers. "Did you get them to agree to a search?" he blurted out as he stalked toward them.

O. T. looked into Dola's eyes and then back at the mine owner. His voice was gentle, yet stubborn. "I didn't ask them. But they said any high-graded ore would be stacked on that platform scale. They want to go home."

"That can't be!" Fleming flailed his hands in the air. "They have to strip. That gold belongs to me. How do I know they will keep their word?"

"How do you know they won't?" O. T. challenged.

"Daddy, did you get to see any gold?" Tommy-Blue interrupted.

O. T. put his hand on Tommy-Blue's shaggy brown hair. "No, son, I didn't."

"Skinner, you go right back in there and tell them Mexicans if they don't agree to a search, I'll—I'll fire the bunch of them!"

"Mr. Fleming, since I don't work for you, I believe you'll need to deliver that remark yourself," O. T. replied.

"They said they would put all the high-graded ore on the scales," Lupe protested. "There will be nothing for you to search for."

"Then they've got absolutely nothin' to worry about strippin' down. Innocent men got nothin' to fear," Fleming raged.

Seeing Rita Ann's wide eyes, Dola stood and walked over to the mine owner. "Mr. Fleming, may we talk in private? This is something I don't want to mention in front of the children."

She led Fleming, O. T., and Lupe over near the door. The toddler tagged along behind his mother.

"Come here, Punky. You can have my jelly biscuit!" Rita Ann called out.

Silas Paul Skinner spun around and ran back. "Rita-Rita-Rita-Rita!"

Dola's voice was barely above a whisper as she stared down at the dry yellow-brown dirt at her feet. "Mr. Fleming, you mentioned that innocent men have nothing to hide and shouldn't hesitate to strip down and be searched. So how about you and these armed men stripping down first?"

O. T. stared at Dola's lowered head.

Fleming's neck flushed. "What did you say?"

Dola Mae Skinner slowly raised her head until she focused on the mine owner's eyes. Then she took a slow, deep breath. "Mr. Fleming, sometimes saving pride and dignity are more important than saving gold. You would not want to strip in front of these men any more than they would want to do so in front of you."

"That's preposterous!" he fumed.

O. T. slipped up beside Dola and put his arm around her trembling shoulders. "Mr. Fleming, until you build a changing room and furnish the men with a set of work clothes, your demands seem a little steep," O. T. explained. "I suggest that until you get the steel gate installed down there on that picture rock, keep everyone out of that tunnel. Wait a few days to be a rich man."

"I'm already a rich man," he huffed.

"Then what is a little gold dirt stuck in some man's pocket?" Dola pressed.

"It's the principle of the matter. It's stealing," Fleming insisted.

"Yes, it is," Dola continued. "And those men will face a much higher judgment than yours for their actions. But is it worth the trouble you are creating?"

O. T. waved toward the open gate. "Mr. Fleming, with so many mines and leases working now in Goldfield, it will be hard for you to find a replacement crew right away. If Lupe's father and the others quit, you'll have to hire the likes of this guard crew to dig your gold. Would that be a better situation?"

Fleming's shoulders slumped. Tension melted from his wrinkled forehead. He rubbed his chin and lips and then licked his fingers again. "I'm tired, Skinner. I get cranky when I'm tired."

"So does Punky," Dola commented.

Fleming tugged his tie loose and unfastened a sweaty shirt collar. "And what do you do when Punky's cranky?"

"Give him a nap," Dola answered.

Fleming took a deep breath. "Skinner . . . never get started in the gold business. It will worry you to death. You'll worry to death about goin' broke, and then you'll worry to death about bein' rich. You can't win." He yelled back at the yard. "Tell the Mexicans they're free to go home. The wagons are over by the cook shack. One of the mechanics will drive them to town."

"Do they still have their jobs?" Lupe asked.

"Or are you goin' to hire these old boys to work in your mine?" O. T. pressed.

Fleming shook his head. A wry smile pierced his face. "Skinner, if you and your wife ever become anarchist union negotiators, mining as we know it today is in real trouble! Tell them . . . they have three days off. When they come back, there will be a changing room and a change of clothes for every worker. Tell them if they don't want to go that route, they can find a different job."

O. T. nodded. "That's a fair deal. I'll tell them that."

"And you and your family are welcome to camp out here as long as you want."

"Thank you, Mr. Fleming," Dola said, "but we'll be leaving soon. We need to get back before dark."

"Could you do me a favor before you leave?" Fleming asked. "I need about an hour of your time. Take your boy and whoever else and take a look at the mine. I'll have Porter give you a tour if you want to go down and see that picture rock. I don't reckon I can hide the news once the Mexicans get back to town anyway. With you inside, I won't worry about what those saloon roaches are doin'."

"What are you going to do, Mr. Fleming?" Lupe Martinez asked.

He stared right at Dola. "I'm going to go into my office and take a nap."

O. T. stopped the wagon at the top of the grade before they dropped back down into Goldfield. Even though town was perched above 5,000 feet in elevation, from the summit it seemed low. The sun hung barely above the distant western mountains, but the temperature didn't lower with it. There wasn't a bit of breeze. The familiar sting of blowing sand and alkali was replaced with suspended dust thick enough that if someone tried to tip his hat, he'd plow a trail through it.

He felt Corrie's hands light on his left shoulder. She stood behind him the whole way from the Pear Blossom Mine. "Look, Daddy, there's Columbia and lower Main Street and all the crib rows. And there's the Northern Saloon and the Stock Exchange and . . . Where's our cafe? I can't see the cafe, Daddy."

Lord, I hope the day doesn't come that I regret exposing them to so rough a town. Little girls should be worried about nothing more than ponies

*and pigtails and penmanship. Soiled doves, saloons, and six-guns are things
of the past. And they all moved to Goldfield to die.*

Dola's head rested on his right shoulder. She and the three-year-
old in her lap were asleep.

"What are you thinkin' about, Daddy?" Corrie pressed.

"I guess I was thinkin' about Dinuba again," he said.

"Are we really goin' to move to California by Christmas?" Corrie
asked.

"I hear it's kind of foggy and cold in the San Joaquin Valley until
after the first of the year. Maybe we'll wait until early spring, darlin'."

Dola's voice was barely a whisper. She didn't raise her head. "I
won't take the children out of school during the year, Orion. Not
again."

"Well, maybe June is a good time. Or maybe August . . ."

Corrie hugged his neck. He could smell rose perfume covering
dirt and sweat. "It's August right now, Daddy."

"Well, what are we waiting for? Let's turn Ida and Ada west right
now!"

"We can't go without Mama's peach tree!" Corrie exclaimed.

Dola sat up. "And we can't pull that auto car all the way behind
us across the desert either."

"In fact we can't pull it anymore at all. I don't trust those brakes
with it behind us," O. T. insisted. "You remember the trouble Hud
had with it in the snow last January?"

"Do you think it will be dangerous in the auto car?" Dola asked.

"Probably not. Hud's got steering and brakes. I just don't want
to get in his way. I'll go unhitch."

"Corrie, come up here and sit with Punky. I'm going to help
Daddy," Dola called.

"I can get it, darlin'," he offered.

"But I really need to stretch. My back and legs are stiff," she said.

At the end of a triple-wrapped rope hitch, the black dust-covered Thomas car loafed like a beached whale in yellow-brown desert

sand. Hud Frazier sat at the steering wheel, Haylee Cox was next to him, and Lupe Martinez was crowded in at the door. In the middle of the backseat, the old Paiute reigned like a king, with Tommy-Blue on one side and Rita Ann on the other.

"What are we stopping for, Daddy?" Tommy-Blue called out. "This is the fun part. I can't wait to feel the wind in my face."

O. T. motioned him out of the car. "The only breeze you will feel is in our wagon. I figure to unhitch and let Hud coast down the hill. I reckon he can travel faster than Ada and Ida can pull. Don't want him behind me and get my mules run over."

"These brakes will hold fine, Mr. Skinner. I fixed them in April, remember," Hud Frazier offered.

"Yep. I believe you fixed them in September and January too. I'd just feel safer with my mules behind you. You don't mind coastin' down the hill ahead of us, do you?"

"No, sir. That's fine. That long grade will be like ridin' a log down a flue," Frazier replied.

"Did you do that?" Haylee asked.

"I did one time up above Carson City. It was a frolic. Nearly broke my neck. There was a turn, and this log I was ridin' didn't make it. I busted through the flue and sailed right off the side of the mountain. Lucky it was spring, and the grass was green. I woke up in a field of poppies! It was quite a ride."

"It sounds very dangerous, Mr. Frazier," Dola said.

"Oh, but this is an auto car with steering and brakes. Ain't nothin' to worry about, Mrs. Skinner. I've been test-drivin' it all summer, you know, just to get the kinks out."

"That's good," Dola said with a nod. "Now, Rita Ann and Tommy-Blue, you get up in the wagon with Daddy and me."

"Mother!" Rita Ann moaned. "Can't I ride back here?"

"No, you may not."

"Mama, it will be a hoot," Tommy-Blue said. "I bet we can go thirty miles an hour. Do you think we'll go that fast, Hud?"

The twenty-one-year-old pushed the leather cap back on his head and nodded. "Might be."

"You, young man, will be in the wagon and will be going about four miles an hour," Dola instructed.

With a just-lost-my-dog expression, Tommy-Blue pleaded, "Mama, please. You just got to—"

"Boy, don't you argue with your mama," O. T. interjected.

"Well," Lupe Martinez added, "I like mules just fine." She opened the door and stepped out on the running board.

Rita Ann slowly climbed out of the car. "I don't know why I have to be treated like a child. Haylee doesn't have to—"

"I'm riding in the wagon," the seventeen-year-old said.

"You are?" Hud Frazier gulped. "But—but—it's perfectly safe!"

"Son, we're just bein' cautious. The grade down Goldfield Summit is kind of steep." O. T. motioned.

Sitting on his mother's hip, with dried jam on the bib of his overalls, Punky threw sticky arms around his mother's neck. "Punky's goin' with Mama!"

"Yes, you are, li'l darlin'."

"How about Fergus? Does he have to ride in the wagon too?" Tommy-Blue asked.

"Fergus is old enough to make his own decisions," O. T. declared.

"'Crabbed age and youth cannot live together; youth is full of pleasance, age is full of care,'" Rita Ann mumbled.

"What did you say?" Dola challenged.

"How old does a person have to be to make her own decisions?" Rita Ann countered.

"Sixty-two," Fergus piped up.

"Are you sixty-two?" Tommy-Blue asked.

"Or perhaps it's seventy-two." Fergus paused and glanced at his fingers. "Perhaps it is fifty-two. I don't remember. I think it is quite old. I don't remember when I wasn't here."

"Ain't anyone goin' to ride with me?" Hud complained.

"I am," Fergus announced. "I like this backseat."

"Well, the rest of you are goin' to miss a great ride," Hud taunted. "Why own an auto car if you don't want to go fast?"

"Like the ride on the log flue?" Haylee asked.

"Even better," Hud said.

"It is not spring, Mr. Frazier, and there are no poppy fields and deep grass to break one's fall," Dola announced. "Please be careful."

"I ain't goin' to crash. But with the right momentum we can roll up right in front of the cafe about twenty minutes before you do."

"Good. Then you can sweep the porch," O. T. suggested.

"And wash the front windows," Dola added.

"I ain't goin' to have that much time." Hudson Frazier grabbed the wooden steering wheel with both hands. "Now if you'll push me over the summit, I'll be on my way."

"Come on, gang. It seems that the pride of modern technology needs a push from strong backs," O. T. called out.

"They won't really get hurt, will they?" Haylee asked.

Lupe brushed back her black bangs off her forehead. "What's the worst thing that could happen?"

Corrie sucked in a deep breath and then exploded. "They could hit a boulder and fly out of the auto car and land in an abandoned mine shaft and plummet 1,000 feet and get stuck heads-down permanently in a narrow pitch-black hole with snakes only inches away."

"Corrie!" Dola snapped.

"That's ridiculous," Tommy-Blue declared. "Who ever heard of snakes 1,000 feet down?"

O. T. puffed as he pushed the Thomas up the last slight incline.

"Maybe snakes was crawlin' on the desert floor and got pulled down by Hud's boot toes when he tumbled into the shaft," Corrie explained.

"Oh, well, that could happen, sure," Tommy-Blue agreed. "But then them snakes would bite their legs and rear ends."

"Tommy-Blue Skinner!" Dola's tone silenced the whole crowd for a moment.

"Eh, what is the second worst thing that can happen?" Lupe asked.

"I don't reckon they will fall out of anything that big and heavy," O. T. said. "They might get jostled, bumped, or bruised. That's all."

"I trust you will be careful," Haylee said to Hud.

"Darlin', I'd be an awful lot more careful if I had someone sittin' by my side."

Fergus pulled his black felt hat so low it came down over his ears. "I'm not going to sit by you. I like the backseat better."

"You don't have to coast up to the cafe. Just stop near the edge of town. I'll hook up and tow you in," O. T. said.

"No, sir," Hud declared. "This is an auto car. It is the techno-logical marvel of the century."

"The century is still young," O. T. said.

"Can you imagine anything more marvelous than an auto car?"

"No, but two years ago I couldn't imagine an auto car," O. T. declared. "Take it easy."

"'I go, I go; look how I go, swifter than arrow from the Tartar's bow,'" Rita Ann droned. She glanced at Haylee. "*A Midsummer Night's Dream*, act 3, scene 2."

"We aren't doin' anything dramatic," Hud maintained. "And we'll be waitin' for you in front of the cafe."

"I'll be waiting in the kitchen," Fergus declared. "Do you have any lonely bear claws?"

"There might be two or three in the basket on top of the china cabinet," Dola informed him.

"There's only one," Tommy-Blue confessed.

"Did you eat those bear claws after church?" Dola probed.

"Just two of 'em."

"That was generous of you. Not overly generous, but generous nonetheless. I will eat it while we wait," Fergus declared. He waved at Hud Frazier. "To the cafe!"

The auto car silently rolled down the dusty grade. It moved so slowly that O. T. pondered whether they should push it again. Finally it picked up speed, and Hud Frazier turned and waved at Haylee. "Don't let modern technology drive off and leave you stranded in the past!" he hollered.

Dola held O. T.'s arm as they watched the descending car. "There are some parts of the past I'd love to be stranded in."

The car spun a tail of dust. "What parts are those?"

Dola stared off in the distance. "My, that auto car does roll smoothly and so quiet."

"That's 'cause the engine ain't runnin'," Tommy-Blue offered.

"What memories do I cling to?" she finally replied. "How about that summer we spent livin' in that cabin on Willow Creek?"

"That was nice," he admitted.

"Where was I that summer, Daddy?" Corrie asked.

"You were still livin' in my heart, darlin'. Me and Mama was jist waitin' for the right time to let you out."

The car was now sailing down the grade.

"Do you think they're havin' fun?" Corrie inquired.

"I think Hud is waving!" Haylee exclaimed. "Maybe I should have ridden with them. Look at how fast they're going."

"It's Fergus wavin'," Corrie Lou said. "Hi, Fergus!" she hollered.

"He can't hear you," Tommy-Blue chided.

Corrie folded her arms across her chest. "Maybe he can. He has very good ears, you know."

Tommy-Blue looped his thumbs in his bib overalls. "He told me he only hears what he wants to."

"Yes, but I just know he wants to hear me," Corrie declared.

Lupe Martinez rested her black parasol on her shoulders and shaded her eyes with her hand. "I think Fergus is hitting Hud with his hat."

O. T. scratched his chin, his eyes tracing the road ahead of the speeding car. "Sort of looks that way, don't it?"

"Why is he hitting Hud? That's not nice." Haylee stood on tiptoes.

"Fergus is funny," Punky declared. He waved at the distant speeding car.

"Maybe they're arguing over that last bear claw," Corrie suggested. "Was it apple or peach?"

"It was the one I dropped on the floor," Tommy-Blue mumbled.

"Young man—," Dola began.

"Look, I think their wheels came off the ground on that corner," Rita Ann called out.

"I didn't see it," Tommy-Blue complained.

"'Like as the waves make toward the pebbled shore, so do our minutes hasten to their end,'" Rita Ann recited. "That's 'Sonnet 60,' you know."

"Their end?" Haylee gasped. "It can't be their end. Why, we haven't even . . ."

"Why doesn't he use the brakes?" Dola interrupted.

"I'm sure Hud has it all in control," O. T. mumbled. *Lord, I'm not very sure.*

"The wheels did come off!" Tommy-Blue shouted.

"The wheels came off?" Haylee wailed.

"Off the ground," Tommy-Blue explained. "When they rounded that corner by the Joshua tree, they raised plumb off the ground. I ain't never been in a rig that raised up like that. I should have gone with them!"

"That was not an option, young man," Dola huffed.

"They're having all the fun," Tommy-Blue complained.

Lupe pointed her closed parasol down the hill. "I think someone's hat blew out!"

O. T. scratched the back of his neck. "We'll pick it up when we get down that far. Come on, we'd better head down too."

"They surely are goin' fast," Tommy-Blue declared.

"Too fast," O. T. mumbled.

"I believe it's time to apply the brakes. They are about to the edge of Seventh Street," Dola observed nervously.

Haylee clutched Lupe's arm and held tight. She seemed to choke out each word. "Hud . . . knows . . . what . . . he's doing."

"Holy hereford!" Tommy-Blue shouted. "Did you see that? Hud done jumped out!"

"Tommy-Blue, you watch your words!" Dola scolded.

"Is he dead?" Haylee sobbed.

"I ain't never seen a man jump out of an auto car on purpose!" Tommy-Blue hollered. "This is like watchin' a circus in Guthrie!"

"He's rollin' into the sage by the stone cabin," Corrie announced.

"There ain't no sage by the stone cabin. Ain't nothin' there but—but—," Tommy-Blue stuttered.

"A big patch of prickly pear cactus!" Rita Ann shouted. "He landed in the cactus! 'To wisdom he's a fool that will not yield.'"

"At least he didn't fall down a mine shaft . . . yet," Tommy-Blue declared.

"Oh, no," Haylee sobbed. "He can't be hurt!"

"Of course he is hurt," Lupe said.

"Why did he jump, Daddy?" Corrie asked. "That wasn't very smart, was it? What's going to happen to Fergus?"

"He'll jump too—won't he?" Rita Ann asked.

Tommy-Blue climbed up on the wagon to get a better view. "What will happen to our motor car?"

"What will happen to the people the motor car runs over!" Dola scurried up into the wagon.

Corrie stood behind her daddy and threw her arms around his neck. "We just have to save Fergus from destruction."

"Where did the auto car go? I can't see it!" Rita Ann cried as she clambered into the wagon.

"Oh, rats, I wish I was ridin' in it! It done zipped behind the bank!" Tommy-Blue hollered.

"On Columbia Street! That will be crowded! Oh, no . . . Lord Jesus, no!" Dola cried.

"Everyone sit down!" O. T. hollered.

Corrie tightened her grip around his neck.

"You too, darlin'. Sit down."

"I'm safe with you, Daddy," Corrie pleaded.

"Punky's safe with Mama," the toddler announced.

"Why did I let him fix that auto car in the first place? He's been workin' on it for over a year. You'd think everything would be fixed by now. How much work does one auto car take?" O. T. fumed as the wagon lurched over the crest of the hill and started the descent. "It wasn't hurtin' anyone parked out behind the cafe. It was fool vanity. Wishin' for somethin' I had no right to wish for. I am a weak and sinful man, Lord. I've always told You that."

"Quit mumbling, Orion, and drive us down the hill. It's not your fault." Dola could feel her voice quiver and break. "Both those men chose to ride in that auto car."

"Yes, but the innocent ones it runs over didn't get to choose," O. T. said.

Ada and Ida lurched forward as the wagon rattled down the long grade into Goldfield.

"Can't you hurry, Daddy?" Rita Ann pressed.

"I'm not goin' to get us all killed like—I mean, injured like those two," O. T. objected. "We are goin' as fast as is safe. We can do no more."

"Look!" Corrie yelled. "Did you see that dust?"

"It's like when the Rokkers' house blew up!" Tommy-Blue added.

"But I didn't hear . . ." Corrie stopped in mid-sentence. A deep crashing rumble rolled like a wave across the desert. "There's the sound! It was late!"

"That's because light travels faster than sound," Rita Ann lectured.

"Well, if we don't travel faster, we'll never find out," Tommy-Blue hollered.

Haylee buried her head on Lupe's chest. "I can't watch. I just can't. I'm so scared."

Every pothole and rock in the dirt road lifted the travelers off their seats and slammed them back into the rough, faded wood. They clutched side rails, tailgate, and each other as Ada and Ida trotted to keep ahead of the farm wagon that seemed to be groaning a death song at every turn of its wood-hubbed wheels.

The pair of mules were lathered but still able to slow the wagon when they reached Seventh Street. O. T. pulled up next to the stone house and the prickly pear patch. A man lay on his stomach, propped up on his elbows, straining to look back at the wagon.

"There's Hud!" Corrie called.

"Go check on Fergus and the auto car!" Hud called out.

"You have blood on your forehead," Haylee cried. "Oh—oh—I'm goin' to faint!"

Lupe grabbed Haylee and pushed her head down on her lap.

"That old fool wouldn't jump," Hud yelled. "The brakes went out, Mr. Skinner. I reckon they ain't made for that steep a grade. At least, not in idle."

"We were afraid you landed in the cactus," Corrie shouted.

"Is anything broken?" Dola asked.

"I don't think so—go on." Hud motioned. "Check on Fergus."

"Haylee, you help Hud," O. T. ordered. "We'll see what happened to Fergus."

"I'll help her," Lupe offered.

"I'm all right now," Haylee insisted as she climbed down. "You go on. Roll over, Hud. I'll help you up."

"I ain't rollin' over," he cried out. "Not until someone pulls out those thorns."

"Thorns?" Haylee asked.

"I didn't miss the cactus patch!" he wailed.

"Oh, dear," Haylee called. "I do think I need some help."

"Or at least a chaperone," Lupe added, as she climbed out of the wagon.

Ada and Ida were too tired to trot and ignored O. T.'s commands. When the wagon finally rounded the corner, dust hung in the air over Columbia Street. A crowd lapped out into the street.

"They're in front of the cafe!" Rita Ann declared.

"We don't serve Sunday supper. Why are they there?" Corrie puzzled.

"That's where the auto car went," Tommy-Blue said as the crowd parted for the wagon.

"Fergus stopped at the cafe?" Dola questioned.

"Looks like he stopped it *in* the cafe!" Tommy-Blue shouted.

Rita Ann leaned into Corrie. "He drove it right up the porch into the window!"

"He wasn't drivin'," Corrie corrected her. "He was in the backseat!"

"He busted up the cafe," Tommy-Blue boomed.

"Cafes can be rebuilt," O. T. said. "Has anyone seen Fergus?"

"My peach tree!" Dola cried out. "What happened to my peach tree? Not my peach tree!"

"It's okay, Mama," Corrie hollered. "It's over on the other side."

Dola threw her hands over her mouth. *Lord, I can't believe I worried about that dumb tree. What's wrong with me? Where's Fergus? Please keep him from mortal harm!*

"Punky wants to see!" The three-year-old stood on the wagon seat, clutching Dola's neck.

A crowd of about fifty parted and allowed O. T. to park the wagon near the cafe. He dropped the lead line, leapt out of the wagon, and scurried up to the auto car that rested half in and half outside the cafe window. Shards of glass and wood splinters littered the porch and cafe floor.

"Where's Fergus? Where's the old Indian?" he questioned as he stared inside the empty car.

"Weren't no one in it when we got here, Skinner."

"I reckon it was a runaway. He must have jumped out."

"Tommy-Blue and Rita Ann, you run back along the street and see if you can find Fergus," O. T. commanded.

"Ain't never seen a runaway auto machine before. Seen many a runaway stage in my day when I was freightin' up in Ideeho," one man remarked.

"Did any bystanders get hurt?" O. T. inquired.

"It didn't hit no one if that's what you're askin'. Don't know if anyone was inside. There's a big poker game over at the Alaskan Saloon. . . . We was all over there seein' if Tex Rickard can outbluff Snake River Johnny," the man said.

Dola raised up her head. "Thank You, Jesus!" she blurted out. *Perhaps in this one case there is redeeming value in a poker game that keeps a crowd from harm.*

Punky reached up and smeared alkali dust across her cheek with his thumb. "My mama's purdy."

"Your mama's a dusty, worried mess, little darlin'. Let's go see if Fergus is inside the cafe."

"You need help movin' that auto car, Skinner?" a big, bearded man asked.

O. T. squatted down and peered under the vehicle. "Not yet, boys. We're lookin' for Fergus first. Besides, this thing's leakin' oil from somewhere. We need to wait until Hud tells us what to do."

Dola, carrying Punky on her hip, emerged from the restaurant dining room. "There's no one in here. Fergus must have jumped." She surveyed the glass on the porch and then walked over and put the toddler back into the wagon. "Corrie Lou, carry Punky up to the apartment and put his shoes on him. We've got to get this glass swept up."

O. T. surveyed the street, watching for some sign of Rita Ann and Tommy-Blue. "Maybe I'd better go help look for Fergus."

"You want me to go get a doc or an undertaker?" the man with the gray beard asked.

"Just go help find Fergus. Please!" Dola pleaded.

Some in the crowd scurried down the street.

O. T. glanced back into the restaurant. "He didn't get thrown out under a table, did he?"

"I don't think so."

O. T. scrambled into the cafe, Dola at his heels. Squatting on his haunches, he peered under the gingham tablecloths. "I don't see him. He must have jumped. I'll go help them look. You try to sweep up this glass. Be careful and don't cut yourself."

She clutched his arm. "What are we going to do if Fergus is . . ."

He brushed a kiss across her forehead and clutched her shoulders. "Darlin', we'll take one step at a time. Right now we have to find that old Paiute."

Dola tossed her hat on a table. "I suppose we can board up the window. Do you think there's any structural damage to the building?"

"The casing is busted—I know that. But that's the least of our worries, darlin'."

"I mean, is it a safe building?"

"This is a sturdy building. You couldn't blow it up with dynamite. Right now we've got to find Fergus. It's all my fault. I knew better than to let him ride. Why didn't I make him stay with us?"

Dola examined the smashed front end of the auto car as it protruded into the dining room. "I suppose this means we will not be driving an auto car when we move to California."

"Nope. I don't reckon we will."

Dola retrieved a broom from the corner of the room. "It was a rather nice-looking auto car when Hud had it all polished."

O. T. slipped his arm around his wife's waist. "Dola Mae, if the Lord is gracious and allows us to get out of this with no injury, I will park that rig. It's too dangerous to drive."

"I believe with a little practice, I could drive the thing better."

The deep, raspy voice sent chills down O. T.'s back. He and Dola spun around.

"Fergus!" Dola called out.

"Yes, it is me. Are you disappointed?"

"We thought you jumped out of the auto car," O. T. blurted out.

"That was the young Mr. Frazier. I didn't want to get my new duckings dirty."

Dola stepped over and hugged the Paiute. "But you could have been killed!"

He patted the top of her head as one would pat a favorite dog. "It was not that difficult to steer, but, as you can see, I was not too good at parking."

O. T. shook his head. "It's a wonder you slowed it down at all. Hud said the brakes were completely gone."

Dola released the gray-haired, hatless old man.

"Oh, they still work," Fergus declared as he licked his fingers. "But they are noisy."

"Noisy?" O. T. asked.

"After the boy foolishly dove out, I crawled up there to steer. I was going good until the goose."

"What goose?"

"The goose in the middle of the street. I swerved to miss it, and the next thing I knew, I crashed through the window. And, since I was in the cafe already, naturally I went to find the bear claw." The old Paiute licked his gnarled fingers again. "It was a good bear claw except for the dirt." Then he glanced out toward the wagon. "I presume you stopped to pick up my hat?"

THREE

O. T. delivered assay reports to the July Extension, the Red Top, and Myers-Hawken Lease mines. Then he stopped by the cafe before noon. He was sweating through his starched shirt, his tie hung loose, and he carried his coat in his hand. A crowd of men clustered on the porch around the black car still parked halfway in the dining room.

A bald-headed man spat tobacco out into the street. "Skinner, you could just build yourself a livery for this motor buggy. No need to park it in the cafe," he chided.

A big man in coveralls, with two upper teeth missing, pushed his tattered top hat back. "Shoot, I got an old barn up at Belmont that I need to tear down. How about you and this here motor car doin' the job? You could contract out in building demolition."

A short little man with a Missouri smile looped his thumbs in his suspenders. "Can a fella jist sit in the front seat and order break-fast, or does he have to come in?"

O. T. grinned at the crowd. He patted the unscathed back fender of the Thomas. "Boys, you surely do seem jealous. But if one of you'd haul it off for me, I'd give it to you."

A man in plaid suit pants and red long-handle shirt rubbed his three-day beard. "You ain't gettin' us to do your work for ya. No sir, Skinner. It's all yours. I've been wonderin' how you'll ever move it."

"Maybe I'll just screen it in and leave it there." O. T. strolled into the dining room.

"You could change your name to the Drive-Through Cafe!" the short man hooted. "You might start a new trend!"

O. T. was surprised to see Rita Ann and Haylee clearing tables. "You girls still at it?"

"'How say you to a fat tripe finely broil'd?'" Rita Ann quipped as she shuffled toward the kitchen with a load of dishes.

"What was that supposed to mean?" O. T. remarked.

"I think she's a little worn out, Mr. Skinner," Haylee explained. "Even her beloved Shakespeare is getting distorted. We served 142 for breakfast!"

O. T. hefted a tub of dirty dishes to his shoulder. "That's double what you normally have. Did a trainload of new gold-seekers hit town?"

Haylee lifted her braids and fanned the back of her neck. "It's the auto car parked in the window. Everyone came to see it, and most stayed to eat."

O. T. sauntered into the kitchen. Dola and Omega had their sleeves rolled up and were scrubbing dishes. Lupe Martinez and a white-aproned Hud Frazier were drying dishes. O. T. set the tub of dirty dishes on the wooden counter.

"This apron ain't my idea," Hud complained.

"I didn't say a word." O. T. opened the lid and stared into an empty coffeepot.

"But you was thinkin' it," Hud groused.

"Love makes a man do strange things."

"Love?" Hud protested. "It's pure guilt for lettin' that auto car get away from me."

O. T. strolled behind Dola. "Looks like you had quite a breakfast, darlin'."

She wiped her forehead with the back of her hand, leaving a narrow trail of soap suds. "We've been scurrying like this since 5:30 A.M. It's crazy, Orion. Everyone in Goldfield wants to see that motor car. You'd think we had an elephant in the yard."

He jammed his hands in his back pockets. "I suppose this is a bad time to ask about some lunch?"

Dola's shoulders slumped. Sharp pains shot down her lower back. *Lord, I just cooked for 142 men I hardly know, and now I'm too spent to cook for the one man on the face of this earth that I dearly love. Now that don't seem right to me.* "Orion, we really need to finish cleaning up a little more. Everything is such a mess."

"Maybe you could just fry me up a piece of meat."

Omega's brown eyes narrowed. "Mister, if you say one more word about wanting something to eat, I will personally pour this pan of dirty dishwater over your head. Is that perfectly clear?"

"Eh, yes, ma'am," O. T. gulped.

Omega winked at Dola. "You see, honey, there are just some times when you have to speak plain—that's all."

He shuffled toward the pantry. "I'll, eh—just fix myself . . ."

"No, you don't!" Lupe insisted. "You will not mess up one dish. Do you understand?"

Dola pointed a big soapy spoon toward the gray metal cash box. "Take a couple dollars and go buy yourself a meal at the hotel. We can afford it today."

"Well, there's no need to—"

White soap suds slithered down Omega's black arms. "It's either that or put on an apron and help out," she barked.

"I reckon I could eat at the hotel." O. T. turned back toward the door to the dining room.

"Take Punky with you," Dola called out.

O. T. spun around at the door. "What?"

Dola stared down at her water-shriveled fingers. "He's been a pill today. He insisted on sitting in the auto car all morning."

O. T. scratched his gray-brown hair. "Where is he now?"

"Corrie took him upstairs to wash his face and hands." Dola plunged her hands back into the nearly scalding water. "Send Corrie

Lou down to help with these dishes. Don't let her sweet-talk you into goin' to the hotel."

"She wasn't very sweet last time I saw her," Omega remarked.

"You know how cranky she can get when she's tired," Dola said.

"Where's Tommy-Blue?" O. T. asked.

Dola squeezed a soapy rag over steamy water. "He took the garbage buckets down to Turnbull's hogs and hasn't come back yet. If you see him, send him home. We've got two more bucketsful ready to haul."

O. T. reached up on the shelf into the biscuit basket. "I presume the novelty of the auto car will wear off soon." The basket was empty.

"If it don't slow down, you'll have five berserk women on your hands," Omega hooted.

O. T. shook his head. "Yeah, well, I appreciate you helpin' out, Hud."

Frazier clattered a plate onto the top of a tall stack. "Ain't nothin' else I can do, Mr. Skinner. I can't sit down. You ought to see how festered them cactus pricks are."

"Oh?" Haylee teased.

"Not you. . . . I meant Mr. Skinner."

"Goodness, you do blush easy," Lupe heckled.

"If I got to do this much longer, I'll turn red permanently," Hud complained.

"Enjoy," Omega called out. "Not many men are surrounded by such a covey of beautiful women."

Rita Ann blurted out, "'Beauty is but a vain and doubtful good; a shining gloss that fadeth suddenly.'"

"You see what I'm dealin' with, Mr. Skinner?" Hud complained.

"Enjoy it, son. There will be way too many days and years you smell nothin' but the sweat of men."

O. T.'s boot hammered the dusty floor of the empty dining room. The wide, wooden stairway to the upstairs apartment echoed each step as he plodded his way up. The pale green door was open.

Silas Paul Skinner sprawled on a hooked rug in the middle of the room, stark naked, playing with a spur and half a peeled carrot.

"Punky, what in the world are you doin'?"

"Punky cook dinner!" he announced. "I'm chopping carrots."

O. T. squatted down and plucked the strapless spur from the toddler's hand. "Don't say that too loud. Mama will sign you up as a cook."

Punky frowned. "My mama's mad!"

"Your mama's tired—that's all." O. T. scooped up the naked toddler who clutched the half-eaten carrot. "Where's your sister?"

"Corrie's tired," Punky declared.

O. T. ambled across the room. Covers from the unmade bed were scattered on the painted wood floor. Curled up like a cat on a cushion was Corrie Lou Skinner.

"Corrie's asleep, Daddy," Punky announced.

"You're right about that, little darlin'. Let's leave her alone. We'll get some coveralls on you, and the two of us will go eat some lunch at the hotel. You want to go with Daddy?"

The three-year-old surveyed the room as if considering the options and then grinned. "Yep!" he replied.

Ten minutes later O. T. waltzed out the back door of the kitchen with a barefoot, coveralled Punky on his hip. When he turned the corner, he thought he heard a voice call out. He stopped to look back.

"Wall Walker!" the rough voice hollered.

Punky held his hands straight out. "Fergus-Fergus-Fergus," he hollered.

The gray-haired Indian scooted up to them. He gently patted the toddler on the back. "Little Skinner, you are friendly enough to be a Paiute. Are you part Paiute?"

The three-year-old's mouth dropped open. "I'm not Paiute. I'm Punky!" he insisted.

"How are you feeling after that wild ride yesterday?" O. T. quizzed.

The old man's leather-tough face showed no emotion. "Not good."

O. T. looked the Indian over, noting the crisp, white cotton long-sleeved shirt and black hat. "You got some bumps and bruises from that collision?"

"I think if I had something to eat, I would feel better. I'm hungry."

O. T. rubbed his clean-shaven chin. "Didn't you have any breakfast?"

"Yes, of course." Fergus slowly surveyed the wagons rolling up the dirt street. "But what does that have to do with me being hungry now?"

O. T. shifted the grinning toddler to his other arm. "Me and Punky are eatin' at the hotel. You're welcome to join us."

"If you insist. But I will buy my own. The bank says I should start spending some of my money."

"Well, now, that is a problem I haven't ever had to deal with."

"Yes," Fergus continued as they strolled down the wooden sidewalk. "I have much to think about. It is not good to think when you are hungry."

Punky pulled off his father's hat and shoved it on his own head. It hung down over his eyes. "It's nighttime," he giggled.

O. T. fingered back his gray-brown hair. "What do you have to think about, Fergus? You're healthy and handsome and have money in the bank."

Fergus stared beyond the western horizon. "Yes, that is all true. Did I tell you my cousin came back to town?"

O. T. retrieved his hat from Punky. "The one who used to own a house in Goldfield?"

"It is still her house. That is the problem. She has come back to town, and the man staying there won't return it to her."

A battered auto car rattled by, backfired, blew smoke across the street, and then lunged on down the road.

Punky clapped and laughed.

O. T. stopped in front of the drugstore. "You mean someone just kicked her out of her own house and moved in?"

"Yes. At first it was four men. She says now only one is left there. And he is using her furnishings and her Winchester rifle as well. She traveled all the way to Washington, D.C., to plead her case—to no avail."

After a green freight wagon groaned past them, they crossed the street toward the Stock Exchange.

"Did she go to the sheriff?" O. T. asked.

"The sheriff said the property was never properly deeded. He can't do anything," Fergus informed him.

"Didn't she file a patent deed on the place?" O. T. pressed.

"She bought the deed from Mr. Stimler. I guess he didn't file a claim, but she thought he had. Sometimes I do not understand white man's government."

"Partner, there are times I don't understand it either."

"It seems it is more important to play by the rules than to do what is right and fair," Fergus added.

"Old man, you keep talkin' like a politician, and you're liable to get elected."

"Can I get elected even if they don't let me vote?"

"I guess not," O. T. replied. "So where does it stand with your cousin? What happens next?"

"This man has filed a proper claim. It will take about thirty days to become legal. After that, there will be no way for her to retrieve her home or any of her things. She is waiting for my help."

"Look, Daddy! A stagecoach to Deadwood," Punky announced.

O. T. watched the Tonopah stage clatter north. "Deadwood? Where does a three-year-old learn about Deadwood?"

Punky nodded his head up and down. "Tommy-Blue's goin' to live in Deadwood."

"Well, not today, he isn't." O. T. turned back to the stoop-shouldered Paiute. "What do you aim to do for your cousin?"

"I told her I would talk to the Wall Walker—that you would know what to do."

"Me? If the sheriff can't do anything, what can I do?"

"You can pray."

Punky squinted his eyes shut and folded his hands.

"Not right at the moment, of course," Fergus added.

A woman came toward them with a grin on her smooth, round face. "Mr. Skinner and little Silas Paul, how are you?"

O. T. tipped his hat. "Very well. Thank you, Mrs. Oatman. And yourself?"

"I'm Punky," the toddler said.

"Oh, you know me. The doctors can never figure out what's wrong. Why, I had this pain in my tailbone just yesterday, and Dr. Ollensby said—he's the young one from Glendale, you know, has blond hair and needs a haircut. He said if I lost a little weight, my lower back wouldn't hurt. Can you believe the nerve of the man? Lose weight! Why, I weigh only a pound or two more than I did the day I married my first husband, Mr. Henley—rest his soul. They forget to teach doctors respect nowadays. I can remember when they always agreed with anything I suggested."

"Eh, yes . . . ma'am," O. T. mumbled.

"I'm heading down to the cafe. I understand you have a very innovative advertising attraction."

"Advertising attraction?"

"I heard that the new proprietor of the Esmeralda Hotel, Mr. Kholler—you know, he's the tall man with the dark brown hair who tries to grow it long so that he can comb it over his bald spot. I heard he said he was goin' to park a locomotive in his lobby just to see if he could get as many customers as the Newcomers' Cafe. Isn't that a bear's den of an idea?"

"Eh . . ."

"Well, I really must go on. So nice to talk to you and Silas Paul." She strutted on down the boardwalk.

"That is a large woman," Fergus commented.

"She certainly likes to talk," O. T. put in.

"I'm medium," Punky insisted.

"What were we talkin' about?" O. T. said.

"Large women."

"Before that."

"My cousin."

O. T. started to stroll on down the sidewalk. "Have you gone by to talk to this guy in your cousin's house?"

"He stuck a gun out the door and threatened to shoot me before I entered the yard."

"What's he look like?"

"How would I know? He just hurled a few obscenities from behind a screen door, and I decided to come see you."

O. T. studied a group of men on the sidewalk who were staring into a large glass window of the hotel. "That's not a happy situation."

"He is not a very happy man. Why does he want a house that does not make him happy? It made my cousin happy."

"Maybe we'll ask him," O. T. suggested.

Fergus pointed to the hotel door. "Not until after we eat. I would hate to get shot and die on an empty stomach."

The lobby of the Colorado Hotel was packed with men peering into the dining room. O. T. turned to the first one who looked faintly familiar. "What's the commotion in there?"

"Ain't no commotion yet," the broad-shouldered man replied. "The Wilkins brothers are sittin' on one side of the big table, and Lucky Jack Gately and them is on the other. We was waitin' to see if they're goin' to kill each other."

"No one else is eatin' in the hotel?" Skinner probed.

"Are you kiddin'? I figure lead will fly any minute now."

O. T. strolled toward the dining room carrying the toddler, Fergus at his heels. A waiter in a starched white shirt met him at the wide archway.

"Mr. Skinner, what am I goin' to do? I've got the Wilkins-Gately feud in my dining room. None of my customers will come in."

A deep voice shouted from inside the dining room, "My Punky!"

A tall, thin, blond-headed man held his arms out. O. T. set the toddler down on the polished hardwood floor, and Punky ran into the room shouting, "Lucky-Lucky-Lucky-Lucky!"

O. T. and Fergus strolled over to the table. "Lucky Jack, Wasco, Charlie Fred . . . I thought you were all still in San Francisco!"

Lucky Jack plucked up the barefooted boy, straddled him over his knee, and began to bounce. "Just got in, O. T. Tell Dola Mae we'll be there for supper."

O. T. glanced at the other side of the table. "I haven't seen all three Wilkins brothers in town for weeks."

"We've got important business," Ace reported.

"Skinner, you got any idea in the world why everyone in town is hangin' out at the door peekin' in and not comin' in to eat?" Charlie Fred asked. "I'm startin' to think that they're all jealous of my permanent tan."

"They think you're goin' to start shootin' each other."

"The Wilkins-Gately feud ended over a year ago between your tent and the privy," Trey Wilkins declared. "You're goin' to join us for lunch, ain't ya?"

Fergus pulled up a chair and sat down at one end of the table. "If you insist." He picked up a fork and knife and stared at an empty place setting. O. T. proceeded to the other end of the table. Punky remained in Lucky Jack's lap. The moment O. T. Skinner sat down, the crowd surged into the dining room. Soon each table was filled.

Within minutes big plates of steaming beef chops were set on both ends of the massive oak table. Boiled potatoes, gravy, sweet potatoes, corn, coffee, and little cakes shaped like the state of Nevada completed the menu. For several minutes the main focus of attention was eating, except for Punky who made the rounds of everybody's laps.

O. T. sat back and sipped his coffee from a china cup with red roses. "Boys, if you don't mind me askin', I'm as curious as the next guy why Lucky Jack and Ace Wilkins are lunchin' in the Colorado Hotel together. Last I knew, Lucky Jack, you boys sold that big mine lease and were retirin' to San Francisco. Ace, you and your brothers told me just two weeks ago you were selling out to Wingfield and Nixon and movin' to Denver."

"We did," Ace reported. "Made more money than we can spend."

"Shoot, O. T., we had to hire accountants just to count it and tell us how to spend it," Deuce added.

"It feels kind of illegal," Wasco piped up from the other side of the table. "I keep thinkin' a U.S. marshal will show up at the door and make me give it all back."

"You're right. It was too easy," Trey said. He stared out the window. "Too easy," he mumbled.

"The challenge is gone, O. T.," Charlie Fred said. "I'm thirty-eight years old, and I don't have to work another day in my life. It ain't what I thought it would be."

"Rich food don't taste so good if you have it all the time," Trey added.

"And the only women that get close to ya are the ones tryin' to steal your fortune," Lucky Jack said with a frown.

"And you cain't trust nobody," Ace complained, "unless it's some other rich fool, like Gately and them."

O. T. glanced at Lucky Jack. "You didn't like city livin'?"

Gately shook his head. "It was nice for a few weeks. We ate at ever' fancy spot in San Francisco. We rode down there and looked at John Muir's Yosemite Park and swam in the Pacific Ocean."

Wasco shivered. "It's too salty and cold. When I got out of there, you couldn't tell me from Charlie Fred."

"I'm tired of watchin' them race track ponies and little men dressed in silks," Charlie Fred added.

"I ain't a farmer," Wasco said.

"Or a rancher," Lucky Jack admitted.

Charlie Fred shook his head. "Or a businessman."

"Or even a mine owner anymore," Lucky Jack added. "O. T., a man's got to stay where every day is a challenge, where the elements summon courage and skill and bring a tad of danger. That's all we've ever known."

O. T. set down his coffee cup and lifted Punky to his lap. "Are you boys sayin' that after a few months of easy livin' you're bored?"

"Bored is too good a word. I'd rather be dead as to live the rest of my life in some gingerbread house on Nob Hill with a British-accented butler answerin' my door," Gately griped.

"Amen to that!" Ace boomed.

"So what's the remedy, boys? You goin' to give your fortunes to an orphanage and go back to gunslingin'?" Skinner queried.

Gately roared with laughter. "We're bored, O. T., but we ain't dumb. We'll bank our money and let the interest pay our bills. But we're selling them houses in San Francisco. We don't need to own a house."

"We never bought places in Denver," Ace remarked.

"The second week we rented an entire floor of the Premble Hotel in Denver. They was havin' a society doin', and three ol' biddies from the committee came to invite us to a fund-raisin' tea," Deuce said.

"A tea?" O. T. grinned.

"That's exactly what I said, O. T.," Trey murmured, rolling his brown eyes to the ceiling.

"We looked at each other and said, 'What in tarnation are we doin' here?'" Ace continued. "Checked out of Denver that afternoon. I wired Lucky Jack from the train station in Colorado Springs."

"A telegram?" O. T. asked.

"All it said was," Lucky Jack reported, "'Sierra Madre gold. You in or not? Meet us in Goldfield next Friday. Ace.'"

O. T. buttered half a biscuit and handed it to Punky. "So you're going after the Mexican gold?" he questioned.

Ace Wilkins nodded. "Yep."

"I hear it's dangerous." Skinner retrieved the buttered biscuit from the floor and handed it back to Punky. "Those mountains are full of bandits."

"Not to mention a revolution brewin'," Ace said.

Lucky Jack stared out the window. "I reckon a man could get himself killed."

"It beats chokin' to death on that blasted caviar," Charlie Fred blurted out.

"Well, boys, I ain't never been rich, and I ain't never been bored." O. T. took the linen napkin and tried to wipe the butter off Punky's forehead. "And I didn't know there was a connection between the two."

"I was bored once," Fergus blurted out.

All seven men stared at the white-haired old Paiute, still wearing his black felt hat.

"It was the September the Truckee River froze. We had enough beef jerked and fish pounded for the entire winter. We pitched a lodge at Pine Meadow near the cottonwood grove. I had seventeen horses and a camel—"

"Wait, wait, wait . . . did you say camel?" Ace probed.

The old Indian glared at Wilkins. "I trust I will not have to repeat the story of Hi-Jolly's camels."

"Go on. You have seventeen horses and a camel," Lucky Jack encouraged.

"And nothing to do." Fergus slowly rubbed the bridge of his large, crooked nose. "I told my wife—"

"Fergus, you were married?" Charlie Fred pressed.

"I have outlived three wives."

"So what did you tell your wife?" Trey Wilkins asked.

"It was the only day in my life I told her I was bored," Fergus explained.

"And what did she say?" Wasco asked.

"She said, 'Don't worry, it won't last, and, oh, by the way, my mother is coming to stay for the winter.'"

"Your mother-in-law showed up?" O. T. repeated.

"Yes, and my wife's two shiftless brothers and a niece and two nephews. And six hungry dogs."

"And you never had another boring day since?" Ace remarked.

"None that I would dare tell my wife about," Fergus grunted. "Now if you are going to just talk, you can pass the chops down here."

"Anyway," Ace broke back in, "we're all headed down to look for the Mexican gold."

"As soon as we get a lawyer to draft up some partnership papers," Gately said. He surveyed the Wilkins brothers, then stared at Charlie Fred and Wasco, and finally nodded toward Skinner. "Are you all thinkin' what I'm thinkin'?"

"Jist 'cause we can afford a lawyer don't mean we need to pay one," Deuce suggested.

Ace tapped his fork on the table. "If you three try to cheat us, we'll chase you down and shoot you dead."

"And, of course, if the situation was reversed, we'd do the same," Charlie Fred replied.

"So why in the world do we need a fancy-talkin' lawyer with a big retainer fee. All we need is one reliable witness," Deuce declared.

All six men stared at O. T.

"What are you sayin'?" O. T. queried.

"We're formin' a six-way partnership. We each put up a similar amount of money and labor, and we split the profit six ways. And you're the witness," Ace announced.

"Why me?"

"'Cause we all trust you. Probably ain't another man in North America that all six of us agree on," Charlie Fred declared.

"I say we split the cost six ways and split the profits seven ways," Ace suggested.

"Now that's a capital idea, Mr. Wilkins," Lucky Jack concurred.

"Skinner gets a seventh. It's his witness fee," Trey said.

"No sir, boys, you know me better than that. I don't want what I don't earn," O. T. insisted.

"Skinner, you did earn it. Your very reputation makes you the only man we can trust. We're payin' you to watch us and see that we don't cheat one another. It might be a complicated task," Lucky Jack said.

"Besides, O. T., one-seventh of nothin' is still nothin'. There is no guarantee that we will find one ounce of gold," Charlie Fred cautioned.

"And no guarantee that we'll even live through the snakes, heat, scorpions, and banditos," Trey Wilkins added.

O. T. wiped a smear of butter off the end of Punky's nose. "It sounds dangerous, boys."

"Yep, it does, don't it?" Wasco's eyes danced as he spoke.

"But it won't be borin', O. T." Ace said.

"I reckon not. What do you want me to do?"

"Just witness this," Ace explained. He stood and stretched out his hand to Lucky Jack Gately.

The entire restaurant seemed to hold its breath.

With a dimpled smile and blond hair flopping down on his forehead, tall, slender Gately glanced at Charlie Fred and Wasco and nodded. As he slowly scooted his chair back and stood, some patrons scurried out of the restaurant. Others dropped down behind their tables.

Deuce, Trey, and then Charlie Fred and Wasco all stood to face each other.

O. T., Punky, and Fergus, who was examining a Nevada-shaped cake as if he were the only one in the room, remained seated. "You folks might want to wait and watch this," Skinner called out to the others in the dining room. "It will be something you can tell your grandkids about."

"I want to stay alive and see my grandkids," one short, bald man bantered.

"Then watch this. It's historic," O. T. said.

Lucky Jack reached across the table and grabbed Ace's hand. The whole restaurant burst into applause.

"What's goin' on, Wall Walker?" the bald man called out as he returned to his table.

"You're seein' the beginnin' of a six-way partnership," he announced.

"They ain't goin' to rob a bank, are they?" a toothless old man probed.

"It's not a six-way partnership," Ace called out. "It's a seven-way partnership."

"O. T. Skinner is the seventh partner," Lucky Jack announced to everyone.

"It's a cinch then you ain't goin' to be robbin' banks," the bald-headed man replied.

O. T. looked up at the standing men. "I really don't deserve a seventh."

"O. T., we probably don't deserve anything we get either. We surely don't deserve the profits from the Corrie Lou Lease, and I know for a fact those bushwhackin' Wilkins brothers don't deserve the profits from the Thomas Motor Mine," Lucky Jack rambled on.

"What are you insinuatin'?" Deuce challenged.

"I'm just makin' a point that Skinner don't need to feel like he

74 ♦ STEPHEN BLY

deserves a seventh of the Mexican mine 'cause none of us this side of Hades get what we deserve," Gately continued.

"Besides he just saved us $500 in lawyer's fees," Trey declared.

O. T. shook his head. "Boys, I couldn't in good conscience take what I didn't earn."

"Skinner, take your seventh and use it to build a church for this town. You could use if for that, couldn't you?" Ace challenged.

O. T. rubbed his mustache with his fingertips. "Yes sir, I reckon I could."

"Then that settles it," Ace declared.

"We'll call it the Oro De Siete Mine," Lucky Jack announced.

"Gold of Seven?" Deuce questioned.

"That's right."

"We haven't found an ounce yet," Charlie Fred cautioned.

"Shoot, we haven't even bought the mules yet," Trey reminded them.

"We'll take the train down to Douglas and then buy the mules and head south," Ace said.

"When do you plan on doin' all this?" O. T. asked.

Ace Wilkins stared at the men facing him. "I ain't got nothing to do the rest of the afternoon. We could head south today."

"It beats goin' to tea," Charlie Fred said. "I can't wait to get out of this suit and tie."

"Before I go anywhere, I'm goin' to sit down and finish my coffee," Deuce Wilkins declared.

He and the others plopped back down just as O. T. stood. Punky didn't bother opening his eyes. "It looks like I better get this young man home for his nap."

Fergus stood at the far end of the table. Cake frosting stuck to his lips and chin. "But first you will go with my cousin and visit the man in her house."

"Where is your cousin now?" O. T. asked.

"Upstairs in this hotel. She rented a room here," the Paiute replied.

"Well, go get her, and we'll trudge over and talk to this old boy."

Fergus wrapped three Nevada-shaped cakes in a linen napkin and shuffled out of the dining room.

"What's the old man talkin' about, Skinner?" Trey Wilkins asked.

"Looks like someone kicked his cousin out of her house here in Goldfield. Just took it by force and threatened to shoot her if she tried to get it back."

"Isn't that a matter for the sheriff?" Ace said.

"She's been tryin' ever' legal way for a year. Fergus said the previous owners didn't file papers on the sale at the courthouse like they promised, and the county considered it abandoned property. These new folks kicked out the cousin, then went and paid back taxes, and now they claim it's theirs. She would have paid the taxes, but no one told her they were due."

"Don't seem fair, does it?" Charlie Fred commented.

"Nope." O. T. took one last sip of tepid coffee and set the cup down with a clatter in his saucer. "I don't guess Paiutes rate too high in legal matters."

"And you're goin' to go talk to the guy?" Gately pressed.

O. T. shifted Punky to his other arm. "Fergus asked me to."

"He chased her off at gunpoint, and you're goin' in there unarmed?" Ace questioned.

"I don't intend to fight him. Just want to remind him to do the proper and decent thing."

"Skinner, I always said you were the bravest or dumbest man I ever met," Ace proclaimed.

"Boys, I'm well aware of the sinfulness of mankind. I jist happen to think folks ought to always have an opportunity to do better. That's all I want—to give him an opportunity to do right," O. T. asserted.

"Well, we'll give Dola Mae your share of the Oro de Siete," Wasco replied.

Punky blinked his eyes open and rubbed his nose with a clenched fist.

"Come on, boys. The worst thing that will happen is that he chases me off. I owe it to Fergus."

"Why's that, Skinner?" Deuce challenged. "Why do you owe anything to that ol' moochin' Paiute?"

"Fergus is my friend!" Punky blurted out.

Lucky Jack stared at the three-year-old and then looked at O. T.

"Couldn't have said it better myself," O. T. murmured.

"Can't argue with the young man's logic. But I don't figure you'll end prejudice in one afternoon," Lucky Jack said.

"If anyone can, it's Skinner," Ace asserted.

"I'd stand up for my friends, but I doubt if I could do it for some Paiutes I didn't even know," Charlie Fred declared.

Fergus shuffled back into the room. A tall young woman with black hair down to her waist and a black lace shawl sauntered behind him.

"This is my friend, the Wall Walker!" Fergus said.

The woman let the lace shawl drop back to her shoulders. Her vibrant brown eyes and soft, easy smile caught O. T. by surprise.

"And this is my cousin, Miss Gerta Von Wagner," Fergus announced.

Behind him O. T. heard six chairs squeak across the floor as the men stood in unison. Once again the restaurant grew quiet.

"Miss Gerta, pleased to meet you," O. T. called out.

"And I, you, Mr. Skinner. You look a bit surprised." Her smile revealed straight white teeth. "You were expecting an old, barefoot, fat woman with a tattered blanket and tangled hair?"

"No, ma'am . . . eh, no," O. T. stammered. "I don't rightly know what I was expectin'."

"But I wasn't it?" she pressed.

"No, ma'am."

The woman laughed and then glanced around. "Well, Mr. Skinner, my former employer insisted that I learn the dress, manner, and vocabulary of an Eastern lady. I am proud of my Paiute heritage, and I am very grateful to her as well."

"Ma'am, you've done a very good job," O. T. said.

"And these men." She pointed to the others. "Do they speak, or are they just your silent bodyguards?"

All six yanked their hats off their heads.

By the time O. T. finished the introductions, Miss Gerta was surrounded by the six adventurers.

"Partner, your cousin is quite a charming lady," O. T. told Fergus.

The Paiute licked frosting off his gnarled fingers but didn't crack a smile. "Yes, and she has my good looks as well."

O. T. surveyed the room and noticed that every man's eyes were on the young Indian woman. "But she is considerably younger than you," he declared.

Fergus pulled a slightly mashed Nevada cake from his coat pocket and took a bite. "I believe I had a very naughty uncle," he mumbled through the crumbs and icing.

The deep laughter of Lucky Jack Gately caused O. T. to look back. Gerta Von Wagner now had one hand resting on Lucky Jack's arm and the other on Deuce Wilkins's sleeve. "Fergus, is your cousin married?" O. T. asked.

The old man held the Nevada cake out for Punky to take a bite. "Why do you ask?"

"I just wanted to know if I should throw cold water on six prancin' stallions," O. T. replied.

Punky strained to lick the frosting off his chin.

Fergus reached over to wipe the boy's chin clean and held the finger out for Punky to lick. "I don't know if she is married or not," the Paiute said.

"What do you mean, you don't know?"

"I've never asked her, and she's never told me."

"Never told you? You have to know whether a relative is married or not."

"I do not understand why this is so important." Fergus gave Punky another bite of cake. "Do you have cousins?"

"Yes, of course," O. T. replied.

"How many?"

"About fifteen, last time I heard," O. T. declared.

"You don't even know for sure how many cousins you have?"

O. T. scratched the back of his neck and peered around the room as if looking for someone. "I've been on the road this year and haven't gotten much mail."

"Are all your cousins married?"

"Well—I—Dola will know. I let her remember all of that."

"Then it is possible you have cousins you don't know about and some that are married without your knowledge?"

"Okay. I get the point," Skinner replied. "Maybe she's married, maybe she isn't."

Fergus nodded. "I was thinking the same thing myself."

"Well, whenever they turn loose of her, we'll go see those folks in her house. Should we rescue her?"

"I know my cousin, and I can assure you, Wall Walker, they will be the ones in need of rescue."

The small wood-framed house stood out because it was the only one on Fourth Street painted white. In fact, it was the only one painted at all. A picket fence surrounded the dirt yard. A long-eared mule was tethered in the yard and had left several days' droppings all over, attracting flies and creating a stench.

"This is horrible!" Gerta moaned. "He has destroyed my house!"

"Do you think the mule will run away if the picket pin got pulled?" Fergus asked.

"I don't think the man inside would appreciate that," O. T. cautioned.

"That's exactly what I was thinkin'." Fergus reached down and pulled the wood stake out of the packed desert dirt and tossed it at the mule's feet.

The animal remained still, his eyes closed.

"So much for chasin' off the mule," O. T. said.

"He must be hard of smelling," Fergus murmured.

"Watch your step, Miss Von Wagner," O. T. cautioned.

"This is horrid!" she seethed.

"Perhaps you do not want this house back after all?" Fergus questioned.

"It's my house. I bought it honestly. I have all my belongings in there, including several volumes of research."

"What kind of research?" O. T. asked.

"I want to write a book about Sara Winnemucca," she declared.

He jiggled the toddler in his arm. "Winnemucca is a family name?"

"Yes, of course," she replied.

"I heard about the town. I always surmised it was just someone's joke."

"Punky's sleepy," the toddler complained.

"Hang on, darlin', we'll be home shortly," O. T. said.

"Would you like me to hold him?" she offered.

"Thank you, ma'am. Little darlin', visit with Gerta."

"She's like Lupe!" Punky declared.

"She has beautiful brown skin like Lupe."

Gerta held the pudgy toddler on her hip.

"I'm Punky, and my mama's purdy."

Gerta jiggled the boy. "With a purdy mama and a handsome daddy, no wonder you're so cute."

O. T. knocked at the door. He glanced back at Gerta, who turned her eyes away. *Ma'am, I've been called a lot of names since I came to*

Goldfield, but no one has called me handsome. You're kind to an old man. Of course, I'm not that old.

"Get off my porch!" a deep voice yelled.

"I need to talk to you," O. T. called out.

"Who are you?"

"O. T. Skinner."

"You the Wall Walker?"

"Yes, I suppose I am."

"Get them Indians off my porch, and I'll talk to you," the unseen man declared.

Gerta and Fergus turned to exit.

"No," O. T. called out. "That's what I want to talk to you about."

"This house belongs to me! I'm warnin' you. Get them off my land, or I'll . . ."

"You'll what?" O. T. said.

The half-round, half-octagon barrel of a '94 Winchester rifle burst through the screen door. O. T. pushed Gerta and Punky to the right and followed her. Fergus fled to the left. The .30 caliber rifle discharged into the dirt of the yard about six feet from the dozing mule. The animal bolted straight through the picket fence and down the street.

A big man waddled out, filling the entire door frame. His stomach lapped down over his beltless trousers. "Hey, that's my mule you chased off!" he screamed.

"You chased him off by firin' the gun," O. T. declared.

"That's my special-order Winchester '94," Gerta asserted.

The gun looked small in the big man's massive hands. "I don't see your name on it."

"Do you know the serial number?" she challenged.

"I don't give a buffalo chip what the serial number is. It's mine."

"The number is 198742."

"Well, I ain't givin' it back," the man insisted.

"Mister," O. T. asserted, "you've got one chance to do the right thing."

"What do you mean?" he growled.

O. T. flinched when the man checked the lever on the rifle. "I mean that this is a test of your character. You have an opportunity to do the right thing. Give Miss Von Wagner her gun and her house and walk away havin' passed at least one test in your life."

"You're crazier than these Indians, Skinner, if you think I'm goin' to walk away from this. I don't care who you are. You have no idea who you're dealin' with. I'm a famous man. Folks don't bluff me. The next shot will be between your eyes."

A deep voice called out behind them, "Mister, the next shot won't come from your gun."

O. T. glanced over his shoulder. Six men in suits and ties stood out at the gate.

"And who the blazes are you? Undertakers?" the big man hollered.

"I'd introduce you," O. T. said, "but I don't even know your name."

"Jeremiah Jolly," the man blustered.

O. T. bit his lip. *Lord, is this as humorous to You as it is to me?* "Mr. Jolly, the tall, blond-headed man with the .45 Colt in his hand is Lucky Jack Gately. Next to him is Wasco, and the bearded man holdin' the double-barreled shotgun is Charlie Fred LaPorte. Over there are Ace, Deuce, and Trey Wilkins, better known just as the Wilkins brothers. Deuce is the one holdin' revolvers in both hands."

Jeremiah Jolly's face went white. The rifle dropped to the porch. "I—I didn't . . . I ain't goin' against the likes of you."

"Pick up the gun and hand it to Miss Gerta," Ace Wilkins called out.

Jolly froze in place.

Gately pointed the revolver at the big man. "Now!"

"I'm a dead man, Skinner. . . . Don't let 'em kill me," he pleaded.

"Pick up the gun and hand it to her," O. T. insisted.

Without takin' his eyes off Lucky Jack's revolver, Jolly bent low, scooped the gun up by the receiver, and shoved it toward Gerta Von Wagner.

She took it and immediately pointed it at him.

"And the house," Deuce Wilkins added. "Give her back her house."

"But—but I paid back taxes. . . . It's mine now."

"I heard you chased her off at gunpoint several times. Is that true?" Wasco pressed.

"What difference does that make? She's an Indian."

"It's her house," Trey Wilkins insisted.

"What about my $196.40 in taxes?"

"Consider it your rent for the last year," O. T. said. "Now get your things and get out of here."

"Eh . . . I, eh, don't have any things. The house came furnished."

"Then go find your mule and get on down the road," Lucky Jack shouted.

"You can't chase me off like this!"

"We just did," Ace announced.

Jeremiah Jolly stomped down the sidewalk toward the gate.

"Those are my brother's boots you are wearing," Gerta called out. "You stole them out of my closet!"

"You ain't gettin' my boots!" He stooped down and pulled a knife from his right boot and waved it at the porch. "I'll be back, squaw lady. . . . I'll be back in the middle of the night, and there won't be any bodyguards in the yard. You'll wish to high heaven you never done this to me."

When he turned back to the gate, Lucky Jack Gately's pistol cracked the man's wrist. The knife fell to the ground. At the same time Ace Wilkins's cocked .45 was shoved into the man's round mouth.

"Mister," Gately growled, "you better pray with all your might that Miss Von Wagner lives to an old age. Because if she dies young, the six of us will track you down anyplace on the face of the globe. You understand? If this woman has a cut, a bruise, or a broken bone ever, you're a dead man!"

Sweat rolled down the man's face as Ace slowly withdrew his revolver.

"But—but—but she's a squaw!" the man blustered.

"What does that have to do with it?" Deuce growled.

O. T. walked back out to the man. "Mr. Jolly, pull off the boots, or you're goin' to have a lot more than a bruised wrist."

"I never figured you'd side with the likes of them gunslingers, Wall Walker."

"You figured wrong."

"I'll be lookin' for you too, Wall Walker."

"I'm not hard to find. You might want to check the Mojave Emporium. They're havin' a sale on boots."

"This ain't no joke, Skinner."

"Neither is a 30 percent discount," O. T. called out.

Jeremiah Jolly waddled with a limp as the hot desert street burned the soles of his bare feet.

"I wonder if he is related to Hi-Jolly?" Fergus pondered. "Perhaps I could sell him a camel."

"Do you have a camel?" Trey asked.

Fergus studied the gunman's eyes. "What does that have to do with anything? I did not say I had a camel. Merely that I would sell him one."

Gerta Von Wagner studied her fouled yard and the broken screen. "I trust this was worth all the effort. I hardly know where to begin."

"Begin by filing the correct papers," O. T. encouraged.

"You need a little help straightenin' up, Miss Gerta?" Wasco asked.

Her waist-length black hair swung around as she studied all six men, guns still drawn. "I could really use the help, but I don't want to take you away from something important."

"We don't have to go anywhere for a day or two," Lucky Jack called out. He turned to the Wilkins brothers. "You three can go on ahead and buy us a pack string in Douglas. We'll catch up with you."

"Oh no, you don't," Ace protested. "We're partners now. Skinner can testify to that."

"So we'll all stay and help fix up the place," Deuce insisted.

"Not me," Fergus announced. "I am not looking to impress a woman, like some I know."

O. T. took the toddler from Gerta. "I'd better put Punky down for a nap. Then I have to go back to work. Unlike these rich ex-mine owners, I work for a livin'."

"I will go with you," Fergus said.

"Do you need a nap too?" Gerta teased.

"Not until I get something to eat. All of this excitement has made me hungry. And Mrs. Skinner is a very fine cook."

"Eat?" Lucky Jack hooted. "Ol' man, you just got up from the dinner table."

The old Paiute slowly shook his head. "I have never understood white man's logic in that matter."

FOUR

"I ain't never seen a peach tree with peach-colored leaves!"

Dola Skinner opened her eyes and tried to focus on the spokesman. It was as if she were standing back looking at herself. It was hot, the sun mostly straight above. The porch was in the shade, but the air hung heavy, still.

Have I been asleep? I didn't know I was that tired. What time is it?

"Mr. Goodwin, please forgive me. I must have nodded off."

"That's all right, Mrs. Skinner." He pushed his glasses up on his nose and stooped down to inspect the tree closely. "I doze off like that myself from time to time."

Yes, but you're a retired seventy-six-year-old former schoolteacher, Isaiah Goodwin. She folded her arms across her chest but remained in the same position as when she was asleep. "What were you saying about my peach tree?"

"The leaves are too yellow." He stood up, but much of the stoop remained in his shoulders. "Too orange. They ought to be green still."

Dola pulled a small cotton handkerchief from her sleeve and patted the perspiration on her forehead and neck. "I know, Mr. Goodwin. I believe it must be the desert climate. Perhaps it's the dry alkali winds or the elevation. We are over 5,000 feet here. I'm not sure how peach trees do in a location like this."

"It's a lack of nitrates—that's what it is." Goodwin walked his finger through his neatly trimmed beard as if chasing a tick.

Dola studied the four-foot tree. "Nitrates? What are they?"

The man rocked back on the heels of highly polished but old black boots. "All fruit trees need nitrates. I read that in the *California Farmer* magazine."

She unfastened one of her combs, pulled back her hair, and reset the comb. "Does it help green up a tree?"

"That article said that peach trees in Dinuba, California, were helped by nitrates."

"Dinuba? The article was about Dinuba?"

"Yes, ma'am. You ever been there?"

"No, but Orion's brother lives there. We're going to move there one of these days."

"Does he have peaches?"

"No, Pegasus, my brother-in-law, grows grapes. At least, at the last report."

"Don't know anything about grapes. Maybe they need nitrates too."

Dola started to lean forward, but a stiffness in her back stopped her. "Where can I get some of those nitrates, Mr. Goodwin?"

His steel-gray eyes danced like a schoolteacher's on the first day of school. "Two sources."

"Oh?"

He held up a gnarled finger. "Fresh steer manure."

Dola took a deep breath and let it out slowly. "Oh, dear, I don't believe that would be too good by a restaurant door, would it? What's the other source?"

"I reckon you could buy them from the drugstore."

"Nitrates, you say?"

"Kind of expensive that way. A person don't want to buy for a whole orchard, but I reckon a big bottle of salt nitrates would go a long way on a little seedling like this."

"Thank you, Mr. Goodwin. I'll look into it."

Goodwin leaned forward. "And while you are at the drugstore, pick something up for yourself, Mrs. Skinner. You are surely looking peaked."

The old man tipped his hat and shuffled on down the boardwalk. He carefully stepped down into the street, holding tightly to the hitching post.

He can barely cross the street, and he thinks I look peaked? I'm just tired, Lord. A good night's sleep, and I'll feel better. I'm just run down. Maybe I'm not cut out for the restaurant business. I worry too much about everything. I worry about whether the meat's overcooked or not cooked enough. I worry about men going hungry. About potatoes scalding. About tough biscuits, like that last hurry-up batch this morning. I worry about whether they can afford a seventy-five-cent breakfast. I worry about the hired girls working so hard at such a young age. Forgive me, Lord.

She brushed down her skirt and noticed a fine frosting of yellowish alkali dust settling back on it immediately.

I'm not trusting You very much, am I?

"Are you awake now, Mama?"

The voice sounded more mature than Dola expected. She craned her neck but remained in the same position. Rita Ann's brown hair was combed out and cascaded across her shoulders. She held her shoulders back, her chin up. Dola stared for a minute.

Rita Ann's blue eyes panicked. "What's the matter, Mama? Did I say something wrong?"

"No, darlin'." Dola patted the bench beside her. "Seeing you standing there looking so mature—it startled me. I forget how you're growing up."

Rita Ann wiped the bench with her open hand and then carefully sat down. "Mature? Do I really look mature, Mama?"

Dola slipped her arm around her daughter's shoulders. "Every once in a while, young lady, I get a glimpse of how you're going to look ten years from now. I predict you will be a very beautiful woman."

Rita Ann leaned back against the bench. "Really, Mama? You aren't just saying that to get me to do something, are you?"

"Honey, you were cute the day you were born. You have been cute every day of your life." Dola's hand slid down her daughter's cheek. "But when you're a grown woman, you'll be more than cute. You'll be beautiful."

Rita Ann kissed her mother's finger. "Mama, I have a question. . . . You know . . . when you catch a glimpse of me at twenty-three, am I, eh, filled out like Haylee and Lupe?"

Dola's hand dropped to her lap as she looked down at her own flat chest. "Darlin', I'm afraid you'll probably look like your mama in that department. But it's your face that will charm everyone in the room. That's much more important."

"'Her face, like heaven, enticeth thee to view her countless glory.' You mean like that, Mama?"

Dola could feel the dimples in her own smile. "Mr. Shakespeare is more eloquent than I, but I suppose that's what I meant."

Corrie burst out the door, stomped passed them, and flopped down on the far side of her mother. Corrie's arms and legs, like her short-cropped, thick brown hair, flailed out in all directions. "I took a nap on the floor. It's hot today. It's always hot in Goldfield. Is it windy today? What are you doin' out here? I wish we could go out to a high mountain lake and go swimming. If we lived next to a lake, we could go swimming ever' day and never need a bath except when it's cold. Hey, where's Punky?"

Dola licked her fingers and tried smoothing the wild cowlicks in Corrie's hair. "Little brother went out to lunch at the hotel," she reported.

Corrie licked her own fingers, made a face, and then wiped her hands on her faded blue dress. "Punky went by himself?"

Lord, how in the world did I have two daughters so exactly the opposite of each other? "No, he took his father with him."

Corrie leapt to her feet and gazed down the street. "My daddy went to the hotel for lunch and didn't take me?"

"You were asleep, remember?" Dola tried to tug down Corrie's skirt, but she couldn't reach it. "You needed the rest, darlin'. How do you feel now?"

"But I never ate in a hotel before. Did you ever eat in a hotel, Rita Ann?"

"Mama cooks better than any hotel," Rita Ann said.

Corrie flopped back down by her mother. "I know, but I hear you get two forks at a hotel."

"Who told you that?"

"Colin Maddison, the third, with two *d*'s. He eats ever' meal at the hotel. He says his mother is the most beautiful woman in Nevada. She used to do trick riding with Buffalo Bill, and she knows kings and queens," Corrie blurted out.

"But she doesn't cook?" Dola inquired.

"When you're rich and pretty, you ain't suppose to cook. Rita Ann told me that."

"Well," Rita Ann sighed, "that's the way it seems in books."

"Anyway I do feel better, Mama," Corrie added. "I was really, really sleepy. Why do I get so sleepy in the middle of the day? Do you think something's wrong with me? Maybe I have growing pains. I ain't growin' very much, but my daddy said maybe I have growin' pains. When I get sleepy, my bones hurt. Do you know what I mean, Mama?"

Dola held her hand against her daughter's round cheek. "Yes, honey, I believe I do."

"You don't look so good, Mama," Corrie said, looking straight into her eyes.

Dola forced her lips to smile. "That's what everyone keeps telling me."

Rita Ann scooted to the front of the bench. "Corrie Lou, Mama's just tired. Some of us don't get to nap when the restaurant is busy."

Corrie lifted her little, round nose. "I was watchin' Punky," she snapped.

"And a fine job you did of that." Rita Ann raised her thin eyebrows.

Dola reached over and patted both their knees. "Girls! I am much too tired to listen to this."

"Here comes Tommy-Blue." Corrie skipped down the sidewalk toward her brother. "Did you find any color? Was there anyone to help you? Do you plan on filing a claim? You goin' to dig it yourself or lease it?" she called out.

"Nah. . . . The lead died. It played out right under the corner of the bank."

Dola thought about standing up.

But didn't.

"You were digging under the bank?" she asked him.

"Just the corner of it," Tommy-Blue explained.

She studied the dirt smeared down her son's cheek. "Didn't anyone complain?"

Tommy-Blue sat down on the boardwalk and started untying his lace-up shoes. "Only Colin Maddison, the third, with two *d*'s."

"What did he say?" Dola asked.

"He said, 'Get away from there, or I'll tell my daddy!' And then he said, 'Where's Corrie Lou?'"

"He asked about me?" Corrie pressed her palms against her cheeks.

"Yeah. Why did he do that? Do you owe him money or somethin'?"

"Ahhhh!" Corrie stuck out her tongue and rolled her eyes.

"If he could see you now," Dola said, "he would never ask about you again."

Corrie's eyes grew big. "Really?"

"Don't you dare, young lady."

"Mama, he's a pest," Corrie complained. "He thinks he's so smart and rich."

"He *is* smart and rich," Tommy-Blue declared. "Did you know his daddy bought him a ranch up on the U.P. line?"

"He's just ten," Dola declared.

"Yes, but he has his own ranch near Winnemucca and Battle Mountain City, or somewhere up there," Tommy-Blue stated.

"How do you know?" Dola watched her son try to stick his tongue out and touch his nose. "Don't do that," she scolded.

Tommy-Blue sucked his tongue back in. "I know he has a ranch 'cause he showed me the patent deed with his name on it."

"He actually carries around the papers?" Dola quizzed. "A ten-year-old boy? That seems a little strange."

Tommy-Blue shrugged. "Not for Goldfield."

"That's true," Dola concurred.

"'Thou gaudy gold, hard food for Midas, I will none of thee,'" Rita recited.

Tommy-Blue rocked back on his heels. "Is it time to eat lunch?"

Dola thought about how much she wanted to just sit there on the bench in the August-hot Nevada sun. For a moment she hesitated, hoping the question would fade away. *Lord, this isn't good. Now I'm resenting fixing meals for my own children. What has happened to me?*

"Mama, can we have bacon and tomato sandwiches?" Rita Ann suggested. "I'll fix them."

"There's a little bacon left from breakfast," Dola offered. "It's under the towel in the white basket."

Rita Ann stood up. "And I can slice some of that sourdough bread. And we have plenty of tomatoes."

"Yes, but don't slice the tomatoes until you are all sitting down at a table. You know how they wither and curl in this alkali breeze."

Corrie stood up. "Can we have a pickle, Mama?"

"You can have half a pickle. They are very big. If your father comes home, Corrie Lou, you take Punky off his hands."

"Aren't you goin' to be here, Mama?" Tommy-Blue asked.

Dola smoothed her skirt down. "I think I'll go down to the drug-store."

"What for? Are you goin' to have one of them sody waters? I wish I could have a root beer. Colin Maddison, the third, says Miner's Fruit Nectar is better than root beer, but he's wrong and just won't admit it."

"No, I'm not going to have a soda water. I just want to buy some nitrates."

"What are those?" Tommy-blue asked. "Will they separate gold from mercury? I wish I had me some mercury."

"Nitrates are a mineral supplement for the peach tree. I under-stand that it will green up these sickly leaves."

"Can I go with you, Mama?" Tommy-Blue pressed. "Maybe they have mercury."

"You're hungry, remember?" Dola said.

"Oh . . . yeah."

Corrie crossed her arms and curled her lip. "I'm goin' to wait right here for my daddy."

"No, you're goin' to go help your sister," Dola instructed. "Daddy will find you when he comes home."

Corrie stomped over to Rita Ann.

Dola sat up on the bench and felt a pain in her tailbone. She started to rock to her feet, and the pain locked in her lower back. She felt as if a hot knife blade had been rammed into her.

"Oh, dear," she cried out.

Tommy-Blue scampered in front of her. "What's the matter, Mama?"

Dola bit her lip and reached out her arm. "Lend me a hand, honey, and pull me up. My back seems to have cramped up or some-thing."

Tommy's dirty hand grabbed hers, and he yanked straight back, hard.

Dola cried out. "Oh, dear Lord . . . oh . . ."

Tommy-Blue loosed his grip and tumbled backward on the raised wooden sidewalk.

Dola could feel tears trickle down her cheeks. She tried to hold every muscle in her body still. Everything ached.

Rita Ann and Corrie huddled around her.

"Mama, what's wrong?" Rita Ann quizzed.

Corrie patted her hand. "It's all right, Mama. . . . It's all right. Don't cry."

"I'm sorry, Mama!" Tommy-Blue sobbed from the porch. "I didn't mean to hurt you—honest!"

"It's okay, honey. You didn't do anything. Help your brother up, girls. Then all of you give me a hand . . . gently. I'm just a little stove-up—that's all."

"But you was cryin'," Tommy-Blue declared. "You are still cryin', Mama."

Dola wiped the tears off her face with her finger. "I think it's just dust in the air."

"That's what my daddy always says," Corrie announced.

Rita Ann took hold of Dola's left hand. Corrie held her right.

"Wait," Dola cautioned. "Let's do this all together . . . one, two, three . . . pull!"

The pain started in the small of her back, shot down both legs until her knees almost collapsed, and rolled right up her spine until her shoulder blades felt as if they were on fire.

Dola bit her lip.

She held her breath.

Tears rolled down her cheeks again.

"Mama?" Rita Ann's face was only inches from hers.

"Fix the children sandwiches," Dola grimaced in a hoarse whisper.

"But . . . but what about . . ."

"Please!" Dola begged.

Thirteen-year-old Rita Ann spun on her heels and waved to

her brother and sister. "Come along. I'm fixing bacon and tomato sandwiches!"

"But . . . but what about Mama?" Corrie protested.

Rita Ann held her head high. "She's going to the drugstore, remember?"

"Like that?" Tommy-Blue gasped.

Dola fought back the pain and tears and stood up straight. "I'm all right," she murmured. "You go on with Rita Ann."

"Have a good time, Mother dear," Rita Ann said. "I'll take care of Punky when Daddy brings him home." She leaned over and kissed Dola's cheek. "Are you really okay?" she whispered.

"Thanks, darlin'. I'll walk off this cramp. It will be all right."

"Don't worry, I'll take care of things here."

"I know you will, honey. I know you will."

Dola didn't move until the children had scampered inside.

Now, Lord . . . I don't need this. I don't know what happened to my back, but I know the Lord "gave, and the Lord hath taken away," and I very much need You to take this away.

She took one step toward the peach tree, braced for the pain, and held on to the back of the bench.

The pain was considerably less than when she had stood up.

But it was still there.

She took a deep breath.

She took another couple of steps and could feel the tears drying on her cheeks.

This is absurd. I must look a fright. I can't go anywhere like this. Why, I don't have my hat or my purse or my parasol. What was I thinking?

She turned back toward the restaurant and shuffled in past the front end of the Thomas car and toward the stairs.

I'll wash my face, put on a fresh blouse, comb my hair, get my things, and then . . .

Dola stopped at the base of the light green stairs and looked straight up to the landing at the top.

It's like climbing a mountain. How will I do it? I go up these stairs a dozen times a day, and now I can't force myself to take one step.

Lord, something happened to my back. Something bad.

I'm scared. Really scared.

I need my Orion. Right now.

"Mama, are you home already?"

She turned to see Tommy-Blue at the doorway to the kitchen.

"I forgot my purse, darlin'," she explained.

"Can I have two sandwiches?" he asked.

"Certainly."

He stuck his head back in the kitchen. "Mama said I can have two sandwiches!"

Rita Ann appeared in the doorway behind her brother. "Mama, didn't you go to the drugstore?"

"She forgot her pocketbook," Tommy-Blue reported.

"Oh," Rita Ann said, "Tommy-Blue, do you still have that assay report from Mr. Tolavitch on your diggings behind the Northern Saloon?"

His blue eyes lit up. "Yep. It's upstairs."

"Well, go get it so you can tell me about it when we eat," Rita Ann instructed. "I want to know all about it."

Tommy-Blue's mouth dropped open. "Really? You never want to read those reports."

There was a tiny, smug grin across Rita Ann's narrow mouth. "I do today."

"You'll like that one!" He trotted toward his mother, who was still at the base of the stairs.

"Oh, by the way," Rita Ann called out, "perhaps Mother would like for you to fetch her pocketbook too."

Dola turned to Rita Ann and managed to mouth "thank you" to her daughter.

"That would be very gentlemanly of you, Tommy-Blue," Dola

commended him. "And bring my cream straw hat, my comb, and my parasol."

"Sure, Mama! Me and Rita Ann is going to study them assay reports."

"You have a very wonderful sister," Dola said.

Tommy-Blue stopped halfway up the stairs and turned back. "Which one?" he pondered.

"Why, both of them, of course!" Dola replied.

"Hurry up, Tommy-Blue," Rita Ann called, "before the tomatoes curl."

He rushed on up the stairs two at a time.

Dola walked from table to table, chair to chair, waiting for Tommy-Blue to return. She pretended to straighten chairs, but she was actually clutching them.

When her son returned, it took her several minutes to comb her hair and pin her hat. By the time she had returned to the sidewalk, she discovered that if she took small shuffling steps, she could move along with a minimum of pain. She slowed and stopped in front of every building as if window-shopping. After a couple of blocks she found she could pick up the pace and proceed without stopping.

Murphy's Drugstore was not her usual stop for drugstore items. Located down a side street, it was neighbored by saloons and gambling halls. But it was several blocks closer than the other drugstore. She caught a glimpse of a heavy-set woman on the far side of the store. Dola scooted to the opposite side.

Lord, it's not that I don't want to visit with Mrs. Oatman. It's just not a good time to try to smile and . . .

"Why, Dola Mae Skinner! I was just on my way to visit you!" the voice boomed across the aisle of stacked dry goods.

Dola turned. "Mrs. Oatman, how are you today?"

"Oh, darlin', you don't want to hear about my ailments! As I was telling your O. T. just a few minutes ago—"

"You were at the hotel?"

"No, I saw him, Silas Paul, and that old . . ."

"Was our good friend Fergus with him?"

"I suppose. Anyway I'm just on my way down to look at your auto car. It's quite the sensation. And I passed by the drugstore and decided to purchase something for my bunions. Have you ever tried Dr. Chinkker's Bag Balm for Feet?"

"No, I haven't." Dola studied the patent medicines on the shelf.

"Mrs. DelGratto simply swears by it. She says it loosens corns, shrinks gout, smooths out wrinkles in her face, and takes the pain out of stiff muscles. I say that if she uses it to smooth out wrinkles, she's not using nearly enough. Am I right? Of course I am, and I think . . ."

Mrs. Oatman stopped as she got close to Dola Mae. "My word, dear, you do look weak. Are you all right?"

"Yes, of course," Dola lied. "We just had a very busy morning at the restaurant."

Isabella Oatman leaned close and lowered her voice. "I ran a restaurant once," she whispered.

"You did? Where?"

"In Creede, Colorado. It was dreadful."

"Creede?"

"No, the work at the restaurant. I'm a good cook, you know . . . and couldn't keep my hands off my own food. I put on a lot of weight. Can you imagine? I was quite heavy back then. Not at all the svelte woman you now see."

Dola bit her lip. *Svelte? She's no taller than I am and weighs 200 pounds!* "Did you say it helps hurting muscles?"

"Oh, yes. Why, my brother Roly just swears by it. He's a faro dealer at the Mispah in Tonopah, and his hands and wrists would cramp up every evening. Since he's been using Dr. Chinkker's Bag Balm for Feet, he hasn't felt a bit of pain in his hands. Do you need some, dear?"

"Some of the girls at the cafe have been havin' a few aches and pains. Perhaps I'll pick some up for them," Dola explained.

"If you want to save money, get the twenty-pound tin. It's quite a bargain."

Dola looked at a tin box the size of a milk bucket. "My word, that's a lot of—"

"Very true, and how do you know it will work for you? Perhaps the four-ounce size is a more reasonable choice." Mrs. Oatman handed Dola one of the small green tins with orange writing on it.

"Thank you," Dola said. "This might do the trick."

"You be sure and let me know if it helps you, dear."

"Actually I've had a little stiffness in the back, and I thought—"

"My word, are you expecting again?" Mrs. Oatman challenged.

"No, of course not. I—we . . ." Dola looked away from the round-faced woman. *Lord, I can't believe that I've been so busy I haven't even considered that a possibility. No, it can't be. . . . Can it?* "It might be time for a checkup. I don't believe I've seen a doctor since Punky was born."

"Well, don't go see that Dr. Ollensby, the young, cute one from Glendale. All he told me was to lose some weight." The woman abruptly stopped talking and surveyed Dola from head to toe. "Now I don't suppose he'd tell you that, but he is too young to know much about medicine. I hear there is a lady doctor in Tonopah, Dr. Cecilia Brewster. I have half a mind to go see her. Say, we could go together. Take the stage up and make a day of it. It would be a girls' day out!"

Dola studied the small tin of salve. "Thank you, Mrs. Oatman. I think I'll give this salve a try first. But I just might want to visit the lady doctor in Tonopah."

Mrs. Oatman's ring-covered hand reached over and patted her arm. "Now don't you go sneakin' up there without me. Promise you'll phone before you go?"

The pain was building again in her back. Dola's smile was more a tight-lipped grimace. "We don't have a phone yet at the restaurant."

"Honey, you just stop by my house and tell me when you want to go."

"Thank you, but really, Mrs. Oatman, I don't think it's that serious." *Not serious enough to spend two dollars for an office visit.* "But I'll let you know if I change my mind and need to go to Tonopah." *Why in the world did I promise that, Lord? I can't think of anything more tiring than spending the day with Mrs. Oatman.*

She watched as the big woman traipsed out the front door.

When Dola reached the back counter, a beardless young man in a starched white apron waited on her. Young Tom Murphy looked a lot like Old Tom Murphy.

Except younger.

The same tiny, round eyes; gold-framed glasses; high, starched collar; tightly buttoned shirt; black and gray silk tie.

"Mrs. Skinner, welcome to our store," he greeted her. "I haven't seen you in here before."

"Thank you, Tom. I've been too busy to stop before."

He stared at the green tin in her hand. "Do you have a sore cow?"

Dola swallowed hard. "I beg your pardon?"

Young Tom pointed at the salve. "Most folks use that Dr. Chinkker's Bag Balm on their cows' udders."

She felt her face flush. "Oh, I understood it was for human use."

He took off his spectacles and held them up toward the electric light bulb as if looking for an imperfection. "Yes, ma'am, it certainly can be. It's been known to help joint muscles, cramps, and trauma. But it's not to be taken internally."

A slight smile touched Dola's narrow lips. "I have no intention of eating it."

"Good. You'd be surprised what some people do. Is there anything else I can get you?"

Dola took a deep breath. The store had a sweet, almost sticky aroma, somewhere between rose water and liver medicine. "Yes, do you have any nitrates?" she asked.

"What kind do you need?" He headed for a tall, narrow oak shelf. "We have sulfur nitrate. Looks like I'm out of potassium nitrate, so you might have to get that at the gunsmith's. I've got ammonia nitrate. Sodium nitrate."

Dola rubbed her narrow, smooth chin. "Goodness, I don't know."

"You want it for yourself? Or for cleanin' pots and pans? Or for your rosebush?" Young Tom asked.

"I have a little peach tree in a half-barrel, and its leaves are turning quite yellow," she reported.

"How often do you water it?" he asked.

"Oh, I suppose not more than, you know, once a day."

"Perhaps it's too wet," he suggested.

Dola threw her shoulders back. "Nonsense, Tom, how can any plant be too wet in this desert?"

"Well, maybe you're right. You'll want the ammonia nitrate salts. Do not take them internally either."

"I won't."

"And don't toss them in the fire."

"All right."

"And don't dilute them and soak your feet in them."

Dola raised her eyebrows. "Will it cause my hair to turn green?"

A wide smile broke across his face. "No, Mrs. Skinner, I don't reckon it would. Just tryin' to be cautious."

"Thank you, Tom."

He lowered his voice to a whisper. "I noticed you were movin' slow when you came in. Would you be needin' any Female Remedy today?"

This time it was Dola who had a wide grin. "You know, Tom, I don't suppose there really is a remedy for being a female, is there?"

The man's round cheeks flushed red. "No, ma'am, I guess there isn't. But some ladies swear by it. Says it takes away the, eh, you know, monthly cramps."

"How much will it cost me for this wonder medicine?"

"Do you want the two-bits size or the six-bits size?"

"How long does it last?"

"Depends on the dosage."

"And what do you recommend?"

"Take a tablespoon every day you are in your womanly way, and for six days after that."

"I'll take the smaller one. Now what do I owe you?"

He looked at the three items. "That's one dollar and thirty-five cents, but for the Wall Walker's wife, make it an even dollar."

Dola dug in her purse and pulled out the coins. "And here's a dollar thirty-five. It's been over a year since Orion carried the water out, and we need to pay our way just like everyone else."

Young Tom took the coins and jiggled them in his hand. "You Skinners aren't just like everyone else. You know that, don't you?"

"What do you mean?"

"You're the only ones in this entire town who aren't lookin' for gold—except that boy of yours."

"Yes, well, if I keep buyin' medicine at this rate, I'll need gold too."

"I hope you get to feelin' better, Mrs. Skinner. You do look a little weak."

"Thank you, Tom. I'm just tired. A good rest will do wonders, no doubt."

Dola walked slowly out of the drugstore. The pain seemed to be all concentrated in her lower back now. Each step it felt as if a branding iron were searing her bones, but no longer did the pain shoot down her legs.

Lord, I thank You that I can at least walk. I don't understand what is happening. I know I certainly could not be . . . I mean, I have planned each child's birth, and I certainly have no plans for more. This is not a good time, Lord. I have to work. I have to take care of my four children. I have to take care of my Orion. I know You understand.

"Now there's a lady who looks like she needs a ride!" boomed a deep voice.

She turned to see a well-dressed black man in a carriage. "Mr. LaPorte!"

"Mrs. Skinner, I'm drivin' up the street anyway. Hop in," Lucian LaPorte called from the front seat of his one-horse hack.

"Oh, I need to walk," she protested.

"Don't you go tellin' me you need to exercise. You're skinny as a possum in spring and weakly lookin' to boot."

Lord, if I hear one more time how horrible I look, I will go to the undertakers and order a coffin.

"Sorry, Dola Mae," Lucian apologized. "That didn't come out right. I'm worried about you. You'll work yourself sick. Won't you please let me give you a lift?"

She held her hand above her eyes, even though the brim of her straw hat blocked the sun. "I really need to stretch, Lucian. I have sort of a cramp in my back, and walking will do it good."

Lucian raised his eyebrows. "Dola Mae, I'm serious. You take care of yourself. Omega says you'll die young at the rate you're goin'."

"Your Omega is working very hard too."

"And my Omega is home in bed asleep. Perhaps you could give that a try."

She continued to walk down the sidewalk as Lucian drove beside her, dodging horses and parked wagons.

"Are you naggin' at me, Mr. LaPorte?"

"Yes, ma'am, I am. Is it workin'?"

"I don't think so."

"Then I'll keep naggin'."

Dola stopped at the corner and braced herself by leaning her hand against the lamppost. The front door of the Vinegaroon Saloon cut diagonally across the corner boardwalk, and the door was propped open with an old, tattered boot stuffed full of rocks.

"Every morning will not be as hectic as this morning. That auto car in the window seems to have attracted half the town."

LaPorte pulled out his red bandanna and wiped his forehead. "You should have set a limit this morning and refused service to the rest."

"I know you're right, Mr. LaPorte. For the life of me, I don't know how to refuse to feed a hungry man."

Dola paused as a tall, thin, unshaven man with hat pulled over his ears staggered out of the saloon. He looked her up and down, rolled his eyes, and then wiped his nose on his blue denim shirt.

She dropped her head so she could avoid his eyes.

"Evenin', ma'am," he said and then staggered backwards all the way into the saloon.

Evening? He's really plastered. She glanced up at the hack driver. "Lucian, what are we doing in this town? Sometimes I feel like a stranger in a foreign land. I'm not sure how I got into this cafe business in the first place."

LaPorte retrieved a toothpick from behind his ear and began to chew on it. "Some hungry men asked you to cook. Remember?"

When she shifted her weight to her left foot, the pain in her back lessened. "It seems like so long ago."

From inside the saloon they heard a shout, then the smacking sound of a fist hitting a face. The same man staggered out, holding his jaw.

Dola turned toward the street. LaPorte stuffed his bandanna into the back pocket of his dark gray suit pants. "Things move fast here, Dola Mae. Lots of folks still movin' into town ever'day. We got six new Chinese families just this mornin'."

"My goodness, I hadn't heard that."

The drunk staggered by her and tried to tip his hat. "Good evenin' again, miss."

Miss? You are so drunk you can no longer distinguish age? "Good morning," she replied.

"And the union organizers are comin' in by the droves," Lucian continued as he surveyed the street. "Dola, they've been waltzin' in two or three at a time all week. But they're easy to spot. Coming down from Idaho, Colorado, Montana, so I hear. There will be trouble."

"Are those the anarchists the mine owners are ranting about?"

"I suppose so. Although I'm not too sure what that word means. Is it good or bad?"

"Depends on whether you own a mine or not."

The drunk sidled up to Dola. "Can I buy you a drink, miss? Anything you please."

Dola winced at the red-eyed man's foul breath. "No, thank you. And you should take better care of yourself. Why don't you go home and sleep it off?"

The man nodded. "I reckon you're right." He glanced her over again. "Where do you live?"

"I meant, to your home!" she snapped.

"Oh, yeah . . ."

Lucian waved toward the empty carriage seat. "Dola Mae, don't be stubborn. Let me give you a ride home."

"You go on, Lucian. I really need to walk. *Lord, I'd love to have a ride home, but there is no way in the world I could climb up into that carriage.*

The drunk staggered off the boardwalk and fell flat on his face in the dirt road.

"I don't believe that ol' boy is long for this world," LaPorte said. "Used to be you didn't see such behavior until after dark. It's not good for you to be over here alone. You know, I could come down there and toss you into this carriage!"

You toss me anywhere, Mr. LaPorte, and it would kill me. "You go on now. I'm goin' to walk, and that's final. You know that there's only one woman on earth more stubborn than me, and you married her."

The big black man twitched his neatly trimmed mustache,

leaned back, and laughed. "Now you're right about that, Dola Skinner."

The drunk sat up in the dirt street. "Is this son of Ethiopia pesterin' you, miss? If so, I'll defend your honor! No beautiful woman should have to take such guff," he shouted. But then he collapsed on his back in the dirt.

Lord, I can't believe this drunk is the first person today who has given me a compliment. If a man's drunk enough, even Dola Mae looks good. Thank you, mister, for not saying I look peaked.

Dola stepped gingerly off the boardwalk and stood over the drunk man. He blinked open one eye.

"He most certainly is not pestering me. In fact, he's—he's my brother!"

The man propped himself up on his elbows, squinted at Lucian LaPorte, and then looked back at her. "Well, I'll be. Your brother? At first glance I didn't notice the family resemblance." Then, as if turned off like an electric lamp, his eyes rolled back, his mouth dropped open, and he passed out cold.

"You lied to him, Dola Mae Skinner," Lucian accused.

"I did not. You do love the Lord Jesus, do you not, Mr. LaPorte?"

"Yes, you know I do, Dola Mae."

"Well, then we are brother and sister in the Lord."

Lucian roared. "That's not what that old boy figured you meant."

"I doubt if this man will remember any words of mine by tomorrow."

"I'm not sure he will live until tomorrow, layin' out there in the street. Now you go on, Dola Mae, and be careful gettin' back to the cafe."

"Thank you, Mr. LaPorte."

He tipped his hat. "You're welcome, Mrs. Skinner."

Two grimy men wobbled out of the saloon and stared down at the man in the dirt. "What happened to Morgan?" the taller one called out.

"I believe he was overcome with Miss Dola Mae's beauty," Lucian declared.

They squinted their bloodshot eyes and leaned close enough for her to smell the whiskey.

"Nope, that ain't it," the shorter one replied.

"Would you please help him off the street?" Dola snapped.

"Yes, ma'am," the tall one said. He grabbed one foot, and the shorter man picked up the other. "Come on, Morgan," one of them mumbled as they dragged the man up onto the boardwalk.

When Dola arrived back at the cafe, Rita Ann met her at the door. "Daddy came back, and I told him you didn't feel well. He said he'd go look for you. Did you see him?"

"No, I didn't. What exactly did you tell him?"

Rita Ann held onto her mother's arm. "I told him that you were tired and hurting some. Was that all right? I didn't know what to say."

Dola patted her daughter's arm. "That's fine, darlin'."

"I told him you went to Fieldstein's Drugstore."

"I went to Murphy's. It's closer." They walked slowly into the deserted cafe.

Rita Ann's voice tightened. "But it's by all those horrible saloons."

"I didn't want to walk too far, so that's where I went."

"Are you better, Mama? What happened? I was so worried."

"I believe I can walk up those stairs now. I think I just had a catch in my back or something."

"But you were crying, Mama. You never cry."

I never cry? How in the world have I kept that from this girl for thirteen years? "I'm tired, baby. It's harder to control my emotions when I'm tired."

Rita Ann heaved a big sigh. "Oh, Mama, you had me so scared."

Dola hugged her daughter's thin shoulders. "You were a real ranger right when I needed you. I believe you grew up some today."

Rita Ann threw her shoulders back and held up her chin. "What do you mean, Mama?"

"Well, for thirteen years I've taken care of you. Today just for a minute you were taking care of me. And it felt very good to have you by my side."

"Mama, are you crying again?"

"Yes, I am."

"Do you hurt?"

"These aren't tears of pain. They're tears of love, darlin'. And a mother is entitled to cry these anytime she wants."

"Mama, you always say things that make me feel good about myself."

"That's what mothers are for." Dola kissed Rita Ann's forehead. "Where is everyone?"

"Corrie and Punky are upstairs. Tommy-Blue went with Daddy. They were going to try to check on you, and then Daddy is riding out to the Little Ophir Lease and take some reports. He told Tommy-Blue he could go along."

Dola stared up the empty stairs. "I don't suppose that set well with Corrie?"

"She's pouting of course. 'Love, thou know'st, is full of jealousy.' Mama, why does Corrie cling to Daddy so?"

"I don't know, Rita Ann. I've never understood that. Each child is made different. The Lord does such a marvelous job that way. I suppose Corrie feels a lot of pressure from you three."

"What do you mean, Mama?"

Dola stopped by a table and rested her hands on the back of a wooden chair. "Well, you are the oldest, the tallest. You are very pretty and smart and confident. Corrie can never be the firstborn, and she doesn't think she can compare to you."

"Yes, but she's second-born."

"But Tommy-Blue is Daddy's oldest boy, so he gets special treatment sometimes . . . like today."

"And Punky's the baby and gets spoiled by everyone!" Rita Ann added.

Dola reached around and put her hands on her lower back and tried to rub it gently. "Exactly. So where does that leave Corrie?" Every touch seemed to ease the pain and aggravate it at the same time.

Rita Ann licked her narrow lips. "I guess she feels she has to strive for attention."

"We are all different and alike at the same time."

"And guess what, Mama? Daddy had lunch with Lucky Jack, Wasco, Charlie Fred, and the Wilkins brothers!"

"My goodness, I didn't know they were all back in town."

"And he said they might be coming here for supper."

"Together?"

"That's what Daddy said. They are in some kind of joint mining deal, and they want to give Daddy a share, and if they find gold, Daddy's goin' to give all his share to build a new church."

"What?"

"Maybe you ought to ask Daddy."

Dola glanced back toward the open double doors that led to the street. "Well, I'm glad to hear they are all getting along. I'm glad they're not gunning for each other anymore."

"I think they are too rich for that," Rita Ann declared.

Dola looked at the clock. "It must have been a rather long lunch."

"After lunch Daddy and Punky went over and threw a guy out of Fergus's cousin's house."

"They did what?"

"I don't know any more than that, Mama. But Daddy told us that Lucky Jack and them are helping clean up the house after throwing some old boy out on his ear."

"It sounds like your daddy had a very interesting day. I believe I'll go up and lie down for a few minutes before we start supper."

"Do you think we'll have as many for supper?" Rita Ann asked.

"I certainly hope not. I think we'll prepare for 100 and turn the rest away."

"Guess what else, Mama. I heard they finally found two more teachers, so school can start next week after all. I can't believe I'm going to the same school for two years in a row."

"That's good, darlin'."

"I can still get up early and help serve breakfast and then after school help with supper."

"We'll see. You'll be busy with studies."

Dola took one step up the stairs and stopped. The pain burned down both legs.

"Are you sure you can make it, Mama?"

"Hold onto my arm, honey."

One step at a time they ascended to the apartment. "My back doesn't hurt nearly as much as it did earlier. I believe I just got it bound in a bad position when I fell asleep on the bench in front of the cafe."

Rita Ann walked over to the open doorway and onto the balcony. "Corrie Lou, what are you doing out here?"

"I'm waiting for my daddy," the ten-year-old replied.

"He went out to Little Ophir. He will be gone all afternoon."

"He'll be back 'cause he didn't find Mama. Then he'll take me with him too," Corrie asserted.

Dola leaned into the dresser, unpinned her hat, listened to her daughters, and ignored the mirror.

"He said it was Tommy-Blue's turn," Rita Ann informed her.

"No, it's not his turn because I traded Tommy-Blue a whole bowl of custard for his next turn to go with Daddy."

Dola craned her neck toward the balcony. "You did what?" she called.

"Hi, Mama!" Corrie called back.

"Answer me, young lady."

"I traded my bowl of custard for the next trip with Daddy."

"Don't you ever trade your food away, young lady."

"Boy, you can say that again. I didn't get to go, and I didn't get to eat the custard."

Dola slowly unfastened the tiny imitation pearl buttons on her perspiration-drenched dress collar.

"Oh, no!" Corrie shouted as she leaped to her feet.

Dola stepped out on the porch. "What's the matter, honey?"

"He's coming here!"

"Who?" Dola asked.

"Colin Maddison, the third, with two *d*'s!" Corrie shouted. "Look!"

Rita Ann stared down the street. "Does he have flowers in his hand?"

"Oh, no. . . . Mama, can I go to Fergus's cousin's house and help them clean?"

"Corrie, if that boy is coming to see you, you cannot run away."

"Why not, Mama? I'm too young to get flowers!"

Dola glanced down the street and spotted a young boy, dark hair slicked back and dressed in white shirt and tie and knickers. He was carrying something in his hands. Then she looked down at Corrie's pleading eyes, bare feet, smudged cheeks, and dust-covered dress. "You're right, darlin', you are too young. Go on out the back way."

"You're the best mama in the world!" she shouted as she sprinted to the stairway.

Rita Ann and Dola walked back into the apartment.

"Is Punky asleep on the comforter?" Dola asked.

Rita Ann rounded the corner of the big bed, then gasped, "Mama!"

Dola ran to her daughter's side. A fiery pain shot up her back with each step. "What is it?"

Rita Ann pointed to the sleeping toddler. "Look!"

"Get me the broom, Rita Ann."

Rita Ann rushed back with a tattered cornstalk broom and shoved it at her mother.

Dola inched closer to the sleeping toddler. Slowly she reached out until the broom was only inches from Punky's arm.

Rita Ann peeked around her shoulder. "Careful, Mama. They're poisonous!"

"I know, darlin'. You grab up Punky and jump on the bed as soon as I sweep him."

Dola swept the toddler's bare arm with a sudden flip of the wrist. "Grab him!"

Rita Ann plucked up her brother and dove on top of the bed.

Dola then slammed the heel of her boot into the painted wood floor. She could feel the pop and crunch beneath her shoe—and a sharp pain in her back.

Punky woke up shouting, "Rita-Rita-Rita-Rita!"

His sister stared at the mangled splotch by her mother's boot. "I think you killed it, Mama."

"If I live here a hundred years, I'll never get used to them. I don't like scorpions," Dola mumbled, "especially ones crawling on my baby's arm."

Punky sat up in the bed. "Bug!" he squealed. Then he flopped on his back. "Rita, Mama killed a bug!"

"Well, why don't you go finish your nap on big sister's bed, darlin'. I don't want you sleeping on the floor anymore."

Rita Ann pulled a pillow out from under the comforter. "I'll put him down, Mama."

"Thanks, honey. I just have to lie down a minute on my bed."

"Can I do anything else for you?" Rita Ann asked.

"I think I hear someone calling out downstairs. I imagine it's Mr. Colin Maddison, the third, with two d's. Would you go talk to him?"

Rita Ann gave the pillow to Punky and walked toward the door. "What shall I tell him?"

"Tell him that Corrie Lou is too young to have flowers. Tell him to come back in six years."

Rita Ann's eyes widened. "Really?"

"Tell him whatever seems appropriate, Rita Ann."

"I think I'll tell him, 'In the morn and liquid dew of youth contagious blastments are most imminent.'"

"That should confuse even a boy with two *d*'s."

"Anything else, Mama?"

Dola glanced over at the drugstore package. "Yes. I have some salve in that sack. I need you to rub it on my lower back."

Rita Ann spun around. "You want me to doctor you?"

"After you deal with the young man downstairs. Darlin', you have to take care of your mama."

"Maybe I am growing up a little."

Indeed you are, young lady. Just like that. How did it happen so quickly, Lord? I'm so happy You trusted me with Rita Ann. Today she is a delight. And there haven't been many delights today.

FIVE

Tommy-Blue stood up as he drove the buckboard into Goldfield. The movement of the wagon created the only breeze. Dust hovered over the hot desert like a wispy fog that couldn't decide whether to come or go. O. T. pulled off his felt hat and ran his fingers through his sweat-drenched hair. He studied the businesses of Goldfield, often five saloons to a block.

Ever'time I roll into town, I keep wonderin' why we came here. Why did we stay? Why don't we push on to California? And I never have an answer.

The snows of last winter seem a long time ago. I don't reckon I remember when it was cold. Or when I felt rested. But I ain't complainin', Lord. We have good meals and a roof over our heads, and my family's healthy. For that I'm grateful. Dola Mae's workin' too hard, I know that. But I can't seem to get her to slow down. Lord, maybe You could talk to her.

"Do you want me to park in front of the Assay Office or in the alley behind it?" Tommy-Blue called out.

O. T. slapped his hat back on and pointed east. "The alley is fine, son. That way we don't clog up the street."

The ten-year-old sat down as he steered the team around a freight wagon and a parked black leather surrey. "I wish I had me a team of horses like these. Do you think we'll ever get some horses? It sure is swell drivin' horses, isn't it, Daddy?"

O. T. held onto the iron rail with his callused right hand. "These two move along good certainly, son. But ownin' two mules is right for us. Don't want any bigger feed bill than that."

Tommy-Blue stopped the rig to wait for a small oriental girl to walk a leashed white goose across the street. "If I had fifty dollars, I'd buy me the best horse in Nevada," he declared.

O. T. stretched out his right foot, wiggled his toe inside his boot, and tried to avoid the hole in his sock. "It would cost a little more than that, son."

"How much, Daddy? How much would the best horse in Nevada cost?" He tipped his hat at the girl with the goose as they drove by. She tugged at her long yellow dress and covered her mouth and giggled.

O. T. slowly cracked his knuckles one at a time. "I reckon it would be closer to $500. But that ain't even includin' racehorses. Lucky Jack said there was a racehorse in Carson City that sold for $2,000."

Tommy-Blue whistled. "For one horse? You can buy a house for $2,000! Oh boy, he must be a wonderful horse."

"He was wonderful to the man who sold him," O. T. laughed.

"Did he do tricks? Mr. Rickard has a white horse that does tricks."

"How do you know that? Have you been hangin' out down at the Northern Saloon?"

"No, sir, I'm temperance, but I heard Doyle Brant say that his cousin's new stepfather lost six dollars on a bet that Rickard's horse couldn't drink a bottle of beer and keep its hat on at the same time. Wouldn't that be a trick to see?"

I will be glad when school starts. Maybe they'll have something else to do besides listen to Goldfield stories. "Son, don't go believin' everythin' you hear in this town."

"If I saved up my money, could I buy me a horse? Then I could ride him when I go prospectin' around town, and he could haul samples for me and be my friend 'cause I ain't had no one to prospect with since Danny Rokker moved to California." Tommy-Blue slowly turned the rig down the alley.

"Didn't I hear Corrie Lou offer to partner with you?"

"She's my sister!"

"I knew that."

"And she's a girl!" Tommy-Blue parked the rig by two broken, empty wooden whiskey barrels.

"Yep, I knew that too."

"They wouldn't take me serious if I had a girl as a partner."

O. T. climbed down from the wagon and pulled a mostly clean gray rag from under the seat. "Who's 'they'?" he asked.

Tommy-Blue jumped off and trailed after his father. "The men at the Mining Stock Exchange."

O. T. began to wipe down the horses. "You reckon to impress the Stock Exchange?"

"Daddy, that's the only way to make it big. A man needs financing. I'd have to sell stock, and they wouldn't want to invest if my sister was my partner."

"Them's mighty big plans for a ten-year-old. Check the hoofs for me, son."

Tommy-Blue asked the lead horse for a hoof and then dug with his finger in the horse's frog. "Say I saved my money, and say I had enough to buy a horse, could I buy one?"

"Nope." O. T. moved over to the other horse and began to wipe it down.

Tommy-Blue proceeded to a rear hoof. "Why not?"

"'Cause you'd need a saddle, bridle, and all the tack."

Tommy-Blue rubbed the horse's leg and then asked for the other rear hoof. "Well . . . well, what if I saved enough for all that, could I buy one then?"

O. T. wiped the sweat off the horse's neck. "Nope."

The ten-year-old dropped the hoof and stood up. "Daddy!"

"You have to pay his monthly feed bill and livery charge."

"What if I had enough for all that? Could I then, Daddy?"

"Maybe."

"Maybe?"

O. T. pulled back the rigging and inspected the place on the horse's nose where the hair had been worn thin. "When you have all that saved, we'll ask your mama what she thinks."

"I think I'll buy a buckskin."

"Just how much money have you saved up so far?"

Tommy-Blue pulled off his flop hat and scratched his mop of brown hair. "You mean cash on hand or countin' my promissory notes?"

O. T. brushed small amounts of caked dirt from the crevices around the horse's eyes. "You been lendin' money?"

"Just thirty-five cents."

"And who did you lend that to?"

"Corrie Lou. She wanted a sody water." Tommy-Blue tugged on a rock stuck in the last hoof.

"Soda water only costs a nickel," O. T. challenged.

"Well . . . she, eh, drank a whole bunch of them."

"Seven?"

"In two days."

"That wouldn't be the time she got sick, would it?"

Tommy-Blue examined the small rock. "No. She drank them sody waters the two days before she got sick."

"Let's say little sis paid you back—then how much money would you have?"

"Includin' my gold dust?"

"Yep."

"I figure I have seven dollars and sixty-three cents."

"That much, huh?"

"Yeah. If I didn't have to go to school, I'd have even more!" Tommy-Blue boasted.

"I certainly can see why so many folks want to go into prospectin'."

"Some of 'em make even more money than me."

"And some make less." O. T. reached into the back of the wagon and pulled out two small tin boxes.

Tommy-Blue held out the stone for his father. "Do you think this rock has some color?"

O. T. didn't look. "Nope, I don't."

He hiked into the back room of the Assay Office and out to the counter. Tommy-Blue followed.

Daniel Tolavitch, his gray hair parted in the middle and neatly combed straight back, glanced up from a stack of papers. "Looks like you had a helper this afternoon."

"Yep, I've got my own driver now." O. T. put his arm on Tommy-Blue's shoulder.

"I'm surprised he took off that long from prospecting." Tolavitch grinned.

"A man needs a break ever' now and then," the ten-year-old declared.

"I agree, Tommy-Blue, especially a prosperous prospector like yourself."

"Well, I ain't had that many big strikes." Tommy-Blue hiked to the back of the room and pressed his nose against the glass case crammed with sample nuggets.

Tolavitch carefully hoisted a glass cover off his largest set of brass scales. "Say, O. T., Jakob Fleming was in looking for you."

O. T. pulled a stack of papers from the top drawer of the counter and sorted through them. "I was just out there the other day."

Tolavitch poured out a small glass vial of gold dust on one side of the scale. "He wants to talk to you real bad. It's a wonder he didn't spot you drivin' up."

"We parked in the alley." O. T. logged his deliveries on the top sheet of paper.

Tolavitch set a very small brass weight on the other side of the scale and studied the balance hand. "Fleming said he'd be cleaning up over at Wilson's Barber Shop, and if you came in to send you right over."

O. T. surveyed what he had written and then filed the papers back in the drawer. "What's this all about?"

"Don't know." Tolavitch wrote down a few words on a scrap of paper, rolled it up, and inserted it in the glass vial along with the gold dust. "But you and I both know he's dancing around like he struck it big. I'm not disclosing his assay, but I don't know why a man as rich as Fleming is still looking for more gold."

"I reckon it's a sickness, Mr. Tolavitch."

The chemist carefully covered the scales with the glass case. "It keeps me working, so I'm not one to complain."

O. T. studied the large map of the Goldfield mining district that covered the top half of the east wall. "Did he get his Mexican minin' crew back to work out at the Pear Blossom?"

"I don't know. I haven't seen them in town the last couple of days, but I don't know where they went."

"You got any more runs you want me to make?"

The chemist pulled a gold watch from his vest. "Look's like it's quitting time for you."

"I could make another stop on my way to the livery to put up the team."

"I'm only paying you for eight hours a day. Don't you go working nine and a half or ten hours on eight hours' pay. I'll start feeling so guilty I won't sleep good at night," Tolavitch lectured.

"I never had a job that only worked me eight hours. Seems like I'm short-changin' you."

Daniel Tolavitch scratched his gray hair. "Go home, O. T. Go help Dola, or play with the kids or something. Or go see Fleming. But work's over."

"I'll take the wagon over to the livery."

"You'll do nothing of the kind," Tolavitch roared. "I'll telephone the livery, and they can send a boy over for the team. That's what I pay them for."

Tommy-Blue spun around from the sample case. "They got a telephone at the livery?" he asked.

"Yes, and it's mighty convenient."

Tommy-Blue scooted over to the counter. "Mr. Tolavitch, did you assay my last sample I brought you yet?"

"Let me look, son." Tolavitch opened a drawer and dug through a thick file of papers.

Tommy-Blue peeked around the corner. "It was sample number 1135."

Tolavitch pulled out a crumpled paper and held it up to the electric light bulb above his head. "Where did you get this sample, son?"

Tommy-Blue's Adam's apple swelled as he swallowed hard. "I ain't sayin' 'cause I ain't filed a claim on it yet."

Tolavitch handed the paper to the boy. "If I were you, I'd file a claim."

Tommy-Blue's mouth dropped open. "Really?"

"You had two dollars and thirty-two cents worth in your sample bucket. That's good diggin's, young Mr. Skinner."

"No foolin'? Over two dollars!"

Tolavitch yanked out a thick black leather-bound ledger. "You want me to credit your account?"

"Yes, sir!"

"Where did you find that sample?" O. T. asked.

"It's a miner's secret, Daddy. I can't tell you."

Tolavitch rubbed his chin. "You won't have to dig very deep, will you?"

"Why's that?" O. T. asked.

"This gold has already been crushed and separated."

"What are you sayin', Daniel?" O. T. inquired.

"This is dropped gold. Fell out of someone's poke, I reckon."

"Where'd you find it, son?" O. T. pressed. "If we knew where you found it, we might be able to figure out who it belonged to and take it back."

"Daddy, I can't do that. It's mine," Tommy-Blue whined.

"He's right, O. T. If a man drops gold and walks away, it belongs to anyone who scoops it up."

"See, Daddy."

"Okay, it's yours, but where did you discover it?"

"Eh, under the sidewalk. There was a loose board, and I reached down and took a representative sampling."

"And just where was that?"

"On Main Street."

"By the Esmeralda Hotel?" O. T. quizzed.

"Down a block or two."

"By the lumberyard?"

Tommy-Blue shifted his weight from one bare foot to the other. "A little lower on Main Street."

"There ain't nothin' lower except saloons, gamblin' joints, and the cribs," O. T. said.

Tommy-Blue looked down at his bare toes and rocked back on his heels. "I didn't go in or nothin'."

"Where were you?"

"At Shotgun Lily's."

"Whoa!" Tolavitch grinned. "Now there's a wild joint. Eh, so I hear tell."

"You aren't goin' down there again, son," O. T. commanded.

"But I ain't sinnin' or anythin', Daddy."

"Your mama would pitch a fit if she knew."

"You ain't goin' to tell her, are you?"

"Are you goin' to sneak down to lower Main again?"

"No, sir."

"Then I won't tell."

"I ain't never goin' to have enough money to buy me a horse if I don't get to prospect the good claims," Tommy-Blue complained.

"You going to buy a horse, Tommy-Blue?" Tolavitch asked.

"Yep. A fast one."

"Well, just how fast is he goin' to be?"

"About two seconds faster than Colin Maddison's horse."

"So that's what this is all about," O. T. remarked. "I thought you and him was buddies."

"He likes Corrie Lou."

"He has good discretion in picking women. Does he know horses?" Tolavitch asked.

"He thinks he does. He's got a long-legged black horse with a blaze on his nose and one white sock that his daddy bought him in Tennessee and shipped out by train."

"Go on home, son," O. T. instructed. "You can help your mama."

"If I had my own horse, I could get home even faster."

"Well, you'll just have to plod home today. Tell Mama I'll be right home. I have to go see Jakob Fleming over at the barber shop. He probably wants Mama's secret recipe for fried chicken."

Tommy-Blue scratched his head. "Really?"

"But I won't give it to him," O. T. laughed, "no matter how much gold he offers me!"

O. T. hiked down the raised wooden sidewalk as the sun was lowering in the west. The thin fog of yellow alkali dust that always hung above Goldfield in the late afternoon gave the scene a sepia look that reminded him of a Matthew Brady photograph of a Civil War battlefield.

Everyone was in a hurry in Goldfield. One set of miners rushed to get to work. Another set hurried to get home. Drunks dashed to get to a saloon. Freighters scrambled to unload. Wagons and stages bolted on down the road. Stock speculators hustled for a sale. Cats ran away from dogs. Dogs ran away from little boys. Little boys ran away from little girls.

The only people not moving fast were the drunks passed out on benches in front of the saloons, older ladies, and pregnant women. When O. T. saw the woman storming his way, his first reaction was to cut across the street near a car that had stalled in front of a tandem freight wagon pulled by sixteen mules.

Instead, he tipped his hat. "Evenin', Mrs. Oatman."

"Mr. Skinner, I am certainly glad to see you again."

The shouting between the teamster and the car's driver caused both of them to stare out at the street. The curses didn't ease until a badged deputy strolled out into the street.

Mrs. Oatman turned back to O. T. "My, I don't believe I've heard some of those terms before." Her mouth was as round as her face.

"Them teamsters have sort of inventive phraseology, don't they?"

She retied her hat bow beneath her chin. "What exactly did he mean when he said the man with the bowtie should take his—"

"Mrs. Oatman, I'm just a simple Oklahoma farm boy. Them descriptions are way beyond me. I surmise it ain't good, and I don't plan on repeatin' it."

With beige-gloved hand she brushed mostly gray curls back. "Yet that's what I like about the frontier. I learn somethin' new almost every day."

"Yes, ma'am," he concurred. "Did you want to see me?"

"Oh, yes . . ." The car in the middle of the street backfired. They both jumped. "Now speaking of something new," she continued, "did you know that Henrietta Brinker's daughter LuAnn ran off to Bakersfield with a man twice her age?"

O. T. thought of LuAnn Brinker and the time she got stuck in the bathtub at the Esmeralda Hotel. They had to call in the doctor and three volunteer firemen to extract her. "No, ma'am, I didn't know that." *He might be twice her age, but I'll bet he wasn't twice her size.* "I surmise Mrs. Brinker is worried sick."

"Who told you that?" she snapped.

O. T. stepped back. "I was just guessin'."

Mrs. Oatman clasped gloved hands around her floral carpetbag purse. "No, no, Henrietta was quite relieved. She was afraid LuAnn was hankerin' for Dill Queen, and you know what a vagabond he is."

Lord, is there a polite way to get out of this conversation? "I don't reckon I know him, Mrs. Oatman."

"He's the one who got his thumb caught in the whiskey bottle and carried it around that way for two weeks last May."

O. T. shifted his weight from one foot to the other. *Lady, is there a purpose in this conversation?* "I guess I didn't hear about that."

"It was quite strange-looking."

O. T. thought he noticed a twinkle in Mrs. Oatman's large brown eyes. "I imagine ol' Dill had a tough time pullin' on his shirt ever' mornin'."

"I don't think Dill Queen has changed shirts in years."

O. T. watched the teamster retreat to his freight wagon. "Why didn't Dill just bust the bottle?" he asked.

With a tone used to educate children, Mrs. Oatman replied, "Because the bottle was almost full."

Now that, Lord, is only obvious in a place like Goldfield. "Nice visitin' with you again, Mrs. Oatman. I don't want to keep Jakob Fleming waitin' for me."

"I heard he was a widower, poor man. Not that I pay attention to such things. Mr. Skinner, I need to speak to you about your Dola."

O. T. could feel his face tense. "Yes, ma'am, what about her?"

Mrs. Oatman leaned forward and lowered her voice. "I saw her at the drugstore this afternoon. She looked just horrid. She needs to go to the doctor, Mr. Skinner. Surely you must see that. I don't believe I've ever seen a woman so haggard, and I told her so. There's a lady doctor in Tonopah. She needs to get up there as soon as possible. I would certainly be willing to go with her if you are unable to get off work."

Lord, I don't rightly know how to answer this lady. I know You cre-

ated her, but she's an obnoxious busybody, and she's got the nerve to say disparaging words about the sweetest woman on earth.

O. T. took a deep breath, and his gaze drifted to the teamster who pulled a shotgun out of his wagon. "Dola Mae's been workin' mighty hard at the cafe, Mrs. Oatman. She surely needs to rest more. I just can't seem to talk her into slowin' down."

"You better do more than talk, Mr. Skinner. That woman will work herself to death at this rate, and you'll be raisin' those wonderful children all by yourself. I don't want to sound like I'm meddlin', but that woman needs help, and you'd better see she gets taken care of."

"Yes, ma'am," O. T. mumbled as he continued to watch the teamster confront the car driver and the deputy. *I really don't need to hear this. Dola and me have had to work hard all our lives. That's just the way life is for some of us. Dola Mae never complains.*

"You take good care of her, Mr. Skinner. She's a dear, precious lady."

"That she is, Mrs. Oatman. I appreciate your concern." O. T. let out a big sigh as the woman started to walk away.

"Certainly. That's what friends are for." She glanced behind him. "Oh, here comes your delightful daughter. I really must run."

O. T. spun around and held out his arms to his ten-year-old. "How's my girl?"

Corrie hugged him and kissed his cheek. "I'm doin' very well, thank you. I've been helpin' Gerta clean her house. You won't believe how much garbage we had to shovel out. And old newspapers. We just buried the spittoon and some of the clothes."

Coming up behind her, Fergus was chewing on a toothpick. "Corrie is a very good worker."

O. T. scratched the back of his head. His hair felt thick and sweaty. "Are we talkin' about my Corrie Lou?"

Corrie stood on her tiptoes and clutched her father's arm. "Gerta asked if she could hire me for ten cents an hour!"

"You cleaned her house?" O. T. pressed.

Corrie nodded, and her bangs bounced up and down on her forehead. "All of us did," she reported.

"Who is 'all of us'?"

"Lucky Jack, Wasco, Charlie Fred, the Wilkins brothers, me, and Gerta."

"And Fergus?"

Corrie shrugged. "He took a nap."

"I did not want to get in anyone's way," Fergus explained.

"Did Mr. Jolly come back and hurrah you?"

"Are you kiddin', Daddy? Ain't nobody in the world that dumb."

"Didn't your mama need you there to help with supper? I heard she was feelin' poorly."

"I don't think so. She said I could go." She tugged on her father's arm as she looked out at the street. "Is there goin' to be a shootin' out there?"

"I don't think so. Just tempers talkin'."

O. T. and Corrie watched the street from the boardwalk. Fergus plopped down on a worn wooden bench.

"How was Mama feelin' this afternoon, darlin'?"

"She was very, very tired and was goin' to lay down and take a nap."

"Good for her. She needs the rest. I'm headin' home after I see Jakob Fleming." He turned to the Paiute. "Is your cousin doin' all right now?"

The old Indian held out his gnarled hand, and Corrie helped pull him to his feet. "She has six men attached to her side. I do not worry about her."

O. T. laughed. "You think she'll renew the Wilkins-Gately feud?"

"I believe this time it is a six-way tie. Only one will win."

"Or none," O. T. added.

"Very true. Now if you would like this young lady to stay with you, I will go to the cafe. I believe it's time to eat."

"I thought Gerta was cooking supper for you," Corrie declared.

"Yes, but I will need something to carry me over until then. Besides, it will be hard to get a proper serving with six other men there."

"All of them are stayin' for supper?" O. T. quizzed.

"They have made no sign of ever leaving," Fergus mumbled as he tucked in his black denim shirt.

"Well, ol' man, go get yourself a snack at the cafe. I'll take li'l sis with me."

All three stared as the deputy yanked a revolver from his holster and cracked it over the raging teamster's forehead. The big man crumpled to the dirt street.

"I bet that hurt!" Corrie gasped.

"Not as much as a bullet," Fergus said. He shuffled down the boardwalk to the east.

Corrie grabbed her father's hand. She almost skipped as she walked. "Daddy, why does a boy want to bring me flowers?"

"I reckon he likes you, Corrie Lou."

"Why?"

"What do you mean, why? Because you are a very bright, cute, winsome young lady."

"Did you ever give a girl flowers? I mean, before you married Mama?"

"Yes, I did," he admitted.

"To Mama or some other girl?"

"Mama's the only girlfriend I ever had. You know that."

"So you married the only girl you brought flowers to?" she pressed.

He squeezed her hand gently. "Yes, I did."

Corrie dropped his hand and rolled her eyes. "Oh, rats! You see what I mean? You see?"

"See what, darlin'?"

Corrie shook her head back and forth. "That's why I didn't want to take flowers from Colin Maddison. I'd have to marry him then."

"Well, it doesn't have to work that way. Some boys are taught that if you go visitin' a young lady, you should take a present. It's just bein' polite."

"Does the girl have to give the boy a present back?" she asked.

"No, she doesn't."

Corrie rubbed her nose on the sleeve of her dress. "I don't think Hud knows that rule about giving a girl presents, Daddy."

"Why do you say that?"

"'Cause he never gives Haylee anything but kisses. On the lips!"

"You watch them kiss?"

"Just with one eye. The one Rita Ann can't see. She says we should close our eyes, but she always knows if I open mine. How do you reckon she does that with her eyes closed?"

"Big sis is a talented girl. But maybe it would be good if you didn't look at Haylee and Hud at all. Sometimes a boy and a girl need some privacy."

"Like you and Mama at night when you turn the lights out and scrunch down in them covers?"

He squeezed her hand. "Yeah, like those times." *We have to get a home with more than one bedroom. Soon.* He stopped by the shop with the red-and-white-striped pole.

Corrie peeked in the window. "Are you goin' to get a haircut, Daddy?"

"No, I just need to find Mr. Fleming."

"Can I read the *Police Gazette?*"

"No, you may not."

"You let Tommy-Blue read the *Gazette*," she complained.

"That's not true, Corrie Lou."

"He said you did," she sniffed.

O. T. held the door of Wilson's Barber Shop open for her, and the bell tinkled as they entered. One man leaned back in a big black leather chair, his face covered with shaving cream, a towel around his shoulders. He signaled with his hand. "Skinner! Boy, am I glad to see you."

Corrie plopped down in an empty chair next to a stack of magazines.

"Mr. Fleming, I trust you have things under control at the Pear Blossom."

"Yes and no." Fleming glanced around. "Pop, can we use your back room?"

"Help yourself." The gray-haired barber motioned. "You want me to finish that shave?"

"Later." Fleming eased out of the chair. "I need to discuss some business."

"Can I come, Daddy?" Corrie called out from the chair.

"No, darlin', you wait here."

"Can I read a magazine?" she asked.

"No *Police Gazettes*," he insisted.

Mr. Wilson smiled at Corrie. "Wall Walker, this girl of yours is entitled to a free haircut."

"No!" she protested. "My daddy cuts my hair!"

The barber laughed. "Yes, ma'am. I was joshin'."

"Well, I wasn't." Corrie shielded her face with a *Harper's Illustrated*.

Jakob Fleming led O. T. into the back room and closed the door. "I didn't want those barber shop lizards listening to us gab."

"So what is happening at the Pear Blossom?" O. T. pressed.

Fleming paced among the dusty crates in the storeroom. "I got those iron doors installed."

"That's good."

"Now the gold's safe, but I can't get it out." Fleming stormed around the room.

O. T. sat on one of the crates. "Why's that?"

"It's those blasted anarchists," Jakob Fleming fumed.

"The union organizers?"

"The W.F.M. I can tolerate, but it's those Wobblies that are goin' to make things miserable."

"I recognize the Western Federation of Miners, but I don't know about the Wobblies," O. T. admitted.

"They call themselves the Industrial Workers of the World. They claim they're goin' to organize every employee on the face of the earth. They're anarchists—that's what they are."

O. T. pulled off his hat and leaned his head against the wall. "I don't know what this has to do with me."

"I'm skirtin' around the pond, but I'll jump in shortly. These Wobblies talked my Mexicans into demandin' more wages, less hours, and no changin' room. Why . . . it's un-American. It's despicable."

"I know hard-rock minin' is difficult work."

"But why should they want more money just because I found a lot of gold? They were happy with those salaries last week."

"I reckon they figure you can afford a raise now," O. T. offered.

Fleming stopped. "Are you sidin' with the anarchists?"

He surveyed the older man. "Mr. Fleming, my opinion is that you can offer anything you want. And they can demand anything they want. You don't have to hire them if you don't want to. And they don't have to work for you if they choose not to. That's about all there is to it."

Fleming continued to pace. "It's not that simple, Skinner."

"I'm a simple man. I guess I can only think in simple terms."

Fleming spun around and marched back over to O. T. "What kind of money would it take for you to come work for me?"

"I wouldn't be a hard-rock miner for all the money in Goldfield. About a month underground, and I'd go crazy. I need the open air."

Fleming waved his hands in protest. "No, no, I don't mean as a miner."

Skinner rubbed his chin and felt the stubble of a two-day beard. "I don't understand. I'm not smart enough for an office job."

"Here's what I need. I have six seasoned guards from Virginia City. With the picture rock locked behind bars, I have two of these boys at a time on guard in eight-hour rotations."

"Then you surely don't need me."

"Yes, I do. Because they're seasoned mine guards, they know the tricks. So Parker, Landusky, and I have been taking shifts down there too."

O. T. leaned forward and rested his elbows on his knees. "You mean, you've been watchin' the guards who are watchin' an iron gate? That's a lot of watchin'."

"That's the picture. It's just temporary, of course. But now I'm needed up top to negotiate with these anarchists. So I want to hire you to take my shift."

O. T. sat straight up. "I have a good job, Mr. Fleming."

"I realize that, Skinner." Fleming pulled a gold watch from his vest pocket, smearing shaving cream on his sleeve. "And this job would only last until that picture rock is hauled out."

With the shaving cream and mashed nose, Fleming reminded O. T. of a circus clown. "How long would that be?"

"About one month of digging after I get men back in there— that's all."

Skinner pulled off his hat and began to flatten the brim. "When will you get men back in?"

"That's what I don't know." Fleming pulled the towel from his shoulders and tried wiping the shaving cream from his shirt sleeve.

"Like I said, Mr. Fleming, I've got a job. It don't make sense to quit a permanent job for a temporary one."

"I wouldn't want you to. I'd need you for the 4:00 P.M.-to-midnight shift. Tolavitch said he could work your hours so you get through by 4:00. I'm askin' you for double-shift work."

"You talked to Mr. Tolavitch?" O. T. stretched his legs out in front of him and pounded on a cramp in his left thigh.

"He did the assay for me, remember? He knows what I have. He pays you $100 a month. Is that right?"

O. T. jammed his hat back on. "Yes, sir."

"I'll pay you $100 a week on top of that."

Skinner laughed and shook his head. "Nobody gets that kind of money, Mr. Fleming."

"Parker and Landusky do."

"Yeah, but I ain't a mining engineer like they are."

"You're the only other man in town I know I can trust."

"But $100 a week is a lot of money."

"Skinner, I will be making you work double-shift, and it's eight more hours a day you are away from your family. It's a horrible thing to ask of a good Christian man like yourself—I know that. You are worth every penny of it."

"I don't know, Mr. Fleming. Dola's feelin' poorly, and I need to be with her, maybe help a little in the cafe."

"If she needs help, I'll pay the salary of another serving girl while you work for me."

"On top of the $100 a week?"

"That's right. It's just temporary. What do you say?"

"Mr. Fleming, never in my life did I ever expect to earn $100 a week. Your offer is generous, but sixteen hours away from the family is tough on a man, what with Dola workin' too."

"O. T., I couldn't agree with you more. I wouldn't press you on this except that I'm in a bind. I don't have another soul in town to turn to. Between you and me, there isn't a man in Nevada I'd trust. It's just a temporary situation. O. T., I don't think you understand your role in Goldfield."

"What do you mean?"

"Findin' gold is like a game. You got teams competing. You got owners and their crews competing. You got owners and unions competing. You got merchants competing. You got saloons competing. It's like a big baseball tournament with everyone wanting to win."

"Is this leadin' somewhere, Mr. Fleming?"

"O. T., you're the only impartial umpire we got. Every side trusts you. Your witness is enough to keep all of us in line."

"I reckon you're exaggeratin' in order to talk me into this."

Fleming slung open the door. "Boys," he shouted to the barber shop crowd, "if the Wall Walker told you the moon was purple, what would you do?"

A big smile broke across the barber's face. "Why, we'd hike out and look at a purple moon!"

An old man with a leathery face as wrinkled as a Fresno prune puckered his lips. "Only two things you can count on in this blasted town, and that's the alkali dust and O. T. Skinner's word!"

Fleming slammed the door shut. "I think I made my point."

O. T. stared down at his boot tops. "I'll have to talk to Dola about it."

"Naturally. I know it will be tough on the family. But it's just for a few weeks, and, well, maybe you can take that money and get that auto car fixed up and take 'em all on a trip or somethin'. Anyway, can you let me know tomorrow?" Fleming held out his hand.

O. T. shook the mine owner's hand. "Yes, sir. I'll do that."

Fleming began to wipe the shaving cream off his face. "O. T., years ago when I just got out of college and started prospectin' up in the Comstock, I worked my fingers raw every day and slept soundly every night. Now look at me. My hands are soft and puffy. My belly's full of biscuits and hangin' over my belt. And I can't sleep for worry that someone is stealin' my gold. I envy you, Skinner. I'll bet you sleep good every night."

"I suppose that's true now, as long as the kids and the wife aren't sick. But, Mr. Fleming, you don't know what worry is until you've laid awake wonderin' how you were goin' to feed that family one more day."

Fleming stared at O. T. for what seemed like several minutes.

Finally he cleared his throat. "You're right, Skinner. I'll give you $200 a week."

"No, sir," O. T. replied. "If I take the job, I'll do it for $100. That's generous. Any more is charity, and Skinners don't need charity."

Fleming led O. T. back into the barber shop. "Skinner, you're like an oasis in a desert. I appreciate you thinkin' about it."

Corrie tossed a magazine down and clutched O. T.'s hand as they exited the barber shop.

"Daddy, did you know that the Albany Arsonist set fire to thirteen houses in one single night?" She skipped along beside him.

"Where did you hear that, young lady?"

She stopped skipping and cocked her head to the left. "Oh, I guess I sort of read it."

"Sort of read it?"

"In the *Modern Crime Magazine*."

"You know I don't want you readin' that kind of stories."

"Mama says it's good to read."

"Do you think your mama would approve of that magazine?"

She hung her head. "Well, I . . . I didn't read the story about three women from Cuba that got killed in the mysterious train wreck just north of Boston. Or the one about how the prisoners escaped and held Miss Randle's third grade class hostage."

"You didn't read those?"

"Not all of them. But I did read about the woman who raised a two-headed dog. She called one head Bow and the other one Wow."

"Do me a favor, darlin', and don't tell Mama what you were readin'."

"I won't if you won't."

They hiked east in the long shadows of a declining sun, stopping at each intersection and waiting for the traffic.

"Daddy, what did Mr. Fleming want to talk to you about?"

"He thinks he needs me to help him out."

"Everybody needs you to help them out."

"Why do you reckon that is?"

"Because you work for next to nothin'. I heard Mr. LaPorte tell Hud that you could get five dollars an hour if you wanted. He said you were workin' for next to nothin'.'"

"No one deserves five dollars an hour."

"Not even the president of the United States?"

"Perhaps the president does."

"And what about Mr. George Wingfield?" Corrie asked.

"I reckon he makes more than five dollars an hour, don't you? But that doesn't mean he's worth it."

They stepped up on the boardwalk in front of the Canary Club Saloon and Gambling Emporium. "Ain't anybody else worth five dollars an hour, Daddy?"

"I can think of only one."

"Who's that, Daddy?"

"Your mama."

"Are you goin' to pay Mama five dollars an hour?"

"There isn't enough money in all of Goldfield to pay Mama what she's worth, so I work hard and give her everythin' I got, and I'm still gettin' a bargain."

"You have a lot of Dola-Mae love, don't you, Daddy?"

He put his arm on her shoulder. "Yes, but I have a lot of Corrie-Lou love too."

"I love you, Daddy. You know that, don't you?"

"Darlin', there has never been a moment since you were born that I didn't feel your love for me."

"Even when I'm naughty?"

"Corrie Lou, is this leadin' to a confession?"

"Eh . . . I hope not. Daddy, are we ever goin' to get the auto car fixed?"

"Are you changin' the subject?"

"Hey, here comes Tommy-Blue!"

O. T. searched the crowd ahead of them. "I don't see him."

"He's runnin'. Maybe somethin's wrong!"

"Tommy-Blue always runs," O. T. reminded her.

"Daddy!" Tommy-Blue shouted from across the street.

"Are you goin' to answer him?" Corrie pressed.

O. T. pulled off his hat and scooted toward Tommy-Blue. "Is there trouble?"

"Mama's hurtin' terrible and can't get out of bed. Punky's cryin', and Rita Ann done burned the supper biscuits! You got to come quick!"

SIX

The heels on his brown leather boots dug into the dry dirt and dung of Columbia Street as O. T. sprinted toward the Newcomers' Cafe.

"Wait, Daddy!" Corrie shouted, but his stride lengthened as he approached the restaurant.

A crowd milled around at the door, waiting for supper. O. T. hurdled the front fender of the Thomas and ducked through the broken window into the empty dining room. He paused at the foot of the stairs when Rita Ann poked her head out of the kitchen.

"Daddy, what are we going to do about supper? I burned the biscuits. 'A heavier task could not have been imposed than I to speak my griefs unspeakable.'"

O. T. jogged over and looked into the kitchen. "Omega, everything all right in here?" Tommy-Blue and Corrie scurried up behind him.

"Go take care of that woman of yours, O. T.," the black lady instructed. "We'll open fifteen minutes late, but we'll manage. I just need a little more help."

Haylee and Lupe, sleeves rolled up to their elbows, had hands flying in flour dough. Fergus rummaged through the cracker basket. "You ol' Paiute, you are officially in charge of pouring coffee tonight," O. T. ordered.

"Do I get tips?" he mumbled through a mouthful of saltine crackers.

Omega wiped her hands on a towel. "Corrie, you help Rita Ann finish setting the tables. Tommy-Blue, you go find Mr. LaPorte and tell him he'd better get himself over here in three minutes to help us serve supper."

Tommy-Blue stammered, "Eh, can I—just tell him to hurry?"

"As soon as Hud comes, I'll put him to work too," Haylee said.

O. T. raced up the stairs two and three at a time. He flung open the door. Dola lay in white petticoats on top of the covers. Her bare feet flagged off the foot of the bed. Punky sat on the pillow next to her head.

"Daddy-Daddy-Daddy-Daddy-Daddy!" he hollered as he slipped down to the floor and sprinted across the room.

O. T. scooped him up with one arm and hurried toward the bed.

"Mama's sick. She was crying," Punky reported and then jammed his right thumb in his mouth.

O. T. hovered over Dola. "It's okay. I'm here now, darlin'. What's the matter?" He took the corner of the pillowcase and wiped the tears from her cheeks. *Oh, Lord, what's wrong with my sweet Dola Mae?*

She reached up for his hand. "I can't get out of bed, Orion. I'm so ashamed." *Oh, look at his face. He's so worried. How can I let him down? He has enough to worry about without me being laid up.*

"If you can't get out of bed, it must be time for you to stay there and rest, sweet Guthrie girl." He brushed the hair back that had been matted to her forehead. *Her face is so sunken. She hardly looks like my Dola.*

She turned her head away. "You haven't called me that in five years."

"It's been a hard five years, darlin'. I'm sorry for that. Tell me where you hurt."

"It scared me, Orion. I panicked. I screamed for the children, and then everyone began to cry. I should have taken it better. Forgive me—I'm such a weak woman."

He rested his hand on her cheek. "Baby, where's the pain?" *Her eyes are so weak. This is not a little thing. Oh, Lord . . . what have I done to her? Have mercy on us.*

"You know how it is when you have a cramp in your leg, and it locks up, and you have to hobble around and work it out? It's as if every muscle in my body from my neck to my toes cramped up all at once," she reported. "Then came a burning pain, like fire in my bones." *If only I were of sturdier stock. Like Lucy McMasters. Or Patricia Vickers. I was weak when I was twelve. I was weak when we got married. Orion, you deserve better than this.*

"Darlin', I'll go get Doc Silvermeyer. He'll know what to do." O. T. set Punky down on the bed. *Her cheeks are so pale. Why didn't I see this comin' on? Skinner, you are a fool.*

Pain shot up her arm and into her shoulder. Dola raised her arm to hug Punky anyway. She could feel the tears burn down her cheek. *He will worry himself sick over me, Lord. Give him peace. I will not cry anymore. I'm just having a bad spell—that's all.*

O. T. studied the tears. Then he stepped over to the sink. He dipped a white flour-sack tea towel into the porcelain basin of tepid water. He began to gently wipe her face. *Oh, Lord, what have I done to this lady? Is this the way I take care of the wife of my youth?*

When his hand whisked across her chapped lips, she brushed on a kiss. *Mr. Skinner, I have to admit, I feel much better just having you in the room. Do you have any idea in the world how much I need you?*

"Darlin', I'll have Corrie come up and sit with you while I go get the doc," he declared. *How did this happen without me knowin', Lord? I knew she was workin' hard, but I didn't figure this.*

Dola tried to take a deep breath, but she had to hold her hand to her chest to ease the sharp pain that seemed permanently locked to her chest bone. "Orion, there's no need for a doctor. If you'd just help me, I can get up now. It's like a cramp. I think it will go away if I move around. It will pass, and then I'll feel better. Besides, I need to help with supper." *There has never been a woman on earth who was better treated than I have been. This man has worked from dawn till dusk every day of his life, just for me. How can I let him down?*

He noticed the strained look in her blue eyes. *What a fool you've been, O. T. Skinner. She will work herself into the grave just for you, and you will never even notice. Dola Mae, do you have any notion how much I need you? You are the reason I get up ever' mornin' and face another hot, dusty day.* "Darlin', you are not gettin' up right now. You just try to find a comfortable position. Omega is in charge of supper and doin' fine. She has plenty of help. Even Lucian, Hud, and Fergus are helpin' her. There isn't room in the kitchen to turn around now as it is."

"How did you round up such a crew so fast?" she managed to ask. *For richer and for poorer, you have been by my side, Orion Skinner. In sickness and in health. I haven't been sick too much. Just when I was carryin' the babies. And that one time in Guthrie. Maybe once in New Mexico when we were camped beside Little Bitterwater Creek, and it snowed on us.* She slowly closed her eyes. *Oh, not a baby. I know, Lord, I'm still of child-bearing age. But I don't . . . I couldn't . . . It would be . . .* She could feel a tear slip down her cheek. *Now, Lord, I feel pain and guilt. Forgive me. Thy will be done. I hurt too much to know what I'm sayin'.*

Punky stared at whichever one was speaking. His thumb never left his mouth.

"They all pitched in and volunteered." *We'll sell out the cafe business and turn the building back over to Mr. Tolavitch and his partners. I'll take that double shift with Jakob Fleming. She shouldn't have to work at all. We'll go back and live in the tent, at least until November.*

"The men volunteered?" *Orion, I've always known I could count on you. I would never have survived this long without you at my side. You are my rock.*

"Sure, I volunteered Fergus, Haylee volunteered Hud, and Omega volunteered Lucian." He tried to grin at her but could muster no more than a pained blink. *Lord, I'm an absolute failure of a husband. She really got a raw deal when she married this ol' boy. I bet Grant Taylor would never have let her run down like this.*

"Please thank all of them for me. I know I'll be feeling fine by morning." *I don't know what's going on in my body, Lord. I hardly know what to tell a doctor. If I could only go to sleep and wake up feeling well. I'll make it. With this handsome gray-haired man at my side, I'll make it. Oh, Lord, how he makes every day worth living.*

O. T. bent over and kissed her perspiring forehead. "Dola Mae, humor me and let me go get a doc. It will make me feel like I'm takin' better care of you. Right now I'm feelin' low 'cause I can't do anything to make you feel better." *Give her strength, Lord—strength of body, soul, and spirit.*

This time the dimples peeked out from her slight smile. "Darlin', things like this happen. No one is healthy every day of their life, except perhaps you. This is just a sickly time for me. Add that to me being a little extra tired, and it's just a collapse. You wait, Orion Skinner. In the morning I'll feel like my old self again, and I'll be baking bear sign." *Lord, not for my sake . . . but for the sake of this strong, shy man and four active children . . . I would ask to be healed.*

"Darlin', I'll be a frettin' nervous wreck if I don't go get the doc."

"We can't afford to do that."

He fought to keep his voice from rising. "What have we been workin' so hard for, if not to use the funds to take care of ourselves?"

"I heard it costs two dollars for a house call."

"Darlin', don't you talk money to me. We're goin' to take care of you."

"Pray for me," she whispered.

He held both of her hands and closed his eyes. "Now, Lord, my Dola Mae isn't doin' too well tonight. *Lord, to be honest, I'm scared to death about her.* She has a lot of pain and a back that is locked up. Now I reckon You know all of that. *Lord, I don't understand why Dola has to go through this.* And the reason I bring it up is because there is nothin' I can do to help her. *I feel like a helpless failure, Lord.* So I'm needin' You to help out really bad. *To whom shall I turn? You have the words of life.* I'm askin' that You ease the pain and bring healin' to her tired and hurtin' body, that You grant her Your peace and understandin', that You reveal Your heart to her. *Oh, Lord, have mercy on all of us*. In Jesus' name, amen." *Please heal her and let me have a chance to treat her better.*

"Amen," the three-year-old added. Then he sat straight up. "Punky's hungry."

"Take him down and feed him, Orion," Dola said. "I'll be all right now that you're home. I just need the rest."

"I'm sending Corrie up. I'll go fetch Doc Silvermeyer."

"No. Not tonight. If I'm not doin' better by mornin', then I'll think about—"

O. T.'s voice was as rigid as his shoulders and neck. "Dola Mae, don't you play stubborn on me. I'm goin' to get the doc, and that's final!"

"Mr. Skinner, I'm beggin' you not to do that," she bawled.

"Mrs. Skinner, I must do what the Lord is tellin' me to do. I'm goin' for the doctor."

"Please, Orion . . . let me wait until morning," she pleaded.

"Sweet Dola Mae, darlin' . . ." His voice broke as he fought back the tears. "Don't ask me to do that. I can't. I just can't do it. Forgive me, but I have to go get the doc."

O. T. Skinner always figured that joy tasted sweet, like an iced slice of watermelon on a dry, hot July day in Oklahoma.

But anxiety tasted tart, like a pomegranate, sweet and sour at the same moment and difficult to eat.

Fear, on the other hand, was always bitter, caustic. Like an unripe persimmon, fear tended to pull the moisture from his mouth and set his jaw on edge. As he sprinted out the back door of the cafe to the alley, there was a bitter, dry taste that made his tongue stick to the roof of his mouth.

He didn't answer when Rita Ann asked, "How's Mama?"

He didn't even look at Corrie when he shoved Punky into her arms.

Someone was crying when he ran through the kitchen.

What have I done, Lord? I've run that woman down, just like a desperate man runs down his horse. A good horse will keep runnin' just to please his master.

Oh, Lord, has she been doin' this just to please me? To feed the family? We just wanted to save a little extra, Lord. For the first time in our life we've saved up a little for that farm in Dinuba.

I can't believe it. What price am I willin' to pay for that twenty acres of grapes? Skinner, you're a fool—a bigger fool than all the gold-seekers in this town.

They are greedy and make no bones about it.

They are ruthless and don't claim to be righteous.

But you . . . you claim you're not interested in money, and you work the best woman God ever created into a sickbed.

O. T. tried to wipe the tears out of his eyes as he ran. The alkali dirt on his shirt sleeve burned more than the tears. Finally he stopped jogging and pulled out his blue bandanna.

Lord, I want You to know I'm surely aware of my failures, so I reckon I can just cast my cares on You. I'll jist never figure out why You wasted such a fine lady on the likes of me.

The banging of the fire bell emptied the saloons behind him. O. T. stepped off the crowded sidewalk and into the street. He, like the others, searched the evening sky for signs of smoke.

"Where's the fire?" he hollered to a man with a purple silk tie.

"No fire. . . . It's a shootout."

"Where?"

"South of here, I reckon."

O. T. brushed past the gawkers. He shoved his bandanna back into his pocket and continued toward the doctor's office. Suddenly a huge, lumbering, barefoot man staggered out of the crowd into the street and blocked his path.

"Here he is, boys!" the man shouted to those hovering on the raised boardwalk.

"Mr. Jolly, I don't have time to talk to you," O. T. barked.

"Did you hear that, boys? He doesn't have time for me!" The man staggered right at Skinner, waving a gun.

"Jolly," a man on the sidewalk called out, "that there is the Wall Walker. You cain't shoot him."

"The blazes I can't! He ain't got no compadres now!"

"He don't even have a gun!" another declared.

O. T. started to push past Jeremiah Jolly, but the drunk shoved the barrel of his single-action revolver into his ribs. "Give him one!" he screamed.

"You need help, Wall Walker?" someone called.

"Jolly, I have to fetch a doc for my sick wife, so don't get in my way," O. T. demanded. "This is not good timing."

"They'll have to—" The fat man began to hiccup. "—fetch the undertaker (hiccup) for you (hiccup)." Jolly sucked in air in an attempt to cure himself and then belched.

With the rancid smell of whiskey filling the air, O. T. hollered, "I don't have time for this!"

The big man sucked in another breath and held it. O. T. cocked his right fist and, with his feet leaving the ground, slammed it into the big man's jaw. Jolly staggered back, fired the gun in the air, and collapsed.

The crowd stared in silence.

An old man shuffled out and peered down at the big man. "The Wall Walker done one-punched Jeremiah Jolly!"

"Is he dead?" someone called out.

"Nope. But he ain't wakin' up for a while."

A cheer rolled through the crowd.

But O. T. was sprinting around the corner to Carson Street by the time the noise quieted down. He banged on the office door.

Lord, I know it's after office hours, but this is an emergency.

He raced around to the back door that led to the doctor's upstairs living quarters and hammered with his clenched hand.

Come on, Doc, be there when I need you.

He banged again.

I wonder how I skinned my knuckles? Lord, I put You in charge here,
but it's like You're too busy or somethin'. I need a doc, and Silvermeyer is
the only one we know.

O. T. bolted up the outside stairway and banged his way into the
small hospital on the second floor. The nurse in a long white dress and
a cap looked surprised as he rushed in. She dropped the folded white
linens she held in her hand. "Mr. Skinner, is something wrong?"

He jerked off his hat. "Yes, ma'am, Miss Greer." O. T. could feel
his breathless voice rising. "I've got an emergency at home. Dola
Mae's in bad shape. Where's the doc?"

"What's the matter with dear Mrs. Skinner?"

"She's in terrible pain, can't get out of bed, can't move or anything! Where's the doc?"

"He was just called out to the July Extension. There was a gunfight between the union men and the guards. We were told six men
were shot, several in critical condition. I'm getting the beds ready for
them. Dr. Silvermeyer went to see what he could do."

"At the July Extension? Are some men dead?"

"I don't know, but if it was half as bloody as we were told, it
would still be horrible."

O. T. jammed his hat back on his head and stared out the sec-
ond-story window. "It's gone to bloodshed already."

"So it seems." The deep-set creases around her eyes revealed her
anxiety. "Please apologize to dear Mrs. Skinner. I would come over
myself, but I have to stay here and assist the doctor when he brings
in the wounded . . . unless, of course, everyone is dead."

"Miss Greer, you wait right here like you're supposed to. I'll go
help the doc."

"But what about your wife?"

"The sooner Doc Silvermeyer gets them patched up, the sooner
he can come see my Dola. So I reckon helpin' him is like helpin' her."

"Thank you, Mr. Skinner."

The July Extension Mine was one mile north of downtown, and O. T. ran halfway, then slowed to a fast walk. He heard occasional gunshots as he got closer.

A crowd of several dozen hovered at the Joshua trees just north of the wash. Another hundred or more crowded around the front porch of the Liberty Saloon perched near the main entrance to the mine.

"Where's Doc Silvermeyer?" he called to the crowd at the Liberty.

"Inside that gate." An old man pointed. "If he ain't dead."

"You be careful, Wall Walker," another shouted. "Both sides is strikin' out like wounded bears."

O. T. marched straight through the gate and into two shots from a carbine and one from a shotgun. Only a quick dive behind a brick guardhouse saved him. Two men hunched behind the brick building—Sheriff Adonijah Johnson and Dr. Hershel Silvermeyer.

"Skinner, what in blazes are you doin' here?" the sheriff demanded.

O. T. flinched as two more shots were fired. "Came to help the doc."

"Help me!" Silvermeyer exclaimed. "I'm just trying to keep from collecting lead."

O. T. peeked out to see which side was shooting. Gun smoke billowed skyward from both buildings. "Miss Greer said you came to bring some wounded back to the hospital." O. T. lay flat on his stomach. "I figured you needed some help."

Dr. Silvermeyer rubbed the sweat and dirt into his thick eyebrows. "In ten more minutes I won't need any help."

"Why's that?" O. T. asked.

"Because neither side will back off and let me remove the wounded." Silvermeyer tugged his black tie loose and unfastened his shirt collar. "In another ten to fifteen minutes, they will all bleed to death."

O. T. peeked back out at the yard. "Sheriff, can't you do somethin'?"

"Skinner, I don't have enough deputies to face both sides. This union thing is gettin' out of control. Two years ago it was Cripple Creek . . . then the riots in Idaho. Now this International Workers of the World moves out here from Chicago. It used to be simple to be sheriff. Just stop runaway carriages, shoot the bank robbers, and string up the horse thieves. The only way I can stop this is to call out the army, and Governor Sparks is not ready to do that. But he's been threatenin' it. Neither side will budge."

O. T. yanked his head back just as dirt flew five feet to the east of him. "How can either side win this way?"

The sun had set. Long shadows melted into twilight. No air moved. The acrid smell of gun smoke mixed with the always-present aroma of alkali.

"I'm not sure they want to win anymore," Silvermeyer said. "They just want to make sure they don't lose."

Skinner peered out at the dirt yard between the shop and the headworks. One man lay in the dirt in front of the office, clutching his bleeding leg. "That looks like Pipestem Drusky."

"He should have been smart enough to stay down at the Northern Saloon and away from this," the sheriff mumbled.

O. T. sat up. "But—but this isn't right. They can't let Pipestem lay out there and die."

"I tried to get them to let the doc look after him, but neither side would back down," the sheriff reported.

O. T. stood up.

"Stay down, Skinner," the sheriff ordered.

"This isn't right. Go get a wagon for the wounded," O. T. replied. "Doc, you go wait over by the Liberty Saloon. I'll carry Pipestem out."

"You are goin' to do what?" the sheriff yelled.

"The only decent thing a man can do." O. T. stuck his head around the tiny brick guard station and cupped his hand around his mouth. "This is O. T. Skinner. I'm comin' in to get the wounded right now!" he hollered.

"You're crazy, Skinner," the sheriff warned.

"Go get a wagon!"

Gunshot sprayed dirt in front of him as he hiked over to Drusky, but none of the bullets hit closer than ten feet.

"I'm bleedin' bad, Skinner," Drusky moaned.

O. T. knelt down beside the man. Two more shots blasted alkali dirt a few feet closer. "I'll get you over to the doc. He's waitin' out there to patch you up."

The injured man chewed on a broken pipe stem. "Get yourself out of here, Skinner. They'll shoot you. Those anarchists will plug you like they did me."

O. T. grabbed Drusky by the shoulder and pulled him up.

"Put me down! They'll shoot me again!" he cried out.

"Doc said you'll be dead in ten minutes if we don't stop the bleedin'. Come on, Pipestem, I'm totin' you out. You ain't dyin' today." Skinner pulled the man over his shoulder like a limp sack of potatoes. He arched his back and slowly struggled to stand.

"What do you think you're doin', Skinner?" someone yelled from the headworks.

"Tryin' to help a man live to see another day. You union men aren't against helpin' an ordinary man, are you? Pipestem isn't a mine owner."

"They shot us first, you know!" a voice called out.

"Just give me a chance, boys. I ain't takin' sides. I'll tote out your wounded too."

"Like Hades you will!" one of the guards screamed. "The only way an anarchist is leavin' here is dead."

O. T. started moving toward the front gate. "Is that you, Mulroney?" he yelled at the men huddled in the shadows behind the broken windows of the July Extension offices.

"Yeah, Skinner, it's me."

"Did you get that stew Dola Mae sent over on Monday when she heard you were sick and didn't show up for supper at the cafe?" O. T. hollered.

"Yeah, tell her thanks. I'm feelin' better. Until today. Are you really goin' to help the anarchists?"

O. T. swayed toward the gate. "No, I'm goin' to help the wounded and dyin', and I promise I won't ask them what their politics is."

Sheriff Johnson had a wagon waiting when O. T. staggered out with Pipestem Drusky. The crowd at the Liberty Saloon cheered when he laid the wounded man in the wagon next to Silvermeyer.

"Sheriff, take this one and the doc down to his hospital. Then come right back for another."

"Do you know the others that were shot?" the sheriff asked.

O. T. rubbed his shoulders and his biceps. "Nope, I don't reckon I do."

"Why are you doin' this, Skinner?" the sheriff hollered. "You ain't gettin' paid for this."

"'Cause men are shot and need a doc."

"You're a fool, Skinner."

"That's somethin' most everyone in town can agree on." O. T.'s mind slid back to Dola Mae lying in agony on top of the comforter. *Lord, I'm even a bigger fool than most of them can imagine. And I wasn't totally honest. I'm helpin' so I can get the doc to go look at Dola. Forgive my motive, Lord.*

No shots were fired when O. T. went back out between the office and the headworks.

"You got any union men wounded?" O. T. hollered at the sheet-iron-covered building.

"Kendall's hurt bad," a voice hollered out.

O. T. trudged toward the door. "I'll come get him."

Someone fired a shot ten feet in front of O. T., and he stopped.

"We ain't goin' to let you turn him over to them guards and have them shoot him," a man yelled.

"Skinner, get out of the way!" someone among the mine guards yelled.

O. T. marched straight up to the broken window of the head-works and hollered past the protruding barrels, "You union men have to start trustin' someone sometime. Ask Kendall if he wants me to tote him to the hospital or not. I won't risk my neck for a man that don't want to go."

The evening darkened as O. T. waited for a reply. Those gathered at the gate were dark silhouettes, looking more like scrub cedars than men.

"Kendall said he wants you to take him to the hospital," a man finally hollered.

The door swung open. O. T. scooted inside the stifling hot building. Fumes of gear oil, gunpowder, and sweat hovered like fog settling on a pond in spring. Several thin, young men hovered around a man lying on the rough wooden floor. Makeshift bloody bandages circled the man's midsection.

Oh, Lord, have mercy on his soul. He's goin' to die.

"You ain't goin' to take him to jail, are you?" a man with a dark beard and shotgun asked.

"I'll see that he gets to Dr. Silvermeyer's hospital. If he gets healthy and he's broken a law, I suppose the sheriff will deal with that. You fellas are welcome to come with me if you want to watch over him."

"They'd shoot us the minute we walk out that door," the bearded one said.

"Lift him up and put him in my arms, boys. I can't carry him over my shoulder without breakin' him in two."

The injured man ground his teeth in pain. He kept his eyes closed as three men lifted him. O. T. cradled the man in his arms.

"How did you boys get in this bind? This isn't organizing; this is a gunfight . . . a war."

"It all blew up on us," the bearded spokesman reported. "We just said a word or two, and someone fired a shot and hit Kendall. Then we dove in here and pulled guns. After that it sort of went berserk."

A short man with a hawk nose scooted up next to O. T. "Mr. Skinner, I'm Peter St. Marie. I was in charge of the riot today. Can you get us out of here without being shot?"

O. T.'s arms were starting to ache. "I might figure out somethin'. You want me to try?"

"We'll vote on it. Would you take us to jail if we go out with you?" St. Marie asked.

"That's not my job to decide. I'll get you out safe. I imagine law-breakers will be jailed," O. T. insisted.

"How about them guards? They started shootin' at us. Are they goin' to be jailed?"

"Boys, I don't know anything about this. You'll have to make your best decision. I know I've got to get Kendall to the wagon before I drop him. You have any other wounded?"

"Pendry took a bullet in the thigh," St. Marie said.

"I'm doin' okay," a man with a belt strapped around his thigh said.

"You're comin' back, ain't you, Skinner?" the bearded one asked.

"Yeah, but it's their turn next. Make up your mind if you want help gettin' out. After dark I won't be much help. It'll be too risky."

O. T. carefully carried the wounded man outside. He could see the streetlights of Goldfield in the distance.

Lord, there's a smell about death, beyond the sweat, and the unbathed body, and the blood. It's like soured milk or the sulfur in the air before lightnin' strikes. It's like wakin' up in a dark room alert and knowin' someone's there, though you can't see or hear a thing.

O. T.'s biceps burned with pain under the weight of the wounded man.

"Are you doin' all right, Kendall?"

The man kept his eyes closed. "I'm dyin', Mr. Skinner," he mumbled.

O. T. tried to shift the weight of the man a little bit to his right arm. "I reckon you could be right."

"I never figured it would happen this way," Kendall said. "Cold, numb, carried by a stranger . . . in a two-bit town . . . without anyone around who cares."

"Do you believe in what you're doin'?" O. T. asked.

The man opened both eyes, but the way he searched, O. T. could tell his vision was limited. "Yes, I do."

"Then you're dyin' for what you believe to be good for mankind. A lot of men die for less noble causes than that."

The man closed his eyes. His head slumped against O. T.'s chest. His voice was so weak that O. T. stopped and lowered his ear to the man's mouth. "I don't suppose nobility gets a man through the gates of heaven."

"Nope. I reckon it don't. You trustin' in Jesus, son?"

Blood now streamed out of the side of the man's mouth. "I never had time for religion."

"Well, Kendall, you're goin' to have a lot of time from now on."

"I ain't sure I believe in life eternal anyway." Kendall choked out each word.

O. T. continued to hike toward the gate. "It don't matter if you believe or not. You're goin' to get eternal life. The only question left for you is, where do you want to spend it?"

"You talkin' heaven or hell, Skinner?"

"That's the only two choices we have."

"There's no way God will let me into heaven."

"Jesus opened the door for all of us."

"Even me?"

"He took the sinner dyin' on the cross next to Him with Him that day. I reckon that means He'll take any of us."

"What did that guy say?"

"'Lord, remember me when Thou comest into—'"

With a voice so piercing and loud that goose bumps popped out on O. T.'s neck, Kendall cried out, "Lord Jesus, remember me . . ." His voice died to a whisper, "Oh, my God . . . remember me!"

O. T. stopped a few feet short of the wagon where the sheriff and a deputy waited.

"What did he say?" the sheriff called out.

O. T. stared at the glazed, unblinking eyes of the man in his arms. "He was just makin' peace with the Lord."

"Is he . . ."

O. T. gently laid Kendall in the back of the wagon. "Take him to the undertaker." He stared back at the mine. "I can talk them out of there, Sheriff. Can you arrest them and keep them safe in jail overnight and then find out who on each side is doin' the killin'?"

The sheriff glanced over at his deputy, then back at Skinner. "If they put their guns down, I reckon so."

O. T. pointed toward the mine company office. "Can you keep those guards from shootin' them as they come out?"

"That's a tougher question. We can stop a gunfight, but we can't stop a war."

"Do me a favor. While I go back for the other injured, send someone to the cafe and tell Lucian LaPorte to bring my children out here. Both daughters and both boys. I need them to help me."

"Even that toddler of yours?" the sheriff asked.

"I want them all," O. T. insisted.

O. T. turned and trudged through the shadows back to the yard. He helped out a short mine guard named August Nascimento, whose entire wrist had shattered when the bullet hit it. Even bandaged, it was so gruesome his friends had tied it behind his back so he wouldn't have to look at it.

Then he hiked back to the union men in the headworks.

"Kendall died in my arms, boys. I'm sorry I didn't get here sooner," he announced.

"They murdered him!" someone screamed.

"I don't know who shot who, but I don't want any more of you dyin' in my arms. I can get you out . . . and the sheriff said he'd protect you overnight in the jail."

"Then what?" someone called out.

"I reckon the judge will try to sort it out. You can explain your case to him," O. T. said.

"They can shoot us, but they can't stop us. The Workers of the World will prevail," someone shouted.

"Save your spiel for the miners, boys. I'm just an old farm boy with no interest in this."

"Whose side are you on, Skinner?" St. Marie asked.

"I'm on Dola Mae's side."

"Who's Dola Mae?"

"She's my wife, and she needs a doctor bad. The doc's tied up with you all shootin' each other. So the quicker you get this solved, the quicker I get help for my wife."

"It's as simple as that?" the bearded one asked.

"I'm a simple man. Family is everything to me, boys. Now do you want me to get you out?"

"How you goin' to do it?" St. Marie asked.

"I've got a team of helpers comin' to lead you out of here."

St. Marie peeked out at the deserted mine yard. "Did you call in the troops?"

"No, sir, I called in my four children." O. T. rolled up the blood-stained, dirty sleeves of his white shirt. "Me and them will lead you out."

"Children?" the bearded man asked.

"I ain't hidin' behind no kids," a man with matted, dirty blond hair declared.

O. T. spun around to the door. "That's your choice, boys. But I'm not hangin' around here for another minute."

"Wait," St. Marie interrupted. "We aren't doin' the union any good if we're all dead."

"I'll be back in five minutes. Be ready, or I'm leavin'. It's the only chance I can give you. I want to get you out before it's pitch black."

The only sound O. T. could hear was the heels of his boots stomping alkali dirt as he marched back to the gate. Everyone in the crowd at the gate seemed to be holding their breath.

Almost everyone.

"Daddy!" Corrie ran to his side and grabbed his arm. "What's the matter? Is that blood on your shirt? Were you shot? Did someone die? Why did you want us here? Where's the doctor for Mama?"

He glanced at Rita Ann. "How's Mama doin', big sister?"

Rita Ann chewed on her lip. "She worried when you didn't come back."

"Daddy-Daddy-Daddy." Punky held out his arms. "My mama's sick."

O. T. pulled the three-year-old into his arms. "I need all of you to help me."

"O. T., what did you get yourself into this time?" LaPorte called down from the carriage.

"They are killin' each other in there, Lucian."

"Maybe some things is just meant to be."

"It's stupid. Life is so fragile. People are the only important thing in life, and they act like it's so trivial."

LaPorte pulled off his round hat and tried to survey the mine. "You talkin' about them union men or about Dola Mae?"

O. T. rubbed the back of his neck and tried to relax muscles as tight as dried rawhide on a saddle tree.

"What are we goin' to do, Daddy?" Tommy-Blue questioned. "Can I carry the shotgun?"

"We don't need guns. I just need you to walk some men from that metal building over here to the sheriff."

"How come, Daddy?" Corrie asked.

"Because they're afraid. You know what it's like when you're afraid. It's nice to have someone to walk with you."

"'To fear the foe, since fear oppresseth strength, gives, in your weakness, strength unto your foe, and so your follies fight against yourself,'" Rita Ann said.

"I like someone to hold my hand when I'm afraid," Corrie added. "Are we suppose to hold their hands?"

O. T. put his hand around Corrie's shoulder. "That might be nice, darlin'."

"Punky will hold Daddy's hand," the toddler declared.

It took several minutes to get everything in position. One deputy held the lead lines of the big wagon. Two more deputies held lanterns at the entrance to the mine. The crowd now circled the gate of the July Extension. Everyone strained in the twilight to see what would happen. Sheriff Johnson hiked over to the building where the mine guards huddled behind the checked levers of carbines and rifles.

Then out of the big tin building came O. T. Skinner leading a parade of anxious Workers of the World. Corrie Lou walked behind her daddy, holding hands with two union men. Rita Ann was behind her doing the same. Tommy-Blue followed his sister. The last man out was St. Marie, who carried Silas Paul "Punky" Skinner in his arms.

No one said a word.

Not a union man.

Not an armed guard.

Not the sheriff.

Not the crowd.

Not the children.

Even though the air was warm and dust-filled, O. T. felt cold sweat on his forehead. *Lord, this is a violent town, and we are a peace-*

ful family. We've got to move as soon as Dola gets stronger. This is like a bad dream. I'm marchin' my children into danger. Please protect us all.

The silence broke into a rolling wave of cheers when O. T. Skinner brought the seven union men to the wagon. The sheriff hustled out to meet them. "Boys, throw your guns to the dirt and get in that wagon in a hurry. I'm going to get you out of here."

"How did you keep them from shootin' at us?" O. T. asked him.

"I cocked my Colt and told them I'd shoot dead on the spot any man that took a shot at one of those Skinner kids. Told them that if one of the kids got hit, all of them would hang and more than likely before they ever see a judge."

"They're goin' to be mad."

"I reckon it's the end of a chapter, but not the end of a book."

O. T. motioned toward the black leather carriage. "Let's load up in Mr. LaPorte's hack and get Doc Silvermeyer for Mama."

It was pitch dark by the time Dr. Silvermeyer was able to ride with them to the cafe. O. T. paced the floor at the bottom of the stairs as the doctor examined Dola. Rita Ann circled one of the empty round tables, the giant Shakespeare book balanced on top of her head. "Daddy, when is the doctor going to be done? I want to see Mama."

"We don't want to hurry him."

Punky rolled over in the center of the table and continued to snooze. O. T. could hear his rhythmic breathing.

"Is the doctor going to give Mama some medicine to make her well?" Tommy-Blue asked.

O. T. gazed up at the empty stairs. "I don't know. Mama needs some rest. It might take a little while for her to feel better."

"What about breakfast? Are we goin' to have to cook and serve breakfast without her?" Rita Ann asked.

"I don't know, darlin'. I don't know."

"Here comes the doctor!" Corrie shouted.

Shirtsleeves rolled up to his elbows, Silvermeyer scurried down the steps.

"Can we go see Mama?" Rita Ann asked.

"Yes, but don't climb up on the bed," the doctor said.

Rita Ann, Corrie, and Tommy-Blue sprinted up the stairs. O. T. lagged back by the sleeping Punky.

"What did you find, doc?" he asked.

"I found a hurting woman, O. T., to tell you the truth, I can't figure it out yet."

O. T. could feel his hand quiver. He jammed it into his pocket. "What do you mean?"

"The symptoms are common to several problems. I haven't isolated which one yet."

O. T. took a deep, slow breath. He could feel his heart race. "What are the possibilities?"

Dr. Silvermeyer slowly rolled down the sleeves on his shirt. "It could be she wore out a disk in her back, and they're grinding on each other. Or it could even be a series of pulled muscles. There is always the possibility she is pregnant and having difficulty, or . . ." Silvermeyer looked down at the sleeping toddler and shook his head.

"Or what, doc?" O. T. demanded.

"It could be she has a cancer."

O. T.'s mouth dropped. His breath stopped. His hand went to his dry mouth. "No . . . no, no, no," he mumbled. "Oh, Lord Jesus, no. It's not that."

Silvermeyer grabbed his arm. "O. T., listen to me. I didn't say it was a cancer. I said, I can't tell. But those are the possibilities. I thought it fair that you know the truth."

"How do you decide which it is?"

"Let her rest up a couple weeks, and we'll look for progress. Cancer won't get better."

"She's got to be in bed for two weeks?" O. T. gasped

"I didn't say that. What I said was, we would evaluate her condition after two weeks. I suspect she might have to be in bed a lot longer than that. But perhaps I will be able to diagnose things better at that time."

"Longer than two weeks? What are you talkin' about here, doc? I don't understand."

"Your wife may have to live with chronic back problems the rest of her life."

"But—that's—that's horrible."

"There are worse scenarios," the doctor sighed. "Look, Mr. Skinner, your wife is one of the most giving, compassionate women I have met in my life. She is a dear lady, and it pains me to tell you this. But you are an honest man, and I need to tell you the honest truth."

"Did you tell her this?" O. T. asked.

The doctor nodded.

"Then I'd better go talk to her."

"Tell her I will check back tomorrow."

"I thought you said two weeks."

"It will take that long to evaluate things, but I intend to stop by most every day."

O. T. gathered a sleepy Punky in his arms and hustled up the stairs. Rita Ann, Corrie, and Tommy-Blue surrounded the bed where Dola lay under the covers.

"We told Mama all about leadin' the anarchists out," Tommy-Blue bragged.

O. T. rested his hand on Tommy-Blue's shoulder. "You would have been proud of them, Mama. They were all heroes today."

"I'm always proud of my children." She didn't look at him. Her eyes were on the children. "Rita Ann, none of you has had supper tonight. Go down and fix them something."

"Do you want some supper, Mama?" Rita Ann asked.

"Not tonight. But fix something for your daddy. He'll be down in a minute or two."

"Punky's hungry," the toddler declared sleepily.

O. T. set Punky down. "Take his hand, Corrie Lou, and stuff this little sausage."

"You're goin' to be all right, ain't you, Mama?" Tommy-Blue asked.

"Darlin', I'm in the Lord's hands. How much better off could anyone be?"

His blue eyes lit up as he spun around and followed his sisters out of the room.

O. T. dragged a chair over to the edge of the bed. Dola reached out her hand. She felt the calluses of his warm hand. "I should be furious at you, Orion Tower Skinner."

"For goin' to get the doc when you told me not to?"

"And for risking your life and the lives of my children. What in the world were you thinking about—having them march into that gunfight?"

"I was thinkin' about you, Mama. I was tryin' to get the doc to come see you. And I knew if they kept shootin' each other, the doc would be busy all night."

"Did Dr. Silvermeyer talk to you?"

"Yep."

"I'm scared, Orion. I know I should have more faith, and I'm so ashamed I can't be the strong woman you deserve. I feel like such a failure."

He glanced over at her and opened his mouth.

But all he could do was cry.

And cry.

SEVEN

When Dola opened her eyes, she could see the tiny spider webs that drooped like Christmas garlands from the dull gray paint on the ceiling. Her neck was stiff. She had a sharp cramp in her left side. Her toes felt ice cold. There was sweat on her forehead. The collar of her thin cotton nightgown was drenched.

She shoved her right elbow out and lifted her head a few inches off the damp pillowcase. Though the room seemed to swim around, she could survey the huge one-room apartment and see that she was alone.

She dropped her head back on the pillow and slowly reached up and flipped the straight brown hair away from her eyes. When she breathed deeply, there was a sharp pain at the base of her breastbone.

Lord, I was really hoping I would wake up and find that yesterday was all a dream. My family needs me, and I'm letting them down. It seems so distant—the pain, the doctor, the worried look on Orion's face. Did it really happen that way? Maybe if I got to my feet . . .

She propped herself up on her elbows and focused on her feet. They twitched. Wiggled. Flexed. But she could not convince them to slide out of bed.

Dola flopped back down on her pillow. Tears trickled down her cheeks.

Not for me, Lord. For the children. For Orion. I have four lovely children and a wonderful husband who need me to take care of them. For their sake, I ask You to heal me. I don't want anything for me, Lord. I just want to take care of them. That's all I've ever wanted in my life—a chance to be the kind of wife and mother that would please You. I don't understand, Lord. How can I be of any value to them or to You while like this?

A gray-headed man wearing a crisp white shirt and leather braces holding up clean denim jeans stuck his head in the doorway.

"Are you awake, beautiful Dola Mae?"

"Orion Skinner, don't you feed me those lies this early in the morning!"

He marched into the room carrying a white-enameled tin basin. "Now, sweet darlin', you know I ain't lyin'. And, besides, it ain't all that early."

Dola could smell the tonic water he had splashed on his cheeks after his shave. "What time is it?"

He set the basin on the wooden orange crate that served as a nightstand. "It's 6:15 A.M."

Dola studied his broad shoulders. "Are the children downstairs?"

O. T. sat on the edge of the bed and plucked up her hand. "Yep. We all pitched in and helped Omega and the girls."

His fingers entwined into hers. "How's it going?"

"Looks like a full house downstairs. The boys are still curious about what we intend to do with the auto car." He laid his other hand up against her cheek. She closed her eyes and could feel her face relax. "Everyone is askin' about you," he added.

Her eyes blinked open. "What did you tell them?"

He squeezed her hand and then stood and strolled to the other side of the room. "I said you were feelin' poorly." He picked up a towel and a cotton washrag from the wooden drying rack and returned to the bedside.

Dola raised her head and peered over at the nightstand. "Just exactly what do you have in the basin, Mr. Skinner?"

He soaked the small rag in the steaming water. "Why, it's your bathwater, Mama."

"But I can't . . ." she protested, clutching the sweat-drenched collar of her cotton gown.

He tugged at her hand. "Well, I can."

She pulled the sheet up to her neck. "But what about . . ."

His easy grin made her relax her grip on the sheet.

"No time to be modest, Dola Mae. I told the kids they couldn't come up for fifteen minutes, that Mama needed time to clean up. And I'm goin' to help you do just that."

She dropped her arms down to her side. "I feel totally helpless."

"The Lord helps the helpless." O. T. pulled the white cotton sheet down below her knees.

Dola turned her head toward the wall. "He didn't answer me today."

"You wanted to wake up healed?" he quizzed as he unfastened a tiny white button on the cuff of her gown.

"Yes, I did." She held up the other cuff for him to unfasten.

"Perhaps there is something better than being healed." He tugged at her high collar.

Dola raised her chin and stared at the ceiling. "What is that?"

"To find yourself exactly where God wants you to be."

She continued to look at the ceiling. "Are you getting spiritual on me, Orion Skinner?"

He unbuttoned her collar and then sat up straight. "I reckon I am."

She folded her arms across her chest, surprised to feel very little pain. "Good," she announced.

He raised his eyebrows and tugged at her arms. "Oh?"

Dola looked right at his blue-gray eyes. "Because I like to know that the man unbuttoning my collar is a spiritual man."

He leaned back and laughed. "I'm not all that spiritual."

She could feel her face blush. "Oh?"

"You are a beautiful woman, Dola Mae. Now come on—let's get this sponge bath over before the children barge in."

"You're embarrassing me, Orion. Give me that sheet back. Then I'll slip this off," she insisted.

He pulled the sheet back up to her chin as she struggled with her gown. "What's wrong with being embarrassed by a man who loves you dearly?"

She raised her hand up above the sheet and brushed her hair back. "Okay, you win. I need your help."

"I hmmmmm."

"Don't hmmmm me, Mr. Skinner. I'm a sick woman."

"Rats." He winked at her.

She made sure the sheet stayed up to her neck even as he pulled the gown over her head. "You're acting foolish, Orion Tower Skinner."

"Dola Mae, darlin', I cried my eyes out last night. I begged and I pleaded and I bargained, and it didn't change one thing. It's no way to live. We'll laugh, tease, and take it one day at a time until we beat this thing. Side by side with the Lord's help, we'll conquer it, but we will not let it worry us sick. You just lie there and blush and let me wash you up."

Dola fought back tears. She turned away when she felt a trickle down her cheek. "I feel so helpless, Orion."

"Darlin', you've been takin' care of this family night and day for years. Now it's your turn to be taken care of. Rita Ann is comin' up to comb your hair. She said she was goin' to braid it with ribbons."

Dola wiped her eyes on the sheet. "Braid it? I haven't braided my hair in fifteen years!"

"Then you're due. Let her play mama. It's good for her to learn to take care of someone other than herself."

Dola sniffed, then took a deep breath. Even in a stuffy room in the Mojave Desert, the air felt refreshing. "And where's my baby?"

O. T. rubbed the bridge of his nose and grinned. "Right now I believe he has maple syrup from his nose to his fingertips."

"Oh, dear." She reached out and stroked O. T.'s clean-shaven cheek. *Lord, You showed Your grace to me so clearly when You gave me this man.*

"And he has a big smile on his face." When she pulled her hand back, he took it and kissed her fingers. "Big sister figured out the schedule. Corrie is watchin' Punky from now till noon. Then after his nap, Rita takes him until supper. While Rita and Corrie are servin' supper, Tommy-Blue will watch him. After supper Corrie will bathe him and put him to bed."

"Corrie Lou puts him to bed? And just where is Daddy going to be while all this is going on?"

O. T. glanced over at the open double doors that led to the balcony. "Darlin', Jakob Fleming is goin' to pay me $100 a week just to sit down in that mine of his and watch his hired men guard that picture rock at the Pear Blossom."

She clutched her hands across her chest on top of the sheets. "You are goin' to work double jobs?"

He gently wiped her face with the washcloth. "Just for a few weeks. Then they'll have that gold sacked up and out of there. It's not permanent. By then you'll be back on your feet."

Orion Skinner, you couldn't tell a convincing lie if your life depended on it, but I love you for trying.

He washed her neck and shoulders. "I figure we can save up the money and get to California before Christmas."

Dola closed her eyes and dropped her hands down to her sides. "I promised the children we wouldn't pull them out of school."

"Some things change, Mama. They'll understand." He continued to bathe her in a soft, circular motion. The warm water was slowly turning cool. He stopped to towel off her face and shoulders.

"But—but what about the cafe?" she pressed.

O. T. soaked the washrag in the water and wrung it out. "We'll all pitch in this week. It will be all right. When the children start school, we'll have to hire someone. Fergus said Gerta might be willing to work."

"We can't afford anyone else, Orion. You know that. We are barely turning a profit now." Dola felt the warm rag on her arms.

"Darlin', all we really need from this operation is for our meals to be provided and this room. I'll be drawin' double wages." When he finished one arm, he proceeded to dry it.

"You said we were savin' those extra funds."

"We'll save all we can."

"Orion, I can't let you work two jobs." Dola felt the warm rag on her other arm.

His voice was deep. Her throat felt a tickle. "Now, darlin', don't go stealin' my praise."

She opened one eye. "What do you mean?"

"I was praisin' the Lord this mornin' that He provided me a job where I sit around and do nothin' and get paid $100 a week."

"But it's not permanent."

"One day at a time, darlin'. We'll praise Him one day at a time."

The warm rag felt good as he continued to bathe her. "I'll be up and around in a few days," she insisted.

"See there . . . and we'll look back and laugh at how anxious we got for nothin'." His voice was now light, almost teasing.

"I love you, Orion Tower Skinner."

He leaned over and brushed a kiss across her chapped lips. "And I love you, Dola Mae Davis Skinner. We'll whip this, darlin'. With the Lord's help, we'll whip this."

She held her breath and fought back the tears. "But what if it's a permanent back injury?"

He sat up and continued the sponge bath. "Then we'll whip that."

"And what if it's . . . you know . . . a cancer?" She turned her head away from him.

"Then we'll whip it together."

"No one whips a cancer."

O. T. put his fingertips on her chin and slowly turned her face back toward him. "Them cancers never faced O. T. and Dola Mae Skinner! They don't have a chance, darlin'. They are whipped already!"

"And what happens if I'm . . . expecting?"

He began to laugh, a deep, tension-relaxing laugh. "Then I'll dance in the dusty streets of Goldfield and howl at the moon!"

She laughed. "You would, wouldn't you?"

"Yep."

She closed her eyes again as the warm washrag reached her stomach. "Dr. Hewitt in Guthrie said the next baby could kill me."

"What does he know? I never trusted a doctor that raised funny-lookin' goats just for the milk. One day at a time, Mama—that's how we'll take it."

Lord, the closer this man is to me, the better I feel. Why is that? I would wither and die in a day without him in my life.

O. T. studied his wife as he washed. *Lord, how I love this woman. Ever' day since we got married, I keep thinkin' You'll send an angel to tell me there's been a mistake, that You had someone much smarter, much more handsome, much wiser in mind for this wonderful woman. She always makes me feel like the luckiest man on earth.*

He washed and dried her toes. "Now do you want a fresh gown?"

"I only have one other."

"Then Rita Ann can wash this one out while you're wearin' the other."

"Oh, I can't ask her to use the washtub and—"

"Ask her, Mama. She's growin' leap and bounds. She wants to take care of you so bad."

She patted his hand. "We have wonderful children."

"Yes, we do. They're just like their mama."

"Not one of them is like me, Orion."

"That's not true," he corrected her. "Tommy-Blue is like you, and you know it."

"Corrie is the exact duplicate of her daddy. Big sister, of course, is unlike anyone on the face of the earth."

"And little dumplin'," O. T. could feel a smile ease across his stiff jaw, "is like all of us rolled into one smilin', chubby body."

"We are lucky people, Mr. Skinner."

He squeezed her hand and then stood beside the bed. "Yes, we are, Mrs. Skinner. Now I suppose you want that clean gown on."

"And the sheet pulled up and the comforter over my toes," she instructed.

She watched as he fussed and fixed everything to make her comfortable.

"Anything else I can do for you, darlin'?"

She studied the creases around his eyes. "Orion, go to work so you can get some rest."

He gently raised her head, fluffed up her pillow, and laid her head back down. "I think I'll do that."

Dola wiggled her toes under the covers and enjoyed the fresh feeling of a clean gown. "Will you come home before goin' out to the Pear Blossom?" she inquired.

"Yep. And I'll come home at lunch if I'm anywhere close to town." He rolled his sleeves back down and buttoned them.

She reached her hand out to him and was surprised that no pain shot up her arm this time. "I feel much better than I did last night. At least, mentally."

He gently rubbed her fingers between his. "Good. What do you think made the difference?"

"Bein' around the most wonderful man on earth helped a lot." Dola could feel her fingers warming up.

He pulled his hand back and scratched the back of his neck. "No foolin'? You'll have to introduce me to him someday."

Dola held up a clenched fist. "You're lucky I'm in bed, Skinner."

He raised his eyebrows. "And you're lucky you're a sick woman, Mrs. Skinner, 'cause I'd . . ."

"Don't embarrass me," she interrupted.

"Darlin', you look good in red."

"I'm glad, because I've been blushing ever since you walked into the room this morning."

"You braggin' or complainin', darlin'?"

"Bragging, of course. Orion, do you have any idea how good being near you makes me feel?"

He studied her from her comforter-covered toes to the top of her long, matted, gray-streaked brown hair. "Dola Mae, I know exactly how you feel."

The wagon seat felt hard, his legs stiff, as O. T. drove out to the Cosmopolitan Lease northeast of Columbia Mountain. High, thin clouds streaked the Nevada desert sky. The air had turned from pleasantly warm to stifling. It was like stepping out of a mountain breeze into a stuffy cabin where too much white pine had been crammed into the woodstove. The back of his white cotton shirt was already plastered to his back. His jeans burned against his legs. In the back of the wagon were six assay reports and six samples of ore, each in its own wooden crate.

As he crested a knoll and dropped into a bone-dry, barren wash, he spotted a man sitting cross-legged by the side of the road, a long Springfield Trapdoor .45-70 musket in his lap.

"You lookin' for a ride, you ol' Paiute?"

"If you insist," Fergus replied.

O. T. pulled off his hat and tried to dry his forehead on his shirtsleeve. "By all means, I insist."

The Indian adjusted his wide-brimmed black felt hat and struggled to his feet, using the long musket as a prop. "If you put it that way, I could help you out."

O. T. jammed his hat back on his head. "Fergus, what are you doin' out here?"

"I was thinkin' about goin' to Arizona."

O. T. looked back over his shoulder. "Arizona is south."

"Yes, I know that." Fergus used his right hand to straighten the fingers of his left. "It is my observation that a man can think of a place without actually going in that direction." He tossed the musket up to O. T. and held out his hand for a hoist.

The wagon jolted forward as the aroma of garlic radiated around Skinner. "You didn't answer my question. What are you doin' out here?"

Fergus stared straight ahead without expression. "I was on my way to Schurz."

Straight ahead O. T. could already see the heat vapors shimmer on the horizon. "That's over 100 miles north of here."

Fergus yanked off his hat, pulled something out of his hair with his fingers, and examined it as if it were a gold nugget. "I was not very far on my way." He dropped the object on the floorboard of the wagon and stomped on it with the heel of his boot.

"Why do you want to go to Schurz? You got family there?"

"Yes. That's why I changed my mind. I think I'll stay in Goldfield."

"You keep avoidin' my question about Arizona. Why is that?"

Fergus dropped the lever on his single-shot musket and stared into the empty chamber. "Your partners have left town."

"My partners?"

"In the Mexico gold mine." Fergus closed the falling block on the Trapdoor and searched the floor of the wagon.

"You talkin' about Lucky Jack, Ace, and all?" O. T. watched the Paiute. "Did you lose something?"

"I thought I had a bullet in this gun. Perhaps I dropped it."

"You don't remember?"

"It has been awhile since I needed one. Perhaps I used it already."

"What about Lucky Jack and Ace?" O. T. queried.

"They are gone. They went to Arizona, then on to Mexico."

"I didn't think they would go off and leave Gerta."

"She told them she has always wanted to go to Mexico and that she'd come visit when they got themselves established." Fergus patted the receiver of his musket. "Perhaps I used my last bullet to shoot that Mojave."

"Old man, you didn't shoot anyone, and you know it. Now which one is Gerta goin' to go see?"

"All six of them, of course. I shot a Mojave once. Perhaps more, but I don't remember."

"Sooner or later they are goin' to want Gerta to narrow the field." Skinner pulled the team to the left as he passed tandem freight wagons pulled by sixteen horses.

"Why should she be choosey?"

"Some men are just that way, I reckon."

"In that case she will choose the tallest."

"Deuce?"

"Whichever one she decides is tallest. I believe she likes tall men. There aren't many tall Paiutes, which might explain why she hasn't married."

"So she isn't married?"

"Yes, I asked her. I told her the Wall Walker wants to know."

O. T. thought about how short Ace Wilkins and Wasco were. "I'm sure she has other requirements besides being tall."

"Why?" Fergus challenged.

O. T. started to reply and then shook his head. "Did Gerta get her house cleaned up?"

"Yes. It is a very nice house." Fergus beamed. "But I hear Mr. Jolly is still in town."

"Yeah, I ran into him last night." O. T. glanced down at the skinned knuckles on his right hand. "I forgot all about that."

Fergus held the .45-70 to his shoulder and tracked an imaginary antelope across the desert. "They say around town that the Wall Walker one-punched him."

"I was sort of in a hurry, and he pulled a gun. I didn't have time to talk him out of it. Him being drunk, I surmise I didn't do too much permanent damage."

"To him or to you?"

O. T. rubbed his knuckles. "Either one."

The Paiute dry-fired the Trapdoor. Skinner heard the musket's loud click.

"I suppose if you hadn't had time to one-punch him, you could have just shot him," Fergus suggested.

"No, you old warrior, I don't reckon I could do that."

"He had a gun pulled on you."

"He was drunk."

"How many murders have been committed by drunks?"

"I suppose most of them."

Fergus stood up as the wagon rambled along and began to stamp his feet.

"What are you doin'?"

"Looking for a bullet." The Indian plopped back down and laid the long musket in the back of the wagon. He tugged off his right brown stovetop boot. "Wall Walker, have you ever shot a man?" he asked.

"Nope. Most times I don't even have a gun. You know that."

Fergus reached inside his boot and pulled out a fat, stubby object. "Aha! My bullet!"

"That's not a 45.-70, partner. It looks like a .44-40."

"That is strange." Fergus stared at the bullet. "I've never owned a .44. I wonder where this bullet came from?"

"Perhaps someone has been wearin' your boots."

"Yes, that must be it." Fergus pulled his boot back on and dropped the bullet to the floorboard of the wagon. "Have you ever shot a woman, Wall Walker?" He tugged on his other boot.

O. T. began to laugh. "No, I've never shot a man, nor a woman, nor a young boy, nor a young girl, nor a baby, nor a priest . . . but I have thought about shootin' a Paiute once or twice."

Fergus flashed a white-toothed grin. "I have had a similar

thought from time to time." The smile dropped off his face. "I think you will have to shoot Mr. Jeremiah Jolly."

O. T. jerked around so quickly his neck popped. "Why do you say that?"

"He is too dumb to change his mind. He has decided he wants to get even. The others have gone, so he will take it out on you." He reached inside his left boot.

"I told you he was drunk last night. Men do irrational things when they are drunk."

"Mr. Jolly seems to stay drunk all the time." Fergus pulled out a bullet about twice the length of the previous one. The brass case was tarnished green. "Aha! I do have a bullet!"

"Looks like an old bullet."

"Well, I am an old man." He pulled his boot back on. "You will have to kill him to stop him."

"He'll stay mad a couple of days, then sober up, and find something more productive to do."

Fergus reached back in the wagon bed and retrieved the musket. "No, you will have to shoot him," he insisted.

O. T. felt his shoulders and neck stiffen. "Why do you keep sayin' that?"

"I know the type of man that is too dumb to walk away." He dropped the block on the single-shot and shoved the big bullet into the chamber. "He is the type that will be waiting for you down some dark alley."

"And just what do you suggest I do?"

Fergus patted the musket lying across his lap. "Hire a bodyguard."

"You wouldn't happen to know a brave warrior, would you?"

"I see him every day."

"I don't have any money to pay the man."

"That is acceptable. I will work for meals," Fergus offered.

"But you get all your meals free at the cafe anyway," O. T. reminded him.

"This way I will earn my meals, and I won't be conscripted to serve coffee."

O. T. leaned back and stared up at the pale blue sky. "I see where this is going. You're still whinin' about havin' to help in the cafe."

"Is it a deal?" Fergus pressed.

"That you are my bodyguard?"

"Yes."

"And you're workin' for meals?"

Fergus was silent for a moment. "And snacks," he finally added.

"That's fine. But you will get bored very, very quick."

"As of this moment, I am on the job," Fergus declared.

"I feel safer already," O. T. laughed.

"Good." Fergus glanced at the crates in the back of the wagon. "I feel hungry. Did you bring any snacks?"

"Mama, your hair looks pretty!"

Dola opened her eyes. All four children huddled around her bed. "I think I dozed off."

"Here, Mama." Rita Ann handed her a mirror. "I'm all done."

"My mama's purdy," Punky squealed.

Dola glanced at her hair and then studied the creases and dark circles around her eyes. "Well, little darlin', big sister combed my hair very nicely and braided it. I like it very much. But I feel rather foolish."

"Why is that, Mama?" Corrie asked.

"Because I haven't braided my hair since I was young."

"You look very young," Tommy-Blue announced. "Except your eyes. Your eyes look old."

"Tommy-Blue, don't say that to Mother!" Rita Ann scolded.

"It's okay, darlin'," Dola soothed. "I like a man who is honest with me."

Tommy-Blue looped his thumbs in his coveralls. "You do?"

"Yes, I do."

"How about Daddy?" Tommy-Blue asked. "He says you're the most beautiful girl on the face of the earth, and you ain't even a girl."

"When your daddy says I'm the most beautiful, he is telling the truth because he's sayin' that in his opinion, in his heart and soul and mind, I am the most beautiful girl in the world. Nobody else might think so, but that man thinks so. And you know what? That's all that matters to me. I really don't care what any other man or woman thinks."

"'Beauty doth vanish age as if newborn,'" Rita Ann recited.

"Daddy says I'm a lucky man," Tommy-Blue spouted.

"Why's that?" Dola asked.

"Because I get to grow up surrounded by beautiful women."

Corrie grinned. "My daddy said that?"

"Yeah. Who do you reckon he was talkin' about besides Mama?"

Corrie stuck out her tongue.

"Children, help me sit up a little more," Dola called out.

"You ain't supposed to get up, Mama," Corrie cautioned.

"I said sit up, not get up. If I'm going to hurt anyway, I might as well hurt sitting up a bit. Tommy-Blue and Rita Ann, pull me forward. Corrie, shove those pillows behind my back."

"Mama, I'm afraid of hurtin' you," Tommy-Blue said.

"Just take it slow. I'll be all right. I won't complain this time."

Tommy-Blue reached out his hand and then pulled it back. "I'm scared of hurtin' you again, Mama."

Dola took his hand in hers and squeezed. "I'll tell you if I'm hurtin'."

Rita Ann tugged on her other arm.

"That's it," Dola encouraged.

Suddenly a pain like a kick from a mule hit her tailbone and flashed straight up her spine. Dola bit her lip. Warm, salty blood trickled inside her mouth. Her head felt light. *I'm goin' to faint. . . . Oh, Lord, not in front of the children. Not with Orion so far away.*

"Mama, are you okay?" Tommy-Blue's voice sounded far away.

"I think I'll take another naaaaap . . ."

The tall man at the door had blond hair like Lucky Jack Gately, but his face looked very different. His shoulders were broad like Orion's, his mustache well trimmed like Deuce Wilkins's. He wore a holstered gun on his hip. He leaned against the doorjamb on the left. His right hand rested on the polished walnut grip on the revolver. His eyes, surrounded by creases, held a soft, kind look like Pop Brannon's.

"Are you comin' with me, Dola Mae?" he asked.

Dola surveyed the room and realized they were alone. "I—eh— I don't know where we're going," she stammered.

"You're goin' home, Dola Mae Davis Skinner."

It was a smooth, gentle voice, and she sat straight up in bed and gazed around the room.

"Now, Dola Mae, you never thought of this apartment as a permanent home, did you?"

She pulled the sheet up to the neck of her gown. "But—but— what about my children?"

"They'll be along shortly. Don't you worry about them. I've got them all taken care of," the man insisted.

"But I can't desert them . . . and Orion." She studied the man's slight smile. He looked familiar. "You're not Orion, are you?"

The man stood up straight and laughed. "No, but I'll take you to him."

"Where? Where is he?"

"At home, waitin' for you, of course, darlin'."

"He is? He's there?"

The man strolled toward her, but his boots didn't make any sound when they struck the bare wooden floor. "Yes, of course. You knew that."

"I think I forgot. I seem to have forgotten lots of things." She reached up and brushed her long, silky brown hair back over her shoulders.

"Come on, darlin', let's go home now." He held out his hand.

"But I'm—I'm not dressed," she protested.

"You look very nice."

She dropped the sheet and glanced down at the smooth, cool white silk gown that flowed across her thin body. "I—eh, I didn't know I had this gown."

He continued to hold out his hand. "That gown has been yours since you were eight years old. What are you waiting for?"

"But . . . my back went out. I can't get up."

"Does it hurt now?" he asked.

Dola scooted around in the bed. "No. No, it doesn't!"

"Then let me take you home." He was by the bedside. His hand clutched hers.

It was a smaller hand than she would have imagined.

Much smaller.

Somewhere a young voice recited, "'Her body sleeps in Capels' monument, and her immortal part with angels lives.'"

"What did Mama say?" Tommy-Blue pressed.

"She wants to take a nap," Rita Ann replied.

"I ain't never seen her fall asleep like that," Tommy-Blue declared. "She's still sittin' up."

Dola blinked her eyes open. Three small heads hovered around hers.

"Hi, Mama. You're sweatin' real bad," Corrie said. "You want me to get you a rag to wash your face? Maybe we ought to get us one of them ceilin' fans like they have at the Northern Saloon. It sure does make a fine breeze, so I hear."

"Are you cryin', Mama?" Tommy-Blue asked.

"Did you bite your lip? There's blood on your lip," Corrie announced.

Dola reached out and put her hand on the back of Tommy-Blue's neck. She was surprised that it didn't cause her much pain. "Could you get me that washrag and towel? I do think I'll wipe my face."

He spun around and raced across the room.

"Would you like a drink of water, Mama?"

"That would be very nice, Corrie Lou."

"I'll bring you a drink," Tommy-Blue shouted from across the room.

"No, I get to fetch the drink." Corrie scampered toward her brother.

Rita Ann leaned close to Dola. "Did you faint, Mama?" she whispered.

"I think maybe I did, just for a moment," Dola whispered back. "How long was I out?"

"Only a few seconds. I was on my second Shakespeare quote when you opened your eyes. I was quite worried, Mama. I didn't know what to do."

"I'm fine now, honey. I don't hurt nearly like I did." *I just had the most frightening or the most peaceful dream in my life. I really can't decide which, Lord. And it all happened in a matter of seconds.*

"Here's your wet rag, Mama." Tommy-Blue thrust the cotton cloth out toward her.

"Thank you, young man."

"And here's your water. Do you want more?" Corrie Lou beamed.

"Oh, my, no. That's quite a full glass." Dola noticed that Corrie's thumb was stuck down in the water.

"I carried it clean across the room, and I hardly spilled any of it."

Dola wiped her forehead and took a sip of water. "I feel quite spoiled. I feel like a queen surrounded by her court."

"'She had all the royal makings of a queen. As holy oil, Edward the Confessor's crown, the rod, a bird of peace, and all such emblems laid nobly on her,'" Rita Ann intoned.

"Now exactly which wife of Henry the Eighth was that about?"

Rita Ann shoved her wire-framed glasses back up on her nose. "Anne Boleyn . . . I think."

"And exactly where is my little court jester?" Dola inquired.

"Punky?" Corrie gulped. "He's . . . out on the balcony."

Dola glanced over at the open double doors and heard a small voice say, "Hi! My name is Punky. My mama's purdy!"

"He's visitin' with someone," Tommy-Blue reported.

"Do you want us to fetch him, Mama?" Rita Ann asked.

"By all means, rescue some poor soul who's been trapped by a three-year-old's charm."

Another voice filtered up into the apartment.

It was older.

A little older.

"And my name is Colin Maddison, the third, with two *d*'s."

The mine tunnel's darkness was pierced by a trail of dim yellow electric light bulbs. The entrance to Lateral 660B differed from the other tunnels; it had heavy steel, jail-like doors bolted into the hard rock wall and padlocked with six staggered locks.

Two suit-and-tie-clad guards tipped their wooden chairs as they waited with dual revolvers in their belts and short-barreled shotguns in their laps. O. T. sat behind a small desk under a bare light bulb and perused a two-week-old Los Angeles newspaper.

One of the guards stood, stretched, and strolled over to him. "Hey, you ain't a bookkeeper, are you?"

"Nope. I've never been mistaken for a bookkeeper. Why do you ask?"

"'Cause them others that Fleming sends down here to watch us all look like bookkeepers."

"My name is O. T. Skinner." He laid the newspaper on the table. "When I'm not down here, I work for an assay office. Deliveries, courier service, mainly."

"I've been an express guard myself," the man replied. "Folks call me Elko. So, Skinner, what are you doin' down here?"

"I needed the money, boys. How about you two?"

The other guard moseyed over to the table. "Yeah, that's why we're here too. I'm Mickey. Did you ever try and buck the tiger?"

"Play faro?" O. T. asked.

"Yeah, did you ever try it?"

Skinner shook his head.

"It's a strange game. It looks easy as can be, but it isn't. You got to work long hours in a hole in the ground just to pay back your losses."

"Speakin' of strange," Elko glanced back at the gated tunnel, "this here is a strange job."

"Mickey, you and Elko have guarded mineshafts before, haven't you?" O. T. asked.

"Yeah, but not because of gold or silver," Mickey reported. "Most times there's a lawsuit goin' on to settle who's the rightful owner of the lead, and the court orders that no diggin' be done until it's settled. And we sit down here just to certify to the judge that no one jumped the verdict."

Elko strolled over to the gate and gazed through the bars into the darkened treasure-laden cave. "I ain't never seen gold like what's in there."

Mickey sauntered up next to him. "I wonder how much a person could carry out in a bucket?"

"Several hundred dollars' worth, I bet," Elko proclaimed. He turned to Skinner. "Not that we're goin' to try it, of course."

O. T. picked his newspaper back up. "Those gates look secure to me."

"You don't have a key?" Mickey asked.

"Not hardly."

Elko began to laugh. "Looks like Fleming don't trust any of us."

Mickey walked back over to O. T. "Did you say your name was Skinner?"

"Are you the guy that one-punched Jeremiah Jolly?" Elko asked.

"I guess I did. He pulled a gun on me, and I didn't have time to—"

"Ain't that somethin', Elko? He didn't have time to pull a gun, so he just one-punched him. Now that's the way a professional operates."

"Actually, I don't carry—"

"Ain't you the one who partners with Lucky Jack Gately and them? Or was it ol' Ace Wilkins and his brothers?" Mickey asked.

O. T. pulled off his hat and laid it on the table in front of him. "They are all friends of mine. With that deal down in Mexico, I reckon I'm partnered with all of them."

"Lucky Jack and Ace both?" Elko asked.

"Yeah, I guess so."

"Did you hear that, Mickey? We're in the shaft with a pard of both Lucky Jack and Ace Wilkins!"

"Good grief, Elko—with the likes of someone like Skinner, what does Fleming need us down here for?" Mickey exclaimed.

"You're right. Havin' Skinner is like havin' Wyatt Earp or Stuart Brannon in their prime."

"You ain't partners with them too, are you, Skinner?" Mickey asked.

"I don't know Mr. Earp. His brother passed away before we got to Goldfield." O. T. tried adjusting the wool suit coat he had borrowed from Jakob Fleming. When he reached inside to straighten his shirt, both men flinched and took a step back. "Pop Brannon is a family friend. He gave my wife that little peach tree out in front of the cafe last time he came through."

"Are you kiddin' us?" Elko asked.

"You really do know Brannon? That's what I like about a boomtown—you never know who you're goin' to rub elbows with. Ol' Jolly was mighty lucky you was in a hurry," Mickey declared.

"I got a question for you, Mr. Skinner, if you don't mind. I'm jist curious. I know a professional like you nowadays carries his pistol concealed. That's obvious. But I was wonderin', do you pack a .44? Or a .38? Or a .45? Do you like them double-actions? I'm still kind of partial to a single-action myself."

"Elko!" Mickey interrupted. "You don't ask a man like Skinner what he's packin'. For pete's sake, show some respect." He turned to O. T. "Sorry about that, Mr. Skinner. Elko don't mean to pry. He's kind of new at this."

O. T. grinned. "Well, actually, boys, you've got me pegged wrong. I—"

"No sir, no sir. Don't say another word," Elko insisted. "I just kind of run off at the mouth. Let's change the subject. You figure Tex Rickard will ever really get one of them big boxin' matches to come to Goldfield?"

"Ain't got no place to hold it," Mickey replied.

"They could build a platform and some bleachers," Elko said.

"Were you in Cripple Creek when they had the big Russian who wrestled a bear?" Mickey asked.

Elko's eyes lit up. "I lost five dollars on it."

"Me too." Mickey strolled back to the chairs by the gate.

"Who would have thought the Russian would win?"

"Just goes to show you."

"Did you see that one, Mr. Skinner?"

O. T. tried to scan the eyes of the guards, but the light in the tunnel was too dim. "I'm afraid I missed that one."

"It took six hours, but the Russian wore him down," Mickey explained.

Elko yawned and stretched his arms. "Is that how long it took?"

"You were there, weren't ya?"

"I passed out after three hours." Elko shrugged. "I woke up with a headache and broke."

O. T. flipped through a large newsprint copy of *California Farmer*. *Lord, this is like a dream . . . a long, borin' dream that I can't wake up from. I'm stuck down here in a hole in the ground with no light except a little incandescent light bulb, listenin' to two men so bored they mumble at the mouth to keep from fallin' asleep.*

Remind me of what I'm doin' here when I could be home with Dola.

I'm glad she was sleepin' when I went home for supper. Let her rest and rest and rest and keep me awake. If I can't stay alert, then I'm not doin' Fleming any good, and I should quit.

"Do you play cards, Mr. Skinner?" Elko asked.

Mickey leaned his chair against the wall of the tunnel. "Of course he don't play cards while he's workin', do you, Mr. Skinner?"

"Actually, boys, I never—"

"See? What'd I tell you?" Mickey declared.

"What are you readin' about, Mr. Skinner?" Elko probed.

"Growing peaches near Dinuba, California."

"Ain't that close to where ol' Evans and Sontag was captured? You didn't know ol' Chris Evans, did you?"

"Nope. How about you boys? Did you know him?"

"I was in Del Monico's in Sacramento one time, and the barkeeper pointed to a tall, bearded man and said that was Evans," Elko declared. "Course how does a man know? I ain't goin' to march up and ask him."

"I once asked Grat Dalton if he was Cole Younger," Mickey admitted. "Course I was just a kid then."

"You did? What did he say?"

"He just laughed and said that Younger got killed in Kansas, and since he was alive, he reckoned he wasn't him."

Lord, this is goin' to be a long evenin'. If You want to speed it up, that's all right by me.

O. T. turned the page and looked at the headline: "South American Bat Droppings Grow Record Fig Crop in Fresno." *Lord, I hope this is where You want me to be 'cause it surely seems like I'm wastin' time. Bat droppings? I wonder how they harvest that stuff?*

The young boy wore knickers, a plaid vest, white shirt, and bowtie. His round cheeks flushed red. Dola could see where the pale snap-brim fedora had creased his greased dark hair. He held the hat in one hand and flowers in the other.

Barefoot, Corrie peeked around the half-open door. "I told you, I don't want you bringin' me no flowers!"

He hung his head and mumbled something.

"What did he say, Corrie?" Tommy-Blue called out from behind the door where he and Rita Ann crouched.

Corrie scratched her hair above her ear. It stuck straight up in the air. "He said them flowers are for Mama 'cause he heard she was feelin' infirm."

"She ain't infirm," Tommy-Blue said. "She's feelin' poorly— that's all."

"My mama's purdy!" Punky spouted as he jogged over toward the caller. "I'm Punky," he announced.

"And I'm Colin Maddison, the third, with two *d*'s," the young boy replied.

"Toodee!" Punky squealed.

"No, I'm Colin—"

"Toodee-Toodee-Toodee!" Punky giggled from across the room.

"Tell young Mr. Maddison thank you very much for the flowers, but I'm not able to have visitors at the moment," Dola called over.

"Mrs. Skinner, my mother said to tell you that she is praying for your speedy recovery."

"Why, please thank her for me. I believe I'm feelin' a little better. I don't think I've had the pleasure of meeting your mother," Dola said.

"She stays at our house in Carson City most of the time. Her name is Tashawna Maddison. Maybe you've heard of her. She was a trick rider for Buffalo Bill in Europe and met the queen of England and everything."

"Mama's a queen!" Punky declared.

Still hiding behind the door, Rita Ann blurted out, "'To be a queen in bondage is more vile than is a slave in base servility, for princes should be free.'"

"Princess Margaret of Anjou to the Earl of Suffolk. *Henry VI*," Colin replied.

"Eh—eh," Rita Ann stammered, "'she had all the royal makings of a queen . . .'"

"'As holy oil, Edward the Confessor's crown . . .'" Colin added.

"'The rod, a bird of peace . . .'" Rita Ann bubbled.

Colin rolled his eyes. "'And all such emblems laid nobly on her.'"

"Oh, brother." Corrie sighed, then marched away from the door toward the balcony.

"'O queen of queens! How far dost thou excel . . .'" Rita Ann challenged.

"'No thought can think, no tongue of mortal tell!'" Colin responded. Then it was his turn to challenge the still-unseen inquisitor. "'As on the finger of a throned queen the basest jewel will be well esteemed . . .'"

"'So are those errors that in thee are seen to truths translated and for sure things deemed,'" Rita Ann replied.

"Which sonnet?" Colin asked.

"96," Rita Ann said.

"No, it isn't. It's 95," Colin insisted.

"It is not."

"It is too."

"I should know!"

"Well, you don't!"

Dola cleared her throat. "Rita Ann, that's enough arguing."

"But I'm right, Mama!"

"No, you aren't," Colin maintained.

"Rita Ann Skinner, apologize to young Mr. Maddison," Dola insisted.

Rita Ann folded her arms around her thick book. "Mama, I can't apologize when I'm right."

"No, you aren't."

"Apologize for your tone of voice, young lady."

Rita Ann took a deep breath, clenched her teeth, and held her breath.

"Rita Ann!"

"I'm sorry for my tone of voice. Even though I'm right, I should learn to be more gracious."

"I accept your admission of error," Colin replied.

"What?" Rita Ann blurted out. "I didn't—"

"Rita Ann!" Dola called.

"But, Mother!"

"Good-bye, Mr. Maddison. Thank you for the flowers. And thank your mother. Tell her I look forward to meeting her next time she's in Goldfield."

He put his hat back on. "Good-bye, Mrs. Skinner." He quickly stuck his head around the door.

Rita Ann raised her thick Shakespeare book above his head as if to strike.

"Good-bye, Corrie!" he called out and then jerked his head back.

There was silence from the balcony.

"Corrie?" Dola pressed.

"Good-bye, Colin Madison, the third, with two d's," Corrie called out.

Dola waved to her ten-year-old son. "Tommy-Blue, walk Colin out to the front door."

Tommy-Blue scratched his head. "Why? He can find the way."

"Because it's the polite thing to do, and I don't feel like getting out of bed and doin' it myself," Dola lectured.

"Hey, your daddy's a banker, isn't he?" Tommy-Blue asked as he strolled over to the door.

"Yes. At the largest bank in Nevada," Colin bragged.

"Good. Maybe he'd like to invest in my latest claim."

"How much per ton does it assay?"

"Mr. Tolavitch says $200-$300 per ton, and that's just the surface stuff."

"No fooling?" Colin's eyes lit up. "I've got some of my own money to invest."

"Really? How much?" Tommy-Blue pressed.

The boys disappeared down the stairs.

Punky strolled out on the balcony with Corrie. Rita Ann returned to Dola's bed.

"Did I just hear two ten-year-old boys discussing a joint mining venture?"

"They were just playing," Rita Ann assured her. "Weren't they?"

"It's a crazy town, darlin'."

"I was right about that quote, Mama. It's from 'Sonnet 96.'"

"I know you're right, but you shouldn't be so argumentative."

Dola glanced toward the balcony. "Who's Corrie Lou talking to now?"

Punky hopped back into the room calling out, "Toodee-Toodee-Toodee!"

She won't talk to him when he comes to the door, but she'll visit from the balcony. Well, Toodee, you were doin' great until you told Rita Ann she was wrong on a quote. You've lost the battle, son.

Dola gazed at the six pink roses. *Lord, I'm humbled to think someone like Mrs. Maddison is praying for me. How did she even know I was sick?*

"Where shall I put them, Mama?" Rita Ann said.

Dola swung her feet to the edge of the bed. "Here, let me . . ."

"Mama! You shouldn't."

"Oh, dear!" Dola gasped. "I forgot I was bedridden."

"Did you hurt yourself?" Rita called out.

"Not nearly as much as I thought I would." Dola lay back down. "Perhaps I should just rest a little more."

"Punky's hungry for beef chops and gravy!" The three-year-old continued to practice his hopping around the room as Tommy-Blue returned.

"I'll take Punky down to find something to eat," Corrie offered.

"You ain't slippin' down there to see Colin Maddison, with two *d*'s, are you?" Tommy-Blue hooted.

Corrie clenched her fist and waved it under his nose. Tommy-Blue back-pedaled across the room.

"Shhhh, Mama's trying to rest," Rita Ann told them.

Her head propped up on several pillows, Dola closed her eyes.

Lord, I don't understand that frightenin' dream. Who was that man at the door? It wasn't O. T. Was it an angel? Or was it one disguised like an angel? Was I being tempted to give up? Do you send angels for Your children, or do You come personally? Are You suggesting that it's my time to leave this earth? I can't go just yet, Lord. I have too many things to complete. I can't leave the children; they're too young. O. T.'s right. We will fight it. Please, Lord, no more scary dreams.

It was after midnight when O. T. left Fleming's carriage at the livery and walked toward the cafe. Shouts and laughter rolled out of every saloon he passed as he hurried home. The streetlamps barely gave enough light to keep him from stumbling. Just past The Idaho Club he thought he saw someone following him.

Lord, if it's Jolly . . . Well, I just don't know what to do. I can't figure him out. I wish he'd just go away.

Half a dozen miners staggered toward him on the wooden sidewalk. As they passed, O. T. ducked into the alley. When the man following in the shadows reached the alley, O. T. grabbed his collar.

The man wheezed. "You scared me, Wall Walker."

"Fergus, what are you doin' followin' me at midnight?" O. T. quizzed.

The old Paiute patted the receiver of his Trapdoor musket. "Protecting you, of course." Then he rubbed his weathered chin. "Is it time for breakfast yet?"

EIGHT

One light bulb illuminated the entire cafe. O. T. left Fergus in the kitchen and shuffled softly across the deserted dining room. An aroma of peach pie, beef chops, and pipe tobacco lingered in the air. When he reached the bottom of the stairs, he sat down and slowly pulled off his boots.

His socks felt damp and dirty as he rolled them down and wiggled his toes. He leaned back against the stairway. His eyelids fell shut, and he slumped like a wind-downed tree.

Lord, I'm tired. Not exhausted from what I've done, but exhausted from doin' nothin'. Nothin' but stayin' awake and listenin' to the borin' banter of Elko and Mickey. I'm so sleepy I could lay on the stairs . . . the floor . . . in a patch of prickly pear. The sight of Hudson Frazier in the cactus flashed through his mind. *Maybe not in a cactus patch.*

O. T. pulled himself up. He padded softly up the stairway and into the apartment. The wood floor felt cool and a little gritty as he stepped across the darkened room. He paused to listen. To the right he heard Rita Ann's nasal breathing and Tommy-Blue's fitful snore.

Lord, those are some of the most satisfying sounds I've ever heard. Help big sister to relax tonight. May her always-anxious brow smooth out, and help her tomorrow to enjoy being herself. And Tommy-Blue—help him to discover treasures that never fade nor rust nor corrupt. Look after my sweet Corrie Lou. Teach her how to be a lady without losing her enthusiasm for life, for people . . . for her daddy. Somewhere over there, Lord,

Silas Paul is asleep with his little, round bottom pointed up in the air. Hold them all tight in your arms tonight, Lord, and give them Your peace.

O. T. felt for the hat rack. He set his boots down, jammed his hat on the rack, and slipped off his denim jeans. He unbuttoned his shirt. He could smell Dola's lilac perfume.

Lord, I really like that smell.

The covers were pulled back even on his side of the bed. He slipped in as quietly as he could. The cotton sheets felt cool and clean as he wiggled his toes and collapsed on the pillow.

Lord, let Dola sleep. Let her have pleasant dreams. Let her have no more pain. Give her exciting visions of the future and sweet memories of the past.

Oh, Lord . . . You know what I want to ask You and am afraid to. I want You to heal her. In Jesus' name, I want her whole and well and without pain. But I'm scared to ask that, scared it's not Your will, scared it's the wrong thing to pray, scared that my faith is so puny my prayers cannot possibly be answered. If I could only be as strong in faith as she thinks I am.

His mind began to drift. He sank into the softness of the feather mattress.

I need the sleep, Lord. Take care of things for me because I'm of no value to anyone when I'm this tired. Oh, how I praise You for sleep, glorious sleep.

O. T. turned to his side, scrunched the pillow beneath his head, and then slowly reached his hand out for Dola. He hardly noticed that his hand was fully extended. He scooted a little toward the middle of the bed and continued to reach until his hand hung off the other side.

He lay there for a minute.

He thought about the picture rock at the Pear Blossom Mine. He thought about Jeremiah Jolly stalking the streets. He thought about an auto still parked halfway in the cafe. He thought about Dinuba, California, and a twenty-acre spread of grapes. He thought about . . . being alone in bed.

With a jolt O. T. sat straight up. The word flew out like a popped balloon. "Dola?"

With the double doors to the balcony open for ventilation, Dola listened to the sounds of the street below. Distant shouts, laughter, an out-of-tune piano, an out-of-sorts dog, an occasional rumble of a car, a whinny of a horse, a muted explosion—maybe a gunshot, a firecracker, a prank with dynamite, or an auto backfire.

She could hear Corrie toss, Tommy-Blue snore, and Rita Ann's funny little breathing noise.

Lord, I'm so proud of them all. They wanted to help me. I'm so fortunate that You allowed them to be my children. How poor my life would be without them. What a blessing they must be to You too. I've been too busy this summer to enjoy them. Lord, for months we were on the road moving west. We had nothing. No home. No belongings except what was in the wagon. We didn't know if we would eat from day to day.

And yet I've never enjoyed my children or my husband as much as during those few months. We did absolutely everything together. All day, every day. I don't want the hardships and worry to come back, but I certainly wouldn't mind the time together. Lord, if You are trying to tell me my days are numbered, well, I want to live each one to the fullest. I can't put anything off till some other day.

Every time Dola closed her eyes, they seemed to pop back open again. She stared at the dark ceiling.

Lord, I've slept for most of the past twenty-four hours. I'm really tired of being in bed. Tired of this stuffy room. Tired of being so helpless. What I really want is to sit out on the balcony and watch the stars and breathe the desert night air. I know, I know, it's fogged with alkali dust . . .

I'm going to get up. What's the worst thing that could happen? I'll faint and collapse back in the bed. That's one way to get some more sleep.

Dola flung back the sheet and slowly kicked the comforter to the floor.

So far the pain isn't bad. Not like before anyway. Now, legs . . . hang

*over the bed. . . . That's the way. . . . Okay, Dola Mae Davis Skinner
. . . can you do it? Don't scream. Don't bite your lip.*

She took a deep breath and then pushed herself to a sitting position. The shadows from the balcony swam back and forth. She felt her head bob in a circular motion.

"Oh, dear." She closed her eyes.

She tried to take a deep breath, but it seemed shallow.

I'm dizzy, lightheaded. Can't get a deep breath.

Dola raised her arms straight above her head.

Did you see that, Lord? I can raise them up without cryin' out in pain. I really am getting better.

Dola let her bare feet drop to the cool, dusty wood floor.

I've got to try it. I've got to know.

She rocked out of bed to her feet. Her head continued to swim. She reached down, grabbed the covers, and pulled them back up on the bed.

There was a dull throbbing pain in her lower back, but that was all.

Lord, I can get up! I can tolerate that pain.

She took a staggering step toward the balcony. Then another and another.

The back pain did not go away.

But it didn't get worse.

Soon she felt a slight drift of an evening breeze on the balcony and reached out for the back of the old rocker. Dola inched her way over to the rough wooden railing. *Lord, even the splintery wood floor feels good on my feet. Just to be standing, breathing, having my head clear up. Lord, something happened, and my body gave out. Something happened again, and it's better. I know it still hurts. But that's just a reminder of what it was like. Did You heal me? Is it just a momentary improvement? Will I make it worse by standing like this?*

One day at a time, Lord.

Right now I feel better than I have in the past two days. So I will enjoy it. Perhaps I feel better than I will for the next week. What a shame it would be to sleep through a good spell.

She stared down Columbia Street. Dull electric lights strained to penetrate the town's dark shadows. Above, a moonless sky dripped with stars and planets. *Most of the defects of this town are muted at night.*

In the distance she heard a woman shout a long string of obscenities.

Dola grinned.

Well, they aren't all muted. What in the world are the Skinners doing in a place like this? When I get an overview like this, it's not a very impressive place. Yet everyone wants to be here. Lucian said a hundred people a week are still moving here. That has to slow down sooner or later.

Doesn't it?

Boomtowns never last, or do they?

"Evenin', Mrs. Skinner."

Dola grabbed the collar of her buttoned gown and stepped back away from the rail. "Eh, good evening. . . . I really can't see who's down there."

"Sheriff Johnson, ma'am. Just walkin' my rounds. I heard you were doin' poorly."

"I'm feeling a little better, Sheriff. Thank you."

"That's mighty fine news, Mrs. Skinner. Good night, ma'am."

"Good night, Sheriff."

Moving slowly, she seated herself in the rocking chair.

He could see me, but I couldn't see him. And I was barefoot and wearing my gown! Dola Mae, don't lose your good sense.

Dola rocked back and forth. There was a slight easing of the dull pain in her back.

Lord, this is so pleasant. I—I was afraid that . . . I wouldn't ever feel pleasant again. I was so scared. I'm still scared. Things that I don't understand frighten me. But I'm in Your hands. I know that. And that's enough.

"Skinner!"

Dola remained seated in the shadows of the balcony. The voice did not sound like the sheriff's.

Maybe it's Mr. Fleming. . . . No, Orion is out at the Pear Blossom. He knows that.

"O. T. Skinner, I know you're up there! I seen you on the balcony."

I may look bad, mister, but I've never been mistaken for a man. You can't see me at all.

"I seen you talkin' to the sheriff."

Dola kept her head against the back of the rocking chair. *Obviously you only saw the sheriff.*

"Don't think you bein' pals with the sheriff will stop me."

Stop you from doing what?

"Do you have any idea who you're dealin' with?"

I do believe you're the one who's mistaken. Last I heard, Jug Cherry was in an Arizona prison. He's the only man in Goldfield who ever got mad at Orion . . . isn't he?

"I ain't no saloon rag."

In that case, it definitely isn't Mr. Cherry. Lord, perhaps I should have stayed in bed. Then I wouldn't have had to hear this.

"You remember what happened to that governor up in Idaho last December?"

Was he the one who was dynamited? Is this man threatening to bomb my husband?

"You think about that next time you throw a punch at me."

Orion in a fight? He never fights. You have the wrong man.

"Your days is numbered, Skinner."

Mister, all our days are numbered.

"And the number is low," he growled.

Is this man serious? Lord, I don't know whether to laugh or cry. Why would anyone be this angry with Orion?

"Mighty low."

The footsteps echoed to the north. She continued to hide in the darkness of the balcony. *Lord, perhaps it's time to move. I don't want to live someplace where people hate my husband so much they want him dead. Orion's right. We will move before Christmas.*

I feel all right.

I can ride.

At least, I can ride a little.

Lord, for the first time in several days I was feeling better. Now this. When does it let up? When is life peaceful? Ordinary? I'm a simple woman, Lord. Married to a simple man. We just want our little corner of Your earth so that we can live a simple life. And here we are in a boom-town.

There's been some kind of mistake.

This can't be our place.

She stared out at the dark street and continued to rock back and forth.

Tears rolled down her cheeks. She let them drip to her gown, unhindered. *I want to go home. I want to round up Orion and the children and go home. And I'm crying, Lord, because I just realized that we don't have any home to go to. A borrowed room above a cafe—that's all we have. This isn't home. It can never be home.*

That dream. The man in the dream said he was going to take me home. He appeared right there at the doorway and asked to take me home. I should have gone with him.

Maybe this man beneath the balcony was a dream too. I never did see him. Maybe I'm hallucinating. Perhaps I will wake up in bed, and all of this was just a dream.

Dola closed her eyes and listened to the faint squeaking of the rocking chair.

After a frantic sweep of the empty bed, O. T. landed on his feet. He sprinted across the dark room toward the doorway to the stairs. His right foot slammed into a hard object. He hopped the rest of the way on one foot. He felt along the wall for the electric wire and then traced it with his hand until he located the switch. He twisted the switch, but the knob merely spun without clicking.

Oh, Lord, I don't need this. Where's Dola? What happened to her? Why didn't someone tell me? They couldn't tell me. I was 600 feet underground.

O. T. heard something rattle to the floor, and he realized that he was holding a small metal shaft.

"I unscrewed the knob?" He crashed down on his knees and felt around on the floor. "Why is this happenin' to me?" he fumed.

"Daddy, is that you?"

O. T. raised up on his knees. "Rita Ann? Where's Mama?"

The reply was soft, yet distinct. "She's in bed."

"No, she isn't. Where is she?" O. T. snapped.

"What do you mean?" Rita Ann's voice softened even more.

O. T.'s didn't. "She isn't in bed, and I want to know where she is!"

"She's got to be in bed, Daddy!" Rita Ann began to sound panicked. "I tucked her in."

"She's not there now."

"Turn on the light."

"I'm tryin' to turn on the light!" he growled.

O. T. heard her sniffle and gasp.

He ran his hands across his face. "I'm sorry, honey. Forgive me. I'm worried sick about Mama, and I can't see anything, and I broke the switch and lost the knob on the floor and can't find it."

"Turn on the hall light and open the doors. Maybe you can see it then."

O. T. struggled to his feet and stumbled out into the hall. He cracked his bare toes against the half-open door. He turned the switch in the hall to the right, and the light above the stair blinked on. For a moment he couldn't see anything. He reached down and rubbed his toes. When he raised his hand, there was blood on his fingertips.

"Here it is, Daddy!" Rita Ann said, wire-framed glasses resting low on her upturned nose and light flannel gown buttoned high on her neck. "Here's the knob. Do you want me to turn on the light?"

"Yes . . . we have to find Mama. Maybe she fell off the bed or somethin'." Rita Ann turned the switch to the right. The bulb clicked on. The dark shadows ebbed in the yellow glow that radiated out to all corners of the room.

"What is that rock?" O. T. pointed to an object the size of a loaf of bread.

"It's Tommy-Blue's latest discovery."

"And he left it in the middle of the room? I just about broke my toe on it."

"Mama said he couldn't take it to bed."

O. T. scurried from one side of the bed to the other. "She's not here!" He dropped to the floor.

"What are you doin', Daddy?" Rita Ann quizzed.

"Lookin' under the bed."

"Mama wouldn't be under the bed."

"Well, she's got to be somewhere! Look over by the couch. If she fell down, she won't be able to get up."

Tommy-Blue sat straight up. "Don't look under the bed!"

"Why?" O. T. mumbled.

"'Cause my rock samples are all under there, and I have them all filed in order."

"Not all of them," O. T. complained. He stalked to the middle of the room.

Corrie, wearing one of her daddy's long-sleeved shirts, meandered over to his side. "Maybe someone kidnapped her."

"Who would want to kidnap Mama?" Rita Ann sneered.

"I would," Tommy-Blue piped up.

"Maybe she got hungry and went down to get something from the kitchen," O. T. suggested.

"But she can't get out of bed!" Corrie declared.

"Well, she did get out of bed 'cause the bed's empty," Rita Ann replied.

"Tommy-Blue, check the dining room. Rita Ann, take the kitchen. Be sure and look on the floor. She could have fallen."

"Where do you want me to look?" Corrie asked.

The voice floated across the room like a warning shot across the bow of a ship. "Why don't you look on the balcony?"

O. T. spun around. A gown-clad Dola Mae stood in the doorway. Tommy-Blue and his sisters swarmed to her side.

"Are you looking for me?"

O. T. hurried over. "What are you doing up?"

"Are you healed, Mama?" Corrie Lou gasped.

Rita Ann retrieved her large book from the orange crate beside her bed. "'My lord Bassanio and my gentle lady, I wish you all the joy that you can wish,'" she said.

It took over half an hour to quiet down and get everyone settled back in bed. O. T. and Dola stood out on the balcony studying the flickering lights of Goldfield. Dola steadied herself as she leaned against the railing.

He put his hand on top of hers. "I still can't believe you're able to get up."

"When the children raised me up and the pain was so sharp, I fainted, but then I think something good happened. It seems like from about that time on, it started feeling gradually better."

"But it still hurts?"

Dola pulled her hand from under his and placed it on top. "It hurts constantly. But it is a pain I can live with." His fingers felt strong, warm.

Her shoulder and arm rubbed against his. "I'll send for Doc Silvermeyer in the mornin'," he said.

Dola's voice was soft, just above a whisper. "You'll do no such thing. I'll go to his office."

"You aren't plannin' on workin' tomorrow, are you? I won't let you."

"No, I think I need to keep from straining my back again."

"Do you have any idea how anxious I got when I couldn't find you?"

"I don't know why you didn't check the balcony." She took a deep breath and let it out slowly. "But I know how you feel. I was a little anxious tonight myself."

"When you got out of bed?"

"No, when a man on the street shouted up threats about my man." She could feel his whole body stiffen. "Man on the street? Who?"

"He didn't mention his name. He just said you had been in a fight with him, and he was goin' to get even. He mentioned the Idaho governor who was blown up. He scared me, Orion. Were you in a fight you didn't tell me about?"

"It wasn't much of a fight; it was only one punch. It was that drunk, Jeremiah Jolly."

"Orion Tower Skinner, I think you better start back at the beginning."

When the dark sky turned to gray, O. T. brought coffee up from the kitchen, and they watched the horizon fade to pale desert blue.

"You can't go to work with no sleep," Dola warned.

"The coffee will keep me awake for a while."

"Are you sure we need to stay here another week?"

"The $100 from Fleming will get us to California. And I need to let Mr. Tolavitch have some time to find someone for the assay job."

"Are you sure it's the right thing to do to move now?" she queried.

"Darlin', in one breath you ask why wait, and with the other why move. We sat right here all night discussin' it. We've tried for over a year to get along with everyone here. It's just not our kind of place."

"I know. In one way I can't wait to get out of town. I will not miss the dirt, the wind, the heat, the snakes, the scorpions, the greed, the crib rows, and gunshots in the night."

"Yet?"

"Yet I will miss the people. Not just Omega and Lucian, Haylee and Lupe, and Fergus—I will miss them dearly—but also the men who come into the cafe . . . worried, tired, hard-working people like us, just trying to survive . . . and they find a good meal and someone to listen to them. . . . I'll miss all of it in some way."

O. T. rubbed the stubble of his two-day beard. "One thing troubles me. If we aren't the ones the Lord sent to this place, who did He send? He wouldn't abandon any town, would He?"

"Are you the one changin' your mind, Mr. Skinner?"

"No, darlin'. We've got to be honest with what we can do and can't do. I would reckon it takes Christian folks a lot smarter than us to understand the way this town thinks and acts. Sometimes I feel like everyone in town knows what's goin' on but me."

"And we need to make sure we are takin' good care of our own family."

"Two members of the family are downstairs helpin' Omega. Tommy-Blue is helpin' Hud remove the auto car from the front window. I told Hud to try and get it runnin' by Saturday."

Dola straightened her back and felt a little relief from the pain. "Did you tell him why?"

"No."

"Are we really goin' to take the auto car to Dinuba?"

O. T. rubbed her forearm. "I think we'll try."

"When should we tell the children about leaving?" *Orion Tower Skinner, you have no idea in the world how good your touch feels.*

"Tomorrow. We've got to get the doc to look at you, and I've got to check on some arrangements first."

Dola patted his hand that still rubbed her arm. "Are we running away from Nineveh, Orion?"

"I've been debatin' that same question, darlin'. How would we know if the Lord really wanted us to stay in Goldfield? Besides letting us be swallowed by a big fish?"

"A dramatic event would have to drop out of the sky, or something like that, I suppose."

"Tell Dr. Silvermeyer we are thinkin' about moving on. Ask whether you should travel. We'll make you a bed up off the hard ground. Tell him we will put you in the auto car."

"Are we really going to take the wagon and the auto car?"

O. T. studied the street below. "Tommy-Blue and Corrie can both drive the wagon."

"Corrie won't want to be separated from her daddy."

"She will if I ask her."

"Yes, she will."

"I'll talk to Mr. Tolavitch and the other owners of this building about allowing Omega to run the cafe. She'd do a good job."

"She would. But do you think there will be a problem?" she asked.

"Why?"

Dola took his hand and placed it in the small of her back. "Just rub real gently right there, darlin'."

"It won't hurt you?"

"It feels wonderful," she sighed.

"So what's this about Omega?"

"Some people will not be too fond of a black person operating a cafe."

"Not in Goldfield. They just want a quick, hot, cheap meal," he answered.

"You forgot tasty."

"Yes, a quick, hot, cheap, tasty meal. Anyway, we haven't had any problems with Omega servin', have we?"

"Not since Lucky Jack threw a couple of them out on their ears." Dola could feel her whole body relax. "Do you think you could keep rubbing right there for about a month?"

"How about for the rest of your life?"

"Hmmmm. I'd like that, Mr. Skinner."

He continued the slow, rhythmic pressure on her lower back. "Darlin', maybe we stayed in Goldfield too long. We are bound to leave some situations unresolved. We should have left last year. We'd have those vines all tied up to wires by now."

"Or you'd be workin' for day wages, and we'd be livin' in Pegasus and Pearl's barn."

"That's a cheery thought." O. T. allowed a tight-lipped grin. "Well, we have $1,200 dollars saved. That's more money than we ever had in our life."

Dola closed her eyes as O. T. continued to softly rub her lower back. "Pearl wrote that the house needs some work."

"I figure $500 down on the place and $300 to fix it up. And the rest is for start-up for the farm. It's not as much as we wanted, but we should do it anyway."

"It is time to go, isn't it?" she sighed.

"Yep." O. T. glanced out at the morning sun just starting to shine across the desert. "And it's time for me to get to work."

"You have to rest sometime, Mr. Skinner."

"I'll sleep in the auto car while you're drivin'."

"Me drive that auto car? I never thought about it, but I'm sure I could do it."

"What?" he gasped.

"It can't be that difficult; I'm sure I can do it," she smirked. "Oh, were you teasing me, Orion Skinner?"

"Couldn't you tell?"

"And I'm teasing you. Couldn't you tell?"

"You're not really going to want to drive the auto car, are you?"

"I promise I will not drive it." Dola paused until his face began to relax. "At least, not downhill!"

O. T.'s eyelids hung heavy. His bones ached from the inside out. He took a deep breath of the night air and coughed as he tramped across the yard to the gate of the Pear Blossom Mine. Jakob Fleming's carriage waited for him to drive back to Goldfield. He coughed up phlegm and spat it into the dry alkali dirt.

Lord, I'm havin' a tough time lastin' a week down in that mine. I wasn't meant to be buried in a shaft. Of course, it might have somethin' to do with not sleepin' last night. This isn't good, Lord. Dola's right. We've got to pack and leave. This is just not our place.

O. T. pulled himself up into the carriage and drove across the yard. He tipped his hat to the guard at the gate and rolled out into the desert. Even in the night shadows he recognized the silhouette that waited for him near the clump of Joshua trees.

"Ol' man, what are you doin' out here?"

"Earnin' my supper," Fergus replied. "I'm your bodyguard, remember?" He handed his musket up to O. T. and waited to be pulled up into the carriage.

"How has the bodyguard business been?"

"Boring, except for Mr. Peter St. Marie's arrival."

"The union man? I didn't see him out here."

"He was turned away at the gate. That was the exciting part. No one got shot though. Other than that, I mostly slept under those Joshua trees."

There was very little breeze and no moon, but the stars were bright enough to give a glow to the barren desert. "I would have slept down there, but Mickey and Elko talk without stoppin'," O. T. reported. "Don't reckon I've ever known men who talk that much and have nothin' to say."

"Obviously you have never negotiated with an Indian agent," Fergus mumbled.

"No, but I did listen to a campaign speech by a man runnin' for mayor of Guthrie, Oklahoma. After an hour and a half the whole crowd agreed to vote for him if he'd stop speakin'."

"What happened to him?" Fergus inquired.

With the rhythm of the wagon like a lullaby, O. T. fought to keep his eyes open. "He never gave another speech and was elected mayor by an 80-percent vote."

"Do you think they will ever let me vote?"

"Dola Mae keeps askin' me the same question. If I could, I'd share my vote with you."

"Thank you. I accept. I think I will vote for the Wall Walker."

Skinner's eyes flew open. He peered through the dark at the old Paiute. "I ain't runnin' for nothin'."

"That's why I vote for you. You don't run. You don't run to the gold. You don't run to the saloon. You don't run away from trouble. The man who does not run would get my vote."

O. T. closed his eyes again and leaned back. *Lord, I don't think I wanted to hear that. I'm tired, Lord. Very, very tired. Tired of bein' tired. Tired of worryin'. Tired of seein' my whole family have to work in order for us to get by. Tired of a one-room place that doesn't even keep out the dirt or the bugs. But mainly just bone-tired. It's just time to leave. But I'm not runnin' . . . am I?*

"Here." He handed the lead lines to Fergus.

"Where are you going?"

"In back to sleep." O. T. stood up. "You're driving."

"There is not much room."

"I'll make do."

"What will Mr. Fleming say about me driving a company rig?"

"If you see Mr. Fleming, by all means, let him drive. I need to sleep."

Fergus kept the horses at a slow trot. "Driving at night makes me hungry."

"Why does that not surprise me? When we get back, you can rummage through the kitchen."

"I wonder how fast these horses will trot?"

"Don't you go runnin' down these horses." O. T. climbed over the leather carriage seat.

"Go to sleep, Wall Walker. Your bodyguard will take care of you."

O. T. stretched out on the narrow luggage bed behind the carriage seat. The rhythm of the rig rocked him from one side to the other. He pulled his light wool vest off and folded it under his head. His long-sleeved cotton shirt was sweat-drenched from collar to tail. The breeze of the moving carriage felt almost chilly against his shirt. The muscles in his neck relaxed.

The line in front of the three-story block building that served as the Mining Stock Exchange stretched down Columbia Street for two blocks. Most were women. Blanket-covered children huddled next to them. All wore hats on their heads and tears on their faces.

And all stood in six inches of fresh snow.

Each woman looked up at O. T. as he walked the line. Each had anxious eyes and desperate faces. He didn't recognize any of them—that is, until he reached a thin woman with sunken eyes.

He tipped his hat. "Mrs. Rokker? Is that you?"

The woman strained to hold back tears. She reached out and grabbed the sleeve of his heavy winter coat. "Mr. Skinner! Oh, you must help me! I have no one to turn to!"

"Nellie, what's the matter? Why are you out here in the cold?"

The woman's weak eyes reflected little life in the overcast winter day. "I'm waitin' to find out."

O. T. looked up and down at the sad faces of the other women in line. "Find out what?" he asked.

"Find out if Elias was one of the miners killed in the explosion."

O. T. glanced around and was surprised that, other than the line of women and children, the street was totally deserted. "How many men were killed?"

Her lower lip quivered. "It was 172."

"Oh, no . . . I—I hadn't heard." O. T.'s breath fogged out in front of him. "Oh, Lord, have mercy on these women."

"They won't tell us which ones, though we are freezing, and our hearts are breaking. We must find out. It's agonizing to know some have died but not know which ones. Mr. Skinner, they will listen to the Wall Walker. Please help us!"

A chorus of wails surrounded him. He threw up his gloved hands. "What can I do?"

"Talk to them. Tell them to do the right thing, the Christian thing to do. You're the only one we have."

He studied the long line of women. "Who should I should talk to? Where are they?"

"Go to the Stock Exchange, past those armed guards," Mrs. Rokker said. "What will I do if Elias is dead?" she moaned.

"But I thought you had moved to California."

"What will I do?"

"Didn't Elias have all that gold he found out on the desert?"

"We will starve," she said over and over. "My children and I will starve."

"You won't starve, Nellie. As long as I have a penny, you and the children won't starve." O. T. took a deep breath. *Lord, I'm so tired. I don't even know what I'm doin' here. I just want to lay down and sleep.* He tugged her hand off his sleeve. "I'll go see what I can do."

"Hurry. You might be able to save his life," she pleaded.

Lord, if Elias is already dead, what will my hurrying accomplish? I can't save anyone's life. What I do is of little consequence. I just want to get home and sleep. When did it start snowing? How did it get so cold so quickly?

As he marched up the line of women, every woman and child clutched his wool jacket.

"Wall Walker, you have to help me."

"Please, Mr. Skinner, don't let it be my Bobby!"

"Hurry, O. T., you must get there quickly."

"Where's my daddy?"

"Why? Why, O God? Why my Richard?"

"You have to help us, O. T.!"

Lord, they want what I can't give them. I don't know what I'm sup-

posed to do. I can't handle this. You have the wrong man. I'm not smart enough. Not strong enough. Not wise enough. Why am I doing this? I'm so tired. I can't even walk. It's like my legs are growin' heavier with each step. Lord, ever'one is countin' on me. I can't let . . . them down.

He was almost at the head of the line when he dropped to his knees in the snow.

"Get up Wall Walker," someone called out.

"Get up," another screamed.

"Keep going!"

"We need you."

O. T. felt tears roll down his face and freeze on his cheeks. *I can't do it, Lord. I can't push myself any further. I've got to get home. Take me home. Take me home now.*

O. T. lay on his side. Snow pressed into his cheek and slid up his back. Cold and icy. The numbness in his feet seemed to slowly roll up his legs and back. He relaxed, and the numbness broke across his whole body like a wave.

He thought he heard an explosion.

But it just didn't matter.

Nothing mattered.

But sleep.

Dola Mae shuffled out of the doctor's office. She tilted her head so that the brim of her straw hat would block the hot afternoon sun.

"Mrs. Skinner, you look like you need a ride. Let me help you up."

She glanced at the black leather carriage. "Thank you, Mr. LaPorte." She held out her hand to the big black man. "I don't suppose it's coincidence that you were parked in front of Dr. Silvermeyer's office."

He almost lifted her into the carriage. "No, Dola Mae. I was instructed by Omega that I had better not let you walk all the way home, or there would be serious consequences to pay."

"Oh my, does she threaten you often?"

"All the time."

"And does she make good on those threats?"

"Shoot, Dola Mae, I ain't dumb enough to ever find out."

"You're a wise man, Mr. LaPorte."

They waited for the dust to settle behind a passing car before pulling back into the street. "What did the doc tell you?"

Dola glanced down at her thin, bony hands. "At this point he's narrowed it down to either my back going out . . . or cancer."

"That ain't very narrow."

"Well, he's pretty sure my problem is a weak lower back."

Lucian stopped the carriage and allowed two women to cross the street. "What does he suggest you do?"

Dola watched the women whose sleeves were pushed up to their elbows. *Some women have such beautiful arms and hands.* "Dollar-a-week pills and lots of rest. He thought that it should take a few weeks, but I might never regain all my strength. He warned that next time my back will go out easier and be more difficult to correct. Someday it will be a permanent condition."

"I surely am sorry, Dola Mae."

"He also said I should quit all work and make sure I have no more children." *Lord, I don't know why I'm pouring all of this out on poor Mr. LaPorte. I should wait and just tell Orion.*

Lucian LaPorte nodded, deep in thought. "I was thinkin' how much you and O. T. are blessed with your children and have to try not to have any more and how Omega and me have been tryin' for years. It's like them angels got the orders mixed up."

"The children situation is fine. Orion and I had come to the conclusion that our family is complete on our own." She turned her head away. "But me not work? How do I raise a family and do no work? He doesn't even want me to lift my baby."

"Dola Mae, that little Punky ain't no baby. He's three years old and as stout as a keg of nails. There is no reason in the world for you to pick him up."

An image of a happy, grinning face came to her mind. "How can I refuse when he asks?"

"Flash him your beautiful dimpled smile and tell him what a big boy he is and how proud you are that he doesn't need to be carried."

Dola put her hand to her mouth. "Well, eh, Mr. LaPorte, I believe you are right. I mean about, you know, making him walk instead of being carried. How is it that a man without children knows so much about child care?"

"My Omega has read every baby book, every kid book, in the state of Nevada out loud. She thinks if we read enough, it's bound to happen."

"It will happen accordin' to the Lord's timing," she assured him.

"I surely hope so. If she reaches thirty and still no kids, she'll be a difficult woman to live with." LaPorte turned the carriage up Columbia Street. "Say, do you think you'll see O. T. before he goes out to the Pear Blossom?"

"I think so."

"Tell him I need to talk to him about the auto car."

"Did you know we decided to go ahead and fix it up?"

"Tommy-Blue told me. I surely am happy to hear that."

"Why is that, Mr. LaPorte?"

"O. T. said if I ever needed to borrow it for a hack, I could do it. Last summer folks was satisfied with any kind of ride. But now lots of them are insistin' on an auto car, and my business is hurtin'. When you folks don't need it, I can ferry people around in it. Until I make enough to buy one for myself, of course."

Dola stared up the street. *Lord, don't do this to us. Don't give us reasons for staying longer in Goldfield. We have to leave. Make it simple, Lord, not complicated. A clean break.*

LaPorte pulled up in front of the cafe. "Can I help you down?"

Tommy-Blue banged out the front door. "Mama, can I—"

"You can help me down," she instructed.

"Yes, ma'am." Tommy-Blue ran over and held up his hand.

"Mama, guess what? Hud said he can fix the auto car without havin' to send to Chicago for parts."

She stepped down on the raised boardwalk and caught her breath. There was a dull pain at the base of her spine. She felt winded as if climbing a hill. *Dr. Silvermeyer is a very nice man, but I wonder if he really knows what's wrong with me?*

She turned back to the carriage. "Thank you, Mr. LaPorte. I suppose you would refuse my offer to pay you."

"Not only refuse it but be offended if you offered."

"Oh, dear, I will not insult such a dear friend as you."

"Good day, Dola. Take care of yourself. You probably don't have any idea how important you are to this town."

Dola watched the carriage depart. *How important I am to Goldfield? Lord, what are You doing to me?*

Tommy-Blue grabbed her hand. "Mama, Hud wants to hire me to help him fix the car. He said he'd give me a whole dollar."

"For doing what?" *Doesn't this boy ever wash his hands unless I force him?*

"When he's under the car and lookin' for a tool or a bolt or something, he wants me to help him find it. That way he don't have to spend his time crawlin' out from under the car."

"This evening?"

"Yeah. Daddy said for him to fix the car by Saturday. So we pushed the auto car over behind the hotel. They have a livery with electric lamps, and they'll let him use it at night. Can I go? Please, Mama."

"I suppose you could go over after supper."

Tommy-Blue held open the cafe door. "It might be late. He said we could just sleep in the straw in the livery and get started again early in the morning. Can I do it, Mama? Can I stay all night with Hud and work on the auto car?"

"Oh my . . . I think so. I'll check with Hud at supper and make sure I have the story right."

Dola strolled into the kitchen. For a step or two she actually forgot about her back and enjoyed the aroma of baked apples. Omega was the first to spot her. "Landagoshen, Dola Mae, what are you doin' waltzin' around? Don't you even think of grabbin' that apron!"

"Oh, Mrs. Skinner," Haylee buzzed, "I'm so relieved to see you up. I was worried about you so much I threw up last night."

"You did?" Rita Ann gasped.

When Haylee shook her head, her blonde hair bounced. Everything bounced. "Yes! It was awful."

"Are you sure it wasn't those dates you ate?" Omega challenged. "The men decided they didn't like them, so we had a lot left over. They were mighty sweet."

"I must have had a dozen of them," Haylee admitted. "But that was only part of it. I really was worried sick."

"Thank you all for your concern."

"What did the doctor say, Mama?" Corrie stirred flour, salt, baking soda, and sugar in a large green bowl.

"He said I had to take it easy for a while, that my back looked like it popped back into place, but it would still be sore."

"That's good news," Lupe said. "Mrs. Skinner, may I talk to you for a moment in private?"

"Certainly . . . eh, where's my baby?"

"He's down here, Mama, sleeping on the potato sacks," Rita Ann reported. "Shall I wake him up? He's kind of sticky."

"By all means let him sleep. What did he get into?"

"Either the molasses or the dates," Rita Ann reported. She turned to Haylee. "Did you ask her?"

"Ask me what?" Dola queried.

"Never mind," Rita Ann gulped. "Eh, Lupe is first."

Dola unpinned her straw hat. "My, there is intrigue when I'm out of the kitchen."

"When you're out of the kitchen, Dola Mae," Omega said, "that's when we can have real girl talk."

"Yes, that's what worries me. Is everything set for supper?"

Omega waved a spatula at her. "Gerta is comin' over to help serve. She seems to be a hit with all the bachelors in town. You get on upstairs and rest."

"Are you kicking me out of my own kitchen?"

"Yes, I am."

Dola smiled. "Good."

She and Lupe walked out into the dining room.

"Mrs. Skinner, this is difficult for me to say, because you've treated me so well for over a year. But Daddy and the other Mexican miners all quit today."

"Quit the Pear Blossom?"

"Quit Goldfield. Daddy said that once the union organizers came in, it is getting too dangerous. Everyone is carrying guns, and everyone is mad at each other. I don't know which side is right or wrong, but Daddy thinks no one will be very careful where they shoot, and innocent people could get hurt, especially if they happen to have brown skin and speak Spanish."

"Are you moving away?"

The round-faced young woman nodded. "We're all goin' back to Mexico."

Dola slipped her arm around Lupe's waist and was surprised that her arm didn't ache. "I certainly understand. Lupe, you are a great worker and a very dear friend. You will be greatly missed, but you have to do what is right. I understand." *I wish I could tell her about us leaving too.* "When will you go?"

"Daddy says Saturday, but I said I can't go until you have plenty of help. I wouldn't do that to you."

"Lupe, you plan on going Saturday. You need to support your daddy."

"Are you sure you aren't mad at me?"

Dola hugged the stocky young woman. "Heavens no, Lupe. It will be just fine."

Lupe gently laid a hand on Dola's shoulder. "I love you and your family, Mrs. Skinner. I always feel good about myself when I'm around you. If it were up to me, I'd never leave you."

Dola kissed Lupe's cheek. "Now I'd better go see what mischief my oldest is concocting."

They headed back to the kitchen hand in hand. "Mrs. Skinner," Lupe added, "if my mother had lived, I know she would have been just like you."

This lady is only nine years younger than me, but she's right, Lord. I do look old enough to be her mother, and I certainly treat them all like daughters. Except Omega. She's that unpredictable little sister. Dola Mae laughed to herself as she entered the kitchen. *Sisters? There isn't a woman on the face of the earth that looks more opposite of me than Omega LaPorte!*

She stopped near Rita Ann. "Now, young lady, just what are you giggling about?"

"Well, Mama, see . . . Haylee's brother Jason went up to Tonopah to meet with some men about a supervisor position in one of the silver mines. And that means Haylee is home alone tonight, and, well, she asked me if I could come spend the night, and we could read Shakespeare and stuff."

When a thirteen-year-old giggles like that, I'm more worried about the "stuff" than I am the Shakespeare. "Is there some kind of conspiracy to have everyone leave home tonight?"

"Why do you say that?" Rita Ann replied.

"Never mind," Dola mumbled.

"Really, Mrs. Skinner, Rita Ann and I have wanted to read Shakespeare for months and—," Haylee began.

"And you've spent every evenin' with Hud Frazier?" Dola interrupted.

"Yes, but he's working on the auto car tonight, so I thought it might be a good time for Rita Ann to come over. After supper dishes are cleaned up, of course."

"Okay, okay. I'm trusting that both of you are grown up enough to act wisely."

Rita Ann twirled across the wide, shallow kitchen. "'If I were now to die, 'twere now to be most happy; for I fear my soul hath her content so absolute that not another comfort like to this succeeds.'"

Dola turned to Haylee. "Are you sure you know what you're getting into?"

Haylee twirled beside Rita Ann. "'We are happy in that we are not over-happy; on Fortune's cap we are not the very button.'"

Dola stared at Omega.

"Good gracious!" Omega yelped. "There's two of them! Heaven help the neighbors tonight!"

"Maybe they could invite Toodee," Corrie said. "Then they could have a trio."

Dola was washing Punky's face when Corrie burst into the room. "Mama, what's Punky's basin doin' up on the table?"

"Punky is hungry for biscuits and gravy," the naked three-year-old declared.

"No, you aren't," Dola corrected. "I put it up here so I wouldn't have to bend down and bathe him. I don't think I'll be able to bend too well for a while."

"How did you get him up there?"

He pointed to the chair beside the table. "Punky climbed the mountain!"

"Mama, I've just got to go to Gerta's house. She has an eagle feather she will give me and moccasins and some other stuff. The feather came off a real eagle!"

"When will you be home?"

"In time to serve breakfast. Can I spend the night? She asked me to. I was complainin' 'cause Rita Ann got to go to Haylee's, so Gerta asked me over to her house. Please, Mama. She has a whole trunk

full of old Indian things. It will be very educational. She's even goin'
to teach me how to clean her gun."

Dola toweled off the three-year-old. "Her what?"

"Her Winchester '94, 30 WCF take-down. You know."

"I don't think you should play with a gun."

"Not play with it, Mama. We're going to clean it. Please, Mama.
She's going to teach me how to make a beaded handbag too. Won't
that be swell?"

"Corrie, you do realize I know what you three are up to?"

The eleven-year-old's blue eyes widened. "You do?"

"You're trying to make sure Daddy and I have some time alone."

"It's kind of obvious, ain't it? It was Rita Ann's idea."

"It's a very nice idea. Now which one of you is going to take little punkin with you?"

"We drew straws."

"And?"

"You won."

Silas Paul Skinner was sound asleep in Tommy-Blue's bed before
Dola turned the light out, his bottom poked up in the air, his head
buried in the pillow, his tiny blanket scrap pulled up to his chin.

Dola tugged back the comforter on her bed, turned the switch
on the electric light, and scooted over to the balcony.

*Lord, three children are gone and one off in sugarplum land. But
Orion will not be home until later. Much later. He should not have to work
so hard. Why does he want this last $100? We can use some of our sav-
ings to get to California. It would be so nice to have him here now.*

*Maybe I'll just take a little nap on top of the covers . . . still in my
dress. Then I'll make us some chocolate, and we'll sit out . . . No, he must
sleep. I will see that he goes to sleep the moment he comes home.*

Her eyes flew open. It was pitch dark in the room.

And someone was whimpering.

She pulled herself out of the bed slowly. Her back ached. "It's okay, darlin'. Mama's here. Let me turn on the light."

"Punky frowd up."

"Yes, it looks like you did."

"Punky's sick."

"It's those dates, young man. You ate too many dates." She scooped up the basin, rag, and towel.

I believe this is my least favorite task of being Mama. She took a deep breath and began to wash him up.

When he was finally clean and smelling like talc powder, Dola said, "It's a good thing Tommy-Blue is not in bed tonight. You'll have to sleep on the girls' bed now."

"Mama, carry me," he insisted.

"No, you're a big boy. You go get in bed on your own."

"I'm medium."

"That's close enough. Now go on."

With the linens soaking in the washtub, Dola glanced around the room one more time. Then she walked over to the electric twist knob.

The voice from the street raised the hair on the back of her neck. "Mr. Skinner? Mrs. Skinner? It's Jared Rokker. Mama's on the train from California. She needs your help. Right now! Please!"

NINE

Dola stepped to the edge of the balcony and stared down into the darkness. "Jared, I'll come down and open the front door."

His voice was high-pitched, and the words ran together. "I've only got twenty minutes until the train leaves. Is Mr. Skinner there?"

She strained to see the young man in the shadows. "No, he's working out at the Pear Blossom Mine tonight. He should be home any minute." *He should have been home by now.*

"I've really got to see Mr. Skinner. It's about Daddy."

"Jared, wait right there. I'll come down."

Dola scooted back into the apartment. Pulling on her lace-up boots, she grabbed a hairbrush. *I will have to leave it down. I know I don't have time to pin it up.* She glanced over at the sleeping three-year-old.

"Baby, Mama will be downstairs," she murmured.

She left the double doors between the apartment and the stair landing open as she scurried down the steps to the darkened dining room. Each stride was a jolt of pain. But it was tolerable pain. She turned on the cafe light and opened the door to a hat-holding, anxious-eyed Jared Rokker, who now stood about two inches taller than she.

She tugged on his shirtsleeve. "Honey, come in. What's wrong? What happened?"

"Mrs. Skinner, we need your help tonight and $800," he blurted out.

Her left hand went to her chest, just below her neck. "What?"

"I got to talk fast. Me and Mama have to be on the California train when it pulls out in fifteen minutes."

"Jared, when did you get to town?"

"Just now. We got to make a turnaround. When did you say Mr. Skinner would be here?"

"I don't know, Jared. Within the hour, I suspect. Tell me about the problem." She motioned him to a chair.

He ran his fingers through his thick brown hair. "Don't have time to sit. Daddy's in a Mexico jail, and we have to have $800 to get him out."

The vision of a drunken, passed-out Elias Rokker flashed through her mind.

"Here's the thing." Jared leaned against the back of a chair as he talked. "We've been living nice for over a year in San Bernardino on the treasure money Daddy found. About May some old pals of Daddy's stopped by and told him of a silver mining deal down in Baja California. If he'd invest $10,000, he could double his money in two months."

"And he believed them?"

"Yeah, he did. When he didn't hear from them by the first of August, he took off to go find them."

Dola folded her arms across her chest. "And he wound up in jail?"

"In some place called Tijuana. I think he got in a fight, and some Mexicans got hurt. They'll keep him there for a year unless we get $800 to bail him out."

"What about your money? The lost Don Fernando gold? It hasn't all been spent, has it?"

"No . . ." Jared Rokker's eyes searched the dimly lit empty cafe, avoiding her probing eyes. "At least, we don't think so."

Dola put her hand on Jared Rokker's shoulder. "What do you mean?"

"Daddy don't trust banks, so he just hid the money."

218 ❖ Stephen Bly

"And you don't know where?"

"No. I guess he don't trust us neither."

Dola tried rubbing her temples, but all her facial muscles remained taut. "Not even your dear mother knows?"

"No, ma'am."

"Could he have taken it all with him?"

"Maybe. We don't know. All I know is, we are down to our last groceries, and we got bills to pay. Mama says we'll pay you back jist as soon as we get Daddy out of jail."

Dola strolled over to the open doorway and stared off into the night. "You said $800?"

"Please, Mrs. Skinner, I'll stand for it myself. I'll work it off no matter what. My word is good."

"Yes, your word is good, Jared Rokker. But that's a lot of money for us. We're not rich folks, you know."

"Ain't the cafe doin' good?" he asked.

"Yes, it's fine, but there . . ." Dola could feel herself breathing hard. *Lord, where is Orion? What should I do? I don't know what to do!*

"Do you have $800?" he pressed.

She faced the dark street. "I think I could grub it up."

"Tonight?"

Dola nodded her head and sighed. "I believe so."

Jared threw his arms around Dola Mae and sobbed. There was a sharp burst of pain when he grabbed her, but she hugged him back anyway.

"I knew you would," he whispered. "Mama got so worried she wouldn't get out of bed, but I told her the Skinners are the best people on the face of the earth, and they'd help us. I just knew you would. God bless you, Mrs. Skinner. I ain't never known folks like you before." He pulled back and wiped his eyes on his shirt. "Don't tell Rita Ann I was cryin' like a baby."

"Rita Ann's spending the night at Haylee's. In fact, everyone is gone but me and Punky."

"We got to hurry, Mrs. Skinner. Mama's on the train waitin'," he said.

"With the other children?"

"No, Danny is watchin' the girls back in California. It's just me and Mama. She was too nervous to leave the train. You know how she gets."

"Jared, this is really something that Mr. Skinner should decide. Perhaps you and your mother could spend the night with us and take a train back tomorrow."

"Mama won't leave that train, Mrs. Skinner. She wants to get back to Danny and the girls . . . and go get Daddy."

"Jared, it's just that I've never spent that much money without discussing it with my husband." *I've never spent that much money in my life!*

"It's just a loan, Mrs. Skinner. You'll get it all back."

Dola's temples began to throb. *I know Jared is completely sincere, but why is it I know in my heart we would never get the money back? In a day or two we could have been gone to California. We'd never have known about this. Why did this happen now? The timing is terrible.*

She stared into Jared's troubled eyes.

Maybe not. Maybe that's Your point, Lord. I hope I know what I'm doing. I can't believe this. Surely, I didn't break my back in the restaurant for a year just to bail a reckless, sloppy, foolish man out of a Mexican jail.

Forgive me, Lord.

That's probably what You said on the cross. And yet You did it.

Dola forced herself to breathe more slowly.

I will trust You in all things, and Your praise will continually be on my lips.

"Mama made me promise to bring you or Mr. Skinner to the train depot. She wants to see you eye to eye," he reported. "It's important to her."

Lord, this is like running downhill. I can't get out. It keeps getting more complicated. I can't seem to get control of the situation. I need Orion here. Right now.

"Please, Mrs. Skinner. It will only take a few minutes. It's just five minutes down there, plus two minutes of conversation, and five minutes back . . . in twelve minutes you'll be home."

She sighed. "I'll go get my hat and purse."

Dola tied on her hat, climbed the steps, and painfully stooped to remove the steel receipt box from the orange crate beside the bed. She set the box on the bed, opened it up, and counted out $800. *Lord, that leaves us only $400 for California. We can't buy a place with that. Of course, if Jared's right and they pay us back, it will just mean a few weeks' delay. Orion, please, please, please come home!*

Dola left the other money in the box on top of the bed. She tucked Punky under the comforter. *Well, little darlin', you're finally asleep. I ought to just leave you sleep. Mama will be home in twelve minutes . . . or so.*

She walked across the room to the doorway and glanced back at her bed. *I'd better put that money box back in the cabinet.*

When she reached the box, she stared at the remaining money. She plucked it up and crammed it into her handbag. She tossed the open steel receipt box down on the bed and hurried back to the door. *Sleep good, baby. Lord, please look after him.*

She took the stairs slowly, trying to keep her back stiff.

"Hurry, Mrs. Skinner," Jared called out from the cafe below.

Dola paused and looked back up the stairway.

Jared scurried to the base of the stairs. "What's the matter, Mrs. Skinner?"

"I forgot something."

"Can I come up and help you?"

"Yes, that would be nice," she replied.

Wearing underpants and a small quilt, Punky Skinner slept in Jared Rokker's arms as they hurried through the night to the train depot.

A frail, panic-stricken Nellie Rokker clutched Dola's hand

through the open passenger car window. She didn't let go until the train pulled away from the station.

Dola walked over to the wooden bench where Punky lay sleeping on his quilt. She watched the train lurch off into the Mojave Desert.

Lord, Nellie and I didn't say a dozen words. But her eyes said it all. I have no idea in the world how to explain this to Orion. No idea what we are going to do now. No idea if they will ever pay us back. All I know is that You wanted me to give it. Oh, Lamb of God that taketh away the sins of the world, have mercy on the Rokkers . . . and the Skinners.

She stared down at the sleeping toddler.

And I have no idea how to get little punkin home. I should have left Orion a note to come down to the depot. I didn't have time.

She thought about her tired husband plodding up the stairs to an empty apartment.

No one's home, and he'll find an empty money box tossed on the bed! He'll think someone broke in and stole the money, and his family is gone. . . . Oh, dear Lord, he'll die of a heart attack. I've got to get home!

She looked back down at Punky. *I didn't even put shoes on the baby or clothes. I can't make him walk in the dark. This is not good.*

Tears streamed down her face even before the pain of lifting the chunky three-year-old kicked in. The dull back pain intensified and then receded with each step. She stopped at the corner and set Punky down on the edge of the boardwalk. She flopped down next to him, her feet on the dirt street, the streetlight glowing above them.

Is this the street that Orion walks home on? Isn't the livery just three blocks over? But what if he came by already? He's probably at home worried sick or still in the kitchen, eating the plate of food I left for him.

She stared down the street three blocks to the dim light filtering out the front of the cafe. "Did I leave a light on? Maybe it's the kitchen light." In the late night shadows she could barely make out the silhouette of her tiny peach tree. *Lord, I don't know why You do what You do. Why tonight of all nights? Why did they need money on a night when Orion is late? Why did I have no kids at home to watch the baby? Sometimes, Lord, Your timing seems so strange.*

She stood up and let out a deep breath. "Come on, Silas Paul."

Punky lifted his chunky bare arms. "Carry me, Mama."

"I guess so, darlin'. I didn't even get your shoes. I'll just have to trust the Lord to give me strength. It's too bizarre to even know what He's doin' tonight."

Dola forced the pain from her mind as she tromped up the empty dirt street. She aimed for the dim glow from the cafe window, only a block away now.

"Looks like Daddy's rummaging in the kitchen, Punky. There's a light on back there."

"Punky's not hungry; Punky's sleepy," the toddler declared.

"Well, isn't that a change?" She hugged him to her chest. He smelled of fresh talc and stale vomit. "I'll get you back to bed soon." *Then I'll sit out on the balcony with Daddy trying to get up the nerve to tell him what I did with our savings.*

She watched the light go out at the back of the cafe.

"Darlin', Daddy's headed up the stairs. We better hurry. I reckon he'll be—"

Everything happened at once.

Like a finely tuned orchestra—a violent deadly orchestra.

A flash of light.

An explosion that would deafen thunder.

The windows of the cafe blew out.

Shattered front doors rained splinters like dry leaves in a windstorm.

The peach tree hurled like a cannonball to the middle of the street.

Dola landed on her rear in the dirt, a wailing Punky in her lap.

"No!" she screamed through the tears. "No! No! No!"

Silas Paul Skinner immediately stopped sobbing and stuck his thumb in his mouth.

Everything blurred in her mind.

Her back throbbed.

Her ears rang.

Her heart raced.

The dark street filled with people.

The air filled with shouts, cries, questions.

Clutching Punky in her arms, she struggled to her feet and staggered down the street now crowded with people and littered with the former contents of the Newcomers' Cafe. She picked her way through the crowd until she stood next to the peach tree, still intact, still in the half-barrel, but now placed in the middle of the street.

Is it time now, Lord? Is this what You meant? The man in the dream said Orion was there waiting for me at Your home. Is he with You now? Are You coming for me now? Is it my turn? Am I already dead? Does Punky go with me? What about the other children? Who will raise them? Oh, Lord, what about my children?

"Oh, Dola Mae . . . oh, sweet mercy, girl . . . what happened, oh, what happened?"

She spun around to see a sobbing Omega LaPorte. Lucian grabbed Punky as Omega threw her arms around Dola and hugged her close.

"I'm too stunned to cry. I—I think maybe this is all a dream."

Omega rocked her back and forth as they hugged. "Oh, dear Dola Mae . . . where are the others?"

"Did this really happen? Did the cafe blow up?"

With long fingers, Omega gently wiped the tears from Dola's eyes. "She's in shock, Lucian. What are we goin' to do?"

"You hold Punky." He shoved the baby at his wife. Then he put one massive hand on each of Dola's shoulders. He leaned down so that his head was squarely in front of hers. "Dola Mae, look at me. Now answer me—where are the other children? Are they upstairs?"

"Rita Ann went to Haylee's, didn't she?" Omega offered.

"Where is Rita Ann, Dola?" Lucian demanded.

Dola nodded. "At Haylee's."

"And Tommy-Blue?" he demanded.

Dola kept pointing to the shattered building. Her lips moved, but no sounds came out.

"Dola?" Lucian repeated.

"Our cafe . . . our house . . . everything . . . it exploded!"

"Yes, it did. Now where is Tommy-Blue?" Lucian shouted at her above the noise of the surging crowd of onlookers.

Her reply was an emotionless monotone. "At the hotel livery with Hud."

"And Corrie—where's that Corrie Lou girl?"

Her hands flew up to her face. "I don't know!" she sobbed.

"Oh, sweet Lord," Omega moaned, "was Corrie Lou in the cafe? Oh, no."

"Think, Dola Mae, think," Lucian prodded. "I need to go help Corrie. Where is she?"

"Orion," Dola mumbled. "Orion!"

LaPorte bent low and put his eyes right in front of hers. "Corrie is with Orion?"

"No!" Dola sobbed. "No! Orion was in the cafe! Corrie's at Gerta's. You have to help Orion!"

"Oh no! No," Omega sobbed.

"I'll go look," Lucian called out. "Omega, you take care of Dola and Punky."

Omega carried Punky and led Dola by the hand through the crowd to the raised boardwalk at the hardware store across the street from the cafe. The black woman sat beside her, rocking the three-year-old. "Dola, did you hurt your back in the explosion? Were you up on the balcony? In your apartment? On the front porch? What happened?"

Dola gasped for breath. "Where's my Orion?" she pleaded.

"Lucian went to fetch him. Honey, how is your back? Do I need to get you a doctor?"

"No!" Dola shouted. "I don't need a doctor! Don't you understand anything?" Then she began to sob. "I'm sorry. . . . I'm sorry. . . . I'm so sorry. . . . I'm so scared."

Omega put her free arm around Dola. "That's okay, Dola Mae. Scream all you want to. It's okay. We're all scared, darlin'."

"Why Orion? Oh, Lord, no!" Dola wailed. "I've got to go find Orion."

She tried to stand, but Omega held her back. "Lucian's doing that."

"Mama! What happened?" Tommy-Blue and Hud sprinted to her side.

"Me and Mama fell down," Punky reported. "House went boom!"

Dola hugged Tommy-Blue.

"Did the anarchists bomb us?" Tommy-Blue gasped.

"Bomb?" Dola said. "Someone bombed us?"

"It must have been a lot of explosives, all right," Hud added. "Look at that building."

"That man! That man in the dark," Dola said. "He did it!"

"What man?" Omega asked.

"The one who was living in Gerta's house. He hated Orion. He said he would get even."

"Jeremiah Jolly?" Tommy-Blue asked.

"He threatened to bomb Orion. I heard him say it. I thought he was drunk!"

"Oh, Mama . . . oh, Mama!" Rita Ann and Haylee, still wrapped in robes, scooted up to them. "Was it another mine explosion?"

"No, the anarchists done tried to blow up our cafe," Tommy-Blue shouted.

"Tried?" Haylee blurted out. "Looks to me like they succeeded."

226 ❖ S<small>TEPHEN</small> B<small>LY</small>

Dola hugged Rita Ann with one arm and Tommy-Blue with the other.

In the roar of the street, one small voice pierced Dola's heart. "Where's my daddy!" Corrie sprinted up to them. Behind her Gerta Von Wagner, in a long black duster, pushed her way through the crowd.

"Where's my daddy?" Corrie screamed.

"I don't know." Dola stared through the dark at the shattered remains of the Newcomers' Cafe. The crowd of mostly men huddled in the center of the street as if waiting for another explosion.

"Lucian went to check on him," Omega reported.

"He was in there?" Corrie wailed. She took off for the now-door-less front entrance of the cafe.

"Corrie!" Rita Ann screamed.

The eleven-year-old kept running.

"What are we goin' to do?" Tommy-Blue moaned as he held his mother's hand. "Mama, what are we goin' to do?"

Dola just shook her head and rocked back and forth. *I'm supposed to be strong. I'm supposed to know. Oh, Lord . . . not Orion . . . please, dear Jesus.*

Lucian LaPorte waded back through the crowd with a kicking, fussing Corrie Lou Skinner under his right arm.

"Put me down," she hollered.

"Not until you promise not to run back in there!" the big black man declared.

"Corrie Lou, you settle down!" Dola snapped. Then her voice softened. "I need you, darlin'. I need you and Tommy-Blue and Rita Ann to stay real close to me."

"But Daddy might be in there!" Corrie cried.

"Yes, but Mr. LaPorte can help Daddy. I need you to help me, please."

Dola looked up at Lucian.

"The explosion seems to have been set in the kitchen or maybe next to the alley door. The back half of the building is destroyed; this half is shattered but still holdin' together in parts. No one was found in the dining room or apartment. The explosion created such a rush of wind, most think the wind put out any fire that might have started. There are some volunteers putting out what blazes did start when the electric wiring shattered. I think it's okay, but a man can't get through from the dining room to the kitchen."

"I'll check around back." Hud Frasier took off at a trot.

"Mama, were you in there when it blew up?" Tommy-Blue asked.

"No."

"Me and Mama were in the street," Punky reported. "We fell down! And I cried, and Mama yelled no!"

"Thank You, Jesus," Omega said. "Dola, what on earth were you and Punky doin' outside on the street at this time of night? And him in his underpants?"

"The Rokkers—it was the Rokkers."

Rita Ann's eyes widened. "Jared Rokker is in town?"

"He and his mother came in on the California train and left with it too." Dola glanced back in the direction of the train station. "I, eh, went down to the station to see them off."

"Why did they come to town?" Corrie asked.

"Was Danny with them?" Tommy-Blue added.

"They were in a hurry." Dola's voice was so soft that she wasn't sure it was audible in the confusion. "And needed some help."

Rita Ann scooted close to her mother. "How much money did they need, Mama?" she whispered. "Daddy always said it wouldn't last them a year."

Tommy-Blue looped his thumbs in his coveralls that rested on bare shoulders. "I surely wish I could have seen Danny Rokker."

"What do we do now, Mama?" Corrie said.

"We'll wait here for Daddy," Dola said.

"But what if my daddy was in the building?" Corrie Lou wailed.

"I said, we'll wait here for Daddy!" Dola snapped. *I will sit right*

here on this wooden sidewalk until Orion comes to us. And if he was in
that building, then I just want to die right here in the arms of my children.

Rita Ann circled her arms around Dola's shoulders, rocking her back and forth. "It will be all right, Mama. . . . It will be all right."

"I know, darlin', I know."

"We're in the Lord's hands, Mama," Corrie declared, her voice cracking.

"You're right, honey. It will be okay. It's got to be okay."

"Mama, I think it's the only night all year that all of us have been out of the house at the same time," Tommy-Blue said. "But—but what about my rock specimen collection?"

"And my new dress!" Corrie yelped. "It's the one my daddy bought me!"

"Some of that stuff might have survived. We'll look around later when it's safe," Lucian offered.

"Here comes Hud!" Haylee yelled.

A somber-looking Hud Frazier signaled Lucian LaPorte. The two men huddled in the dark.

Dola stared at them. *No, Lord . . . no . . . no . . . no . . . oh, no . . . no!*

Lucian marched back. "Dola, we have to talk."

"What is it?" Corrie demanded.

Lucian glanced around. "Hud, you and Haylee get a lantern and take the kids upstairs. Help them retrieve some of their personal items. The stairway turned out to be the sturdiest part of the building."

"Be careful," Dola mumbled as they hiked off into the night. Lucian sat down beside Dola. "Now, girl, before you jump to any conclusions, the sheriff said he couldn't identify the body."

Dola rocked back and forth, eyes clamped shut. *No . . . no . . . no . . . no.*

"What do you mean, they couldn't identify the body?" Omega asked.

"He got blown up with the dynamite. There's only—"

"Lucian LaPorte," Omega shouted, "don't you be tellin' us things like that!"

Lucian took a deep breath and put his muscled arm on Dola's shoulders as she rocked. "When I saw O. T. today, he was wearing denim jeans. According to the scraps found in the kitchen, this man was wearin' duckings."

"Lucian!" Omega hollered.

"I have to find out. Dola, wasn't O. T. wearing jeans today, like always?" he pressed.

"I think so. . . . I don't know! Oh, Lord, no, no . . . yes, denim . . . unless . . . he changed. I can't think. . . . I can't think."

"Fergus was wearing duckings!" Gerta gasped. "Where is he?"

"Wasn't he staying with you?" Omega asked.

"No, not tonight," Gerta said. "That's why Corrie came over. He said he was going out to the Pear Blossom Mine to be with Mr. Skinner and would be back very late. I never heard him come in."

"I saw a light on in the kitchen," Dola said. "Right before the explosion, I saw a . . . If it wasn't Orion, who . . ."

Gerta took off on a dead run toward the back of the building.

Omega LaPorte handed Punky to Dola and grabbed Lucian's hand. "Help me catch her," she shouted.

The LaPortes disappeared into the crowd.

"Punky's house went boom!" the toddler said. "Mama cried."

"Oh, darlin' . . . forget the house . . . the things. . . . None of that means anything. . . . We had nothin' when we came to this town, and we'll have nothin' when we leave."

"Daddy!" Punky cried out.

"You're right, little darlin'." She rocked him back and forth. "All we need now is our daddy."

O. T. hit the hard-packed dirt like a 120-pound sack of oats falling out of a barn loft. He managed to roll onto his back, but he could neither get to his feet nor catch his breath. He wasn't sure where he was, but he knew he wasn't in snow. Sucking in air, he detected a rich aroma of hay, leather, horse sweat, and dried manure. He heard muted sounds of talking, shouting, running.

"Fergus?" he managed to croak out. His eyes adjusted as he finally stood.

Fleming's carriage? The livery? I fell out of the carriage! Fergus let me sleep. Why didn't he wake me up? What time is it? Dola will be worried sick. Fergus will tell her. He was going over to get something to eat. Snow? That was a dream. No one died in a mine?

O. T. retrieved his vest from the back of the carriage. He jammed on his hat and stumbled out to the street. Everyone seemed to be running east. A thin man with a long, dangling mustache stumbled and fell. O. T. helped him up.

"What's happenin' up there, mister?" O. T. asked.

"I heard the anarchists done blew up one of the buildings!"

"The union men? Did anyone get hurt?" *Was this the explosion I was dreaming about?*

The man spat out a chaw of tobacco. "I heard there was one dead."

One? That's better than 172. The man began to tug away. "Was it the Mining Stock Exchange?"

"No, it's way on past there." The man jogged east, then turned back. "I heard it was that there Newcomers' Cafe!"

No one would want to . . . O. T. staggered along on the edge of the crowd. *Jeremiah Jolly! He actually did it. Oh, no! One dead, oh, Lord, no. . . . It's me he wants . . . not them. Not my sweet Dola, not my Rita Ann, not Tommy-Blue, not my darlin' Corrie . . . or my baby. Jolly, you didn't kill my baby, did you?*

O. T. shoved through the crowd. He stumbled and fell and ran some more. He sprinted right down the middle of Columbia Street. He shoved people aside. By the time he reached the front of the cafe, he could see the windows and doors blown out and debris littered everywhere. The crowd of spectators was so thick that he could not see from one side of the street to the other. The balcony doors were flung straight out to the street, taking some of the railing with them.

There was a faint glimmer of a lantern light in the upstairs apartment. He pushed through the crowd again. Someone grabbed his shoulder. "Don't get too close, mister. I heard 'em say there might be another bomb."

O. T. shoved him back. He scooted up just below the broken balcony railing.

"Dola!" he called out. "Rita Ann?"

A small head appeared on the darkened balcony. "Daddy!" Corrie shouted. "It's my daddy!"

"Corrie Lou, where are the others?"

"Up here, Daddy—all except Mama and Punky."

O. T. clenched his fists and gritted his teeth. He wanted to shout, to scream, to cry.

"Can you help us, Daddy?" Corrie called out.

"Sure, darlin', jump down. Daddy will catch you."

"But, Daddy . . ."

"Don't be afraid. Jump, honey . . . come on!"

Corrie looked back into what was left of the apartment and then shrugged. With arms in the air, she leaped off the balcony.

Corrie landed in O. T.'s arms. He staggered back and then fell, still clutching her in his arms.

He kissed her cheek. "Are you all right, darlin'?"

"I am now that you're home. But we really need to go up and help the others. Maybe we should use the stairs."

"The stairs still work?"

"How do you think we got up there?"

"Who's up there?"

"Haylee, Hud, Rita Ann, Tommy-Blue, and me. You ought to see our place. Everything is busted except the clothing and the pans. Even Mama's china and crystal are all broken. She'll be very, very sad. Of course, she already is sad," Corrie reported.

"Where is Mama?" he shouted.

"Didn't you see her?"

His breath was so short and shallow that he felt dizzy. *The one? Not my baby.* O. T. set Corrie down and struggled to his feet. *Not Punky!* O. T. closed his eyes and tried to steady himself. "No, where is Mama?"

"Over on the steps of the hardware."

O. T. squatted down next to Corrie. "And Punky? How about Punky?"

"He's with Mama."

It was like an explosion of beautiful fireworks on a coal-black night. "Is everyone okay?"

"Yes. None of us were home when it happened. We were all gone. Isn't that a miracle?"

O. T. plucked her off her feet, kissed her on the lips, and then danced around in the dirt street. "Oh, yes, darlin'! That might be the greatest miracle in my whole life!"

"You dance good, Daddy."

"Corrie Lou, you don't know how good I feel right now!" he replied.

"Me too, Daddy. But I think someone died. The grownups started whisperin' and shushed us away."

He set her down. "Who?"

"I don't know. Will you help me find my new dress?"

"I'll be along shortly. Go on back up. I'll check with Mama and then come find you."

"I love you, Daddy! Hurry and see Mama. She's worried sick. Just like Mrs. Rokker last year."

O. T. tried to shove his way through the surging crowd, but like swimming in a river of great power, by the time he made it to the other side, he was one building down from the hardware. He hiked back up the street. He stopped to stare at a woman sitting on the edge of the raised boardwalk in her Sunday dress, rocking an underwear-clad toddler below the dim glow of an electric street lamp.

Now that, Lord, is the most beautiful sight in the world.

"Daddy!" Punky hollered.

"Dola Mae!" he called out.

She spun around. Her whole body started to quiver. Her head shook. Her hands shook. Her shoulders shook. She opened her mouth, but nothing came out. He dropped to his knees in the dirt in front of them and circled Dola and Punky with his arms.

He could feel her chest heaving against his. "It's okay, darlin'. I'm here now. Everyone's okay. The kids are upstairs. Baby, it's okay. The Lord took care of us. Oh my, how He took care of us."

It was several moments before she could catch her breath and speak. "What are we goin' to do, Orion?" she murmured. "Everything's gone. The restaurant. Our apartment. Our belongings. Everything."

He released his grip, but she clutched his arm.

"We'll pack up the children in the wagon and leave."

"Tonight?"

"At the break of day."

"Where will we go?"

His answer came like the last hammer blow on a nail. "California."

"O. T.!" a deep male voice hollered in the darkness. "I feel as relieved as Brother Abraham when he spied that lamb caught in the bush! The Lord hath provided!"

Skinner stood and was engulfed in a bear hug. "Lucian! Who did this?"

"The sheriff's tryin' to find Jeremiah Jolly." The smile dropped off the big man's face. "Someone wearin' duckings died in the kitchen."

"Who?"

"Ain't enough parts to tell. But there was a Springfield trapdoor musket in the rubble."

"Fergus!" O. T. closed his eyes and could only see the sly grin of the old Paiute.

"Where's Gerta?" Dola asked.

"She went a little—well, she went on the warpath when we found the Springfield," Lucian said. "She took off to her house to get her Winchester. Says she's goin' to find Jeremiah Jolly and kill him on sight."

"Didn't the sheriff stop her?" Dola asked.

"Nope. He said he was too busy. Sort of like he's just goin' to turn his head."

O. T. paced the dirt street. "But she could get killed herself!"

Lucian shrugged. "Omega ran after her, but I don't reckon any of us could stop her. I don't know if we even want to. Some men give up their right to live."

O. T. glanced down at Dola.

She reached up her hand, and he gently pulled her to her feet. "Orion, you have to try to stop her. Lucian and I will help the children."

"I'll be back. You wait for me!"

She threw her arm around his neck and kissed his lips. "Orion, I thought my whole world was lost, and within a short time I have everything in life I need. I was prepared to sit over on this boardwalk until I died waitin' for you. Oh, we'll be here. Now hurry and help Omega with Gerta."

O. T. broke free from the crowd and jogged down a narrow dirt street. He turned right at the brick brewery and ran up to the top of the knoll where the streetlights ended. As he approached the house with the picket fence, he heard two women yelling in the moonlit yard.

"Turn loose of my gun!" Gerta yelled.

Omega LaPorte held the other end. "Don't you tell me what to do! I ain't goin' to let you go get killed."

"Ladies!" O. T. called out.

Both of them leaped back and then faced him.

"Skinner! Don't you go sneakin' up on us and scarin' us," Omega complained.

"I'm going to kill him. He has killed his last Indian!" Gerta wailed. "The big, dumb anarchist blew up the kindest Paiute in Nevada! I'm going to shoot the—"

"Wait until mornin'," O. T. cautioned. "Don't go runnin' in the dark after a man who has dynamite."

She yanked the gun from Omega's grip and trained it on Orion. "I'm not going to wait until morning!"

The voice was deep. Slow. Drowsy. "Listen to the Wall Walker. Whatever it is can wait until daylight. An old man is trying to sleep in the back room! For the life of me, I don't know why anyone wants to live in a town. No one ever sleeps."

"Fergus, is that you!" O. T. hollered.

There was a pause, then a quiet reply. "Yes, I believe it is. Were you expecting President Roosevelt?"

"I like Gerta's house, Mama," Corrie murmured as she and Rita Ann were tucked into pallets stretched out on the living room floor.

"It has two bedrooms, a kitchen, plus this nice-sized living room," Dola agreed.

"I like the yard!" Tommy-Blue called out. "We ain't never had a yard with a fence. Are we goin' to build a fence in Dinuba?"

"If we want one, we'll build one," O. T. said.

"Daddy, do you think it was the Lord leading us all to be away from the cafe tonight?" Corrie asked.

"Yep."

"And I thought it was mostly my idea," Rita Ann replied.

"Well, darlin', who's to say the Lord didn't use you to accomplish His will?" O. T. said.

Rita Ann slid her glasses down on her nose and peeked over the gold frame. "Really?"

O. T. turned to Dola. "What do you think, Mama?"

"I want to know something, Mr. Skinner. A couple of hours ago someone tried to kill all of us with a huge bomb. In the process, he destroyed our business and our home and 90 percent of our meager belongings."

"Including Grandma Davis's china and crystal," Rita Ann called out.

Dola's voice was soft. "I had forgotten about that."

"Does it change your point, Mama?" O. T. said.

"No." Her reply was firm. "For a moment I thought I had lost some of you. And the thought was absolutely unbearable. I don't believe I could live through that. But the Lord was gracious to me."

O. T. patted her hand. "Darlin', we rolled into this town with a wagon, two mules, and an empty water barrel. When we leave in the mornin', the barrel will be full. Not only that, we have some funds."

"Not nearly what we thought we were goin' to have," Dola replied.

"Dola Mae, if I had been here, I would have done exactly the same. Especially after that dream about Nellie Rokker," O. T. contended. "I believe the Lord was softenin' my heart."

"Is your heart really soft, Daddy?" Corrie called out in the darkness.

"Your Daddy just might have the softest heart in the whole world." Dola clutched his hand.

"Daddy's arms aren't soft. They are very strong. Tommy-Blue said you are the strongest man in the world," Corrie reported.

"Did you say that, son?"

"Yeah, sort of. But I ain't exactly seen every man in the world."

O. T. chuckled and then cleared his throat. "I think maybe we ought to get an hour or two of rest before daylight."

"Are we goin' to leave the auto car here in Goldfield?" Tommy-Blue asked.

"Yep. I'm goin' to give it to Mr. LaPorte for free, but he has to pay Hud for the most recent repairs."

"For free?" Tommy-Blue gasped. "You gave away an auto car for free?"

O. T.'s voice rolled across the room like a wave. "What did it cost us, son?"

Tommy-Blue's reply was scratchy, tight-sounding. "Eh, nothin'. The Wilkins brothers sort of gave it to us, busted."

"And we're givin' it to the LaPortes for nothin' and busted." O. T. settled in on the mattress next to Dola.

"Hud and me almost had it runnin' tonight," Tommy-Blue informed him.

"What time are we goin' to leave, Daddy?" Corrie quizzed.

O. T. laid his head back on the borrowed pillow and closed his eyes in the darkness. "Any minute now if we don't all get some sleep."

"What road are we going to take, Daddy?" Corrie asked.

"Toward Gold Point and then across the desert. Now, everyone, go to sleep."

"Can we swing around and drive up Main Street from one end to the other first?" Rita Ann asked.

"Why do you want to do that?"

"Because it might be our last time to see it. I want to look at it one more time," Rita Ann replied.

"We are not drivin' to the lower end of Main Street," Dola insisted.

"Mama, we all know what the cribs look like," Tommy-Blue said.

"And we know what goes on in there," Rita Ann added.

"Well . . . well, I don't know what they do in them, and I don't want you to tell me!" she blurted out. "Now . . . just think—tomorrow we'll be on our way to California. Won't that be grand?"

None of the children replied.

After a while Corrie mumbled, "Goldfield is okay. I liked school last year. Ever'one treats us right, and there's always somethin' excitin' goin' on."

"Treats us right!" O. T. exclaimed. "Someone blew up our cafe and house and tried to kill us tonight."

"Well, other than that," Corrie mumbled.

"But he blew himself to kingdom come!" Tommy-Blue blurted out. "I bet no one will try that again."

Dola reached over for O. T.'s hand. "Is the sheriff positive it was Mr. Jolly?"

"The sheriff told Lucian that he had a positive identification of the man as Jeremiah Jolly but would rather not describe it."

"Oh, ugh!" Corrie gasped.

"I'm glad I recovered our things in the dark," Dola said. "I don't think I want to go back in daylight."

"'I cannot but remember such things were, that were most precious to me,'" Rita Ann said.

"What do you mean by that?" Tommy-Blue asked.

"Every day we've been in Goldfield I've had exciting things to write down in my journal."

"Dust storms, scorpions, rattlesnakes, shootings, explosions, drunks asleep on the sidewalk—you mean things like that?" Dola challenged.

"Yes, Mama, that's exactly it," Rita Ann replied. "Life is raw and alive here in Goldfield, and neither sin nor virtue are carefully concealed."

"Who said that, Rita Ann?" O. T. asked.

"I just made it up, Daddy."

"It's a good sayin', darlin'. Write it down. Maybe someday little girls will tote around the writings of Rita Ann Skinner and memorize quotes like that."

"Really?" There was a young woman's lilt in her voice.

"You just might be a fine writer someday."

"I don't think so."

"Why not, darlin'?"

"Because we're leaving Goldfield where there are so many good and horrible illustrations to choose from."

"Children, when we left Guthrie, Oklahoma, I promised you that we were going to Dinuba, California. And I haven't gotten you there yet. So at 7:00 A.M. we'll be on the road. I trust you all remember how to set up the tent. Now no more talking."

"Good night, Daddy. I love you."

"Corrie Lou!"

"I can't help it, Daddy! It's in my bones. I just have to say it, or it burns all night long!"

"And I have a burnin' question," Tommy-Blue added.

"This is absolutely the last one!" O. T. warned.

"I cain't figure out if this is the worst day of my life or the best day of my life."

"Both," Dola replied. "Now no more talking because your daddy wants to kiss me."

Suddenly the room was dead quiet, except for one muted voice giggling under the covers.

O. T. whispered in her ear, "I can't believe you said that."

"And I can't believe you're taking so long!"

O. T. had harnessed Ada and Ida to the old farm wagon and parked in front of Gerta Von Wagner's house by 6:00 A.M. He sat on the back porch of the little wood-frame house and watched the sun rise over the distant bare brown hills.

Carrying two cups of coffee, Fergus came out and sat beside him.

"Thanks, partner. You're welcome to come to California with us," O. T. said.

"I like the invitation, but it is not good for a Paiute to leave the Great Basin."

"Why is that?"

"I do not know. My father never told me, but I will stay anyway. When are you leaving?"

"In about an hour, I reckon."

Fergus stuck a bony finger in his coffee and then noticed O. T. staring at him. "My finger was cold," he explained. He pulled it out and licked it. "You have not heard of my plan."

"What plan are you talkin' about?"

"Gerta wants you to live in her house for a while."

"We're leavin' town in an hour."

"Sometimes people change their minds when the sun comes up," the gray-haired man commented.

"We're not going to change our minds."

"You did not hear the rest of my proposal."

"Okay, tell me the rest."

"I am going to take my money from the gold mine and move up north to Battle Mountain to take care of my mother."

O. T. took a swig of coffee and then coughed it back up. "Take care of who?" he croaked.

"My mother," Fergus declared. "Every man has a mother."

O. T. stared at the Paiute. "Your mother is still alive?"

"Yes."

"But . . . you never told me that before."

"You never asked."

"But you are—you are so very old."

"My mother is even older than I am. She needs me to help her, and Gerta is going with me."

"Why is that?"

"Because Sarah Winnemucca's family lives near my mother."

"The one Gerta wants to write about?"

"Yes. She is very excited about going but worried about leaving her house vacant again."

O. T. glanced back at the wood-frame house. "I'm sure she can get someone to live here. Housin' is scarce."

Fergus took a slow, noisy sip of coffee. "She doesn't want someone. She wants the Skinners."

"That's a very nice gesture. If we were stayin', we'd probably accept."

Fergus stood. "Good. I'll tell her."

"But we aren't stayin'. We're on our way to California. You know that."

The Paiute sat back down on the step. "Is California where the weather is perfect?"

"So I hear."

"And the crops grow easily?"

"I reckon they do."

Fergus cleared his throat. "And the neighbors are always agreeable."

"My brother and his wife will be my only neighbors."

The Paiute threw up his hands. "What is the challenge in that? It sounds boring."

"Are you tryin' to talk me into stayin' in this godforsaken place?"

O. T. had to lean toward Fergus to hear his reply. "It will not be godforsaken as long as the Skinners stay here."

O. T. set his empty coffee cup down and gazed at the sunrise in the east.

Lord, this should be the easiest decision in my life. Why do You keep interfering with it? I'm too tired to figure this out. Just lead us where You want us to be.

"Is it time to go, Daddy?"

O. T. looked around in time to catch a leaping Corrie Lou. "I reckon it is, darlin'."

After kissing her smooth, slightly sticky cheek, he set her down and stood up. "I've got ever'thing loaded except for you kids and Mama."

"Gerta surely has a good view of the sunrise, don't she, Daddy?"

"There is one every morning!" Fergus said.

O. T. grinned at the Paiute and shook his head. "Old man, you are really tryin' to get us to stay, aren't you?"

"Did it work?"

"Nope."

"Well, if a sunrise won't convince you, I suppose nothing will."

O. T. surveyed the wagon before he climbed aboard. Wearing her church dress, Dola sat in the wagon seat with Punky next to her. Behind them on a makeshift bench, Rita Ann sat with back straight and head held high, her straw hat neatly tied under her chin, Shakespeare book in her lap. Behind O. T.'s place Corrie sprawled across the bench. Her beige dress hung as straight as her thick, floppy brown bangs. She was licking her fingers and trying to clean some of Gerta's strawberry jam off the front of her dress. Tommy-Blue, barefoot and wearing coveralls and a big felt hat, sat on a water keg at the back. Next to him the half-barreled peach tree waved its green leaves at the desert breeze.

Dola studied her husband. *He's so tired, so very tired. This year has been tough on him. If we find a nice, cool meadow on our way to California, we will camp there several days and let him sleep.*

O. T. pulled himself up in the wagon beside her. "I guess we aren't forgetting anything."

"Nellie Rokker once told me that the good thing about having nothing is that it's always easy to pack," she replied.

"Mama, we have healthy kids and a peach tree. What else could any family want?"

"I wasn't complaining," she murmured.

"I know, darlin'. You never complain. How's your back this mornin'?"

"If I have many more nights like last night, I'll be back in bed permanent. But really it's just a dull pain. As long as I do things slowly, it will be fine."

"Anytime you need to stop and stretch out, you let me know."

She patted his knee. "Let's get rolling, Mr. Skinner, while the sun is low and there's a desert breeze at our face. And I don't think about friends we're leaving."

O. T. looked up at the clear, pale blue Nevada sky. "Lord, we're in Your hands. Lead us on to the place You have called us to and keep us safe. In Jesus' name—"

"Amen!" Fergus added. "I think I will ride this mule with you to the edge of town."

"You don't plan on turnin' us around, do ya, you ol' Paiute?" O. T. called out.

"No, I have already admitted defeat in that matter." Fergus pulled himself up and hung off to the side of the tall, stout mule. "I believe I need a push."

O. T. swung down off the wagon and shoved the old man up on the back of the mule.

"Thank you very much. Now if you'll hand me my musket."

O. T. plucked the long gun off the fence. "Anything else you want?"

"I would like one of Mrs. Skinner's bear claws and a cup of her coffee—not your coffee," the Indian declared.

"I'm sorry, dear Fergus," she called out with a wide smile, "I have retired from the cafe business."

"You are not nearly as sorry as I am." He straightened his wide-brimmed black felt hat.

When Dola sat up straight like Rita Ann, the dull pain in her back almost disappeared. "Are you ready, young man?"

"Punky's goin' to Californy with a bronco on my knee!"

"A banjo!" Tommy-Blue corrected.

The wagon lurched out into the rutted dirt street.

"Can we sing, Daddy?" Corrie asked.

"Not until we get out of town!" Rita Ann insisted.

Dola hugged the bare shoulders of the coverall-clothed three-year-old. "We are all going for a long, long ride, Silas Paul. Just maybe this will be our last move."

"But what if we don't like California, Mama?" Rita Ann asked.

"Did you ever in your life meet anyone who didn't like California?" O. T. challenged.

"Colin Maddison, the third, with two *d*'s, doesn't like California," Corrie Lou blurted.

"Toodee!" Punky cried out.

"Oh, what doesn't he like about it?" Dola asked.

Corrie stuck her tongue out and tried to touch the end of her nose. "He says it's too green in the spring."

Dola chuckled. "Too green? I've never heard that complaint before."

"Mama, you didn't answer my question," Rita Ann insisted.

Dola turned around and patted Rita Ann's knee. "Well, if we all agree that the Lord doesn't want us in California, then we'll just have to press on."

"We could go to Alaska!" Tommy-Blue called out from the back of the wagon. "I heard they was pickin' up nuggets off the beach at Nome."

"That was several years ago," Rita Ann said. "The boom is all over now."

"Good. It won't be so crowded," he called back.

"We can't go to Alaska," Corrie said. "Mama's peach tree would freeze."

"Li'l sis is right. We aren't goin' to Alaska," O. T. replied.

"Daddy, look up there on Main Street. It looks like trouble!" Tommy-Blue shouted.

O. T. stopped the wagon.

"My word, Orion, what is it?" Dola asked. "The street is filled with people."

Rita Ann stood up and adjusted her glasses. "They're not in the street, Mama. They're all on one sidewalk or the other."

"I think it's the anarchists on one side and the mine guards on the other!" Tommy-Blue called out.

"Well, we are not subjecting the children to the danger of a union riot," Dola insisted. "We'll just go around."

"But, Mama, you promised that we could have one more look at town," Corrie fussed.

"That promise was made with the assumption that it would be safe. I do not intend to subject my children to possible harm. Orion, turn the wagon around," Dola insisted.

O. T. stood up and stared at the intersection. "Fergus, what's goin' on up there?"

The old Indian turned around and rested his right hand on the mule's rump. "It looks like a parade."

"A parade!" Tommy-Blue called out. "How come we didn't know anything about it?"

"Maybe they just decided today to have a parade," Fergus hollered back.

"It's not a parade," Dola declared. "Turn around, Orion."

"Maybe it's someone's birthday," Corrie suggested.

"It's August 17," Rita Ann informed her. "Nobody famous was ever born on August 17."

"Well, kids, Mama says turn around, so we'll turn around," O. T. declared. "Remember last year in Tonopah? I stopped so we could watch the men fight, and Mama wanted to go on. If we had listened to Mama, we would never have met Lucky Jack and never had a lot to pitch our tent on in Goldfield and would have pushed on through town and never stayed, and we would have gotten to California a year ago."

"And be livin' with Uncle Pegasus and Aunt Pearl," Corrie said.

246 ❖ STEPHEN BLY

"Well . . . that could be. Or maybe out in their barn."

"All right!" Dola shook her head. "What you're sayin' is, I'm too cautious."

"Only once in a while. We don't want you to change," O. T. insisted.

"But you want to drive on up into that rabble?" she asked.

"I'd like to at least know what I'm runnin' away from." O. T. slapped the lead lines. "Okay, Fergus, we're going to check it out."

"I am glad."

"Why is that?" Dola shouted.

"Because it looks like someone did a lot of work. I would not want them disappointed."

She turned to O. T. "What did he mean by that?"

"I don't know, but it does look like a parade."

As they turned into the intersection on Main Street, crowds on both sides of the street started to cheer.

"We must have gotten at the head of the parade by mistake," Dola said. "They think we're a part of it."

"Daddy, I'm so embarrassed I could die!" Rita Ann moaned. "'What fools these mortals be!'" She ducked down behind her mother.

The people in the crowd waved and shouted.

"Orion, get us out of here," Dola insisted under her breath.

"The crowd closed in behind us, Daddy," Tommy-Blue reported.

O. T. glanced back at the surging mob. "We'll have to ride it out," he said. "There's no way back."

"I suppose we could all pull blankets over our heads," Dola grumbled.

Punky giggled and began waving at the crowd.

O. T. shook his head. "He thinks it's all for us."

They could hear some of the voices.

"Wish you would stay awhile longer, Wall Walker!"

"We're goin' to miss the Skinners of Goldfield!"

"Don't forget us, Skinner!"

Corrie wrapped her arms around O. T.'s neck. "Are they yellin' at you, Daddy?"

"I reckon they heard we were leavin'."

Tommy-Blue hollered as he waved to the crowd. "I ain't never been in a parade before. This is fun!"

"Tommy-Blue, stop waving. You're embarrassing me. This is not our parade!" Rita Ann hissed.

He continued to wave. "Maybe not, but I don't reckon I'll ever get to be in another one."

The crowd followed them, still shouting, clapping, cheering. Corrie had to shout to be heard. "Look, Daddy, it's Mr. and Mrs. LaPorte!"

Lucian and Omega LaPorte drove their black carriage up beside the wagon.

"What's goin' on here?" O. T. shouted.

Lucian got down and started to transfer two wooden crates from his carriage to the back of the farm wagon.

"What's in the crates?" Dola asked.

"Shoot, Dola Mae, we weren't goin' to let you leave town without a good-bye gift," Omega said. "Haylee, Lupe, Gerta, and me chipped in. It's a new set of china and some crystal glasses."

"But I can't take that," Dola said.

"Oh, yes, you can, honey. You are too gracious a woman to crush us by a refusal."

"But . . . you didn't have to."

"That's the point," Omega shouted. "We did it because we love you and will miss you."

"You're making me cry," Dola said.

Omega pointed her long index finger at Dola. "Good. I've been cryin' all night."

"I think we'll pull in behind and follow you awhile," Lucian told him.

"Mr. LaPorte, did all these people come here to see us off?" Dola asked.

"Yep, I surmise they did. You can't leave without sayin' good-bye to your friends!"

"But we don't know most of them," Dola shouted back.

"They know you, Dola Mae. Ever'one of them knows the Skinners of Goldfield."

Four men marched over to them carrying big brown paper bundles. David St. Marie led the troupe.

"You got room for a few packages in your wagon, Mr. Skinner?" the union organizer called out.

"I—I suppose," O. T. stammered. "What is this, Mr. St. Marie?"

"Some new bedding and linens, Mr. Skinner." He tipped his hat. "Mrs. Skinner, these are from the union men. We don't know what side you folks are on, but we know good, brave people when we see them. Heard one of our former members got drunk and bombed you out. We want you to have this. It's important to us to give it to you."

"Thank you very much, Mr. St. Marie," O. T. acknowledged.

The honking of a rubber-bulbed brass horn split the crowd as the wagon rolled slowly south. Hud Frazier drove out, Haylee beside him. The backseat of the auto car was piled with a new oak table and chairs.

"I got it runnin' again," Hud hollered.

"Well, join the parade," O. T. offered.

"The table and chairs are for you," Hud said. "The mine owners are sorry to see you go. Wanted you to have a new oak table for your home in California."

O. T. looked over at Dola.

"We don't even have a home, but we have a new oak table for it!" she declared.

"I'll stop the wagon and repack it north of town," O. T. said.

"And this trunk is for you, Rita Ann." Haylee pointed to a large gray suitcase beside her.

Rita Ann stood up and stared down into the car. "What's in it?"

"All my dresses that are still pretty but don't fit me anymore," Haylee announced.

Rita Ann's mouth dropped open. "Really?"

"I'm goin' to miss you, little sister," Haylee called out.

Rita Ann nodded and began to cry.

After another 200 feet of boisterous well-wishers, Daniel Tolavitch marched out, leading a haltered, long-legged black horse.

O. T. stopped the wagon. "Mr. Tolavitch, did you get a new horse?"

"It's not my horse. The bill of sale says it belongs to Tommy-Blue Skinner, the most enthusiastic prospector Goldfield has ever seen."

"For me?" Tommy-Blue gasped.

Tolavitch tied the horse to the tailgate of the wagon. "Yep, son. You reminded every man in town that gold prospectin' is just a game to be enjoyed, win or lose. When we forget that, we are a sorry lot. We'll miss you, all of you."

"You ain't makin' this easy, Mr. Tolavitch," O. T. blurted out.

"Good. Leavin' friends shouldn't be easy," the gray-haired man declared. "O. T., you know you got a job with me any day of the year."

O. T. noticed the tears rolling down Dola's cheeks. He slapped the lead lines, and the wagon rolled on up to the next block. A small boy in knickers ran out of the crowd carrying two dozen red roses. He stumbled, but he kept the roses held up as he fell to his knees. The crowd roared when he got back up and trotted over to the wagon.

"These are for you, Miss Corrie," he said.

Wide-eyed, she took the flowers.

"Tell Mr. Maddison thank you," Dola instructed.

"Thanks, Colin," Corrie said. "They're the purdiest roses I ever saw in my life."

"I'm goin' to miss you, Corrie Lou."

"I'mgoinamissyoutoo," she mumbled.

"What did you say?" Colin inquired.

She looked up and chewed on her lip.

"She said she was goin' to miss you too!" Tommy-Blue hollered out. "Colin, did you see my new horse? I bet he's the fastest horse in Nevada. I'm goin' to name him Edison 'cause Daddy says that electricity is about the fastest thing on earth."

Colin trotted alongside the rolling wagon. "He's not faster than my horse."

"He is too."

"Is not."

"Is too!"

"Prove it!" Colin declared.

"Come to California and race against him," Tommy-Blue said.

"Why not in Goldfield? You're going to come back and visit, aren't you?" Colin dropped back and climbed on the running board of the car. Behind the car the crowd marched in haphazard fashion.

Sheriff Johnson stopped them at the next intersection, where each corner was anchored by a saloon.

"Sorry about this crowd, Sheriff. I didn't stir it up," O. T. apologized.

"Well, I did . . . or helped do it anyway. The boys and me bought you a present, O. T."

"A gun? You know I don't—"

"It's a huntin' rifle, Skinner. A Winchester '95 rifle, .405 caliber. It's a take-down, so it won't occupy much room. But there's still plenty of good huntin' in California, and you need somethin' besides that old shotgun to bring in the meat."

"I—I don't know what to say."

"Don't need to say anything. Having you in town is like havin' six more deputies. These miners seem to want to do their best around you Skinners. You stopped more than one crime in this town by just being you and expectin' the best from others."

A woman in a bright red dress yelled from across the street, "Don't stop prayin' for us, Mrs. Skinner!"

Dola waved to the woman and then turned to the sheriff. "I don't even know who she is."

The sheriff pushed back his stiff felt hat with its Montana crease. "She goes by Lola Toledo. She works the cribs."

"Oh, my."

"They all know you pray for them," the sheriff said.

"Well, yes, I do, especially when my back hurts and I can't sleep nights."

The sheriff walked along beside the wagon as it continued to roll through the town. "You Skinners got to realize you're the picture rock of virtue in our dusty, dirty town."

"Picture rock of virtue?" Dola repeated.

"I reckon most folks have some good in them. The Lord put it there, but some of 'em don't assay out very high. Just a tiny speck or two of goodness in their whole miserable lives. But your family— well, it's like stumblin' onto a treasure of goodness. We all hate to see you leave. With you here, we were all able to say, Goldfield ain't too bad. After all, we've got folks like the Skinners livin' here."

Dola reached over and wiped a tear from the corner of O. T.'s eye. "It must be dusty today, Orion," she said.

They drove another block. People crowded close to the wagon. Dola took O. T.'s arm. "What are we doing, Orion?"

"We asked the Lord to show us a startlin' sign, and we almost got killed when our house and business blew up."

"That was surely a sign to quit the cafe business," she said.

"I was thinkin' it was more demonic than anything else."

"But today . . . this crowd—this is a startling surprise, isn't it?"

When O. T. pulled off his hat, Dola thought his eyes looked younger than they had in months. "I ain't never heard of anything like it."

"How can we tell them all thanks? What can we do?"

O. T. let out a long, slow sigh and squeezed her hand. "Only one thing that I know of, Dola Mae Davis Skinner."

He took the new rifle, pointed it out across the empty Malpais Mesa, and pulled the trigger. The recoil knocked him back down on the wagon seat, but the explosion quieted the crowd. He stood back up. "Folks, I have an announcement to make. As you know, we were bombed out of our home and business last night. But the Lord's justice is sometimes swift, and the bomber died in the explosion. That left us with next to nothin'—"

Dola stood up slowly. "With nothing but our dear friends."

"But what you might not know is that Dola Mae has been in fierce pain with a bad back. We thought maybe she was well enough to make the trip to California today. But it looks like I was wrong. Isn't that right, Mama?"

Dola slowly stood beside her husband. "Well, actually . . ." She glanced up at O. T. "I still have quite a bit of pain. This might not be a good time to travel."

"So," O. T. shouted, "the Skinners are goin' to stay in Goldfield until Dola Mae's back is completely cured."

Women applauded.

Men shouted.

Dogs barked.

Cowboys shot their pistols in the air.

Miners beat on their lunch buckets.

Some danced in the dusty street.

Tommy-Blue crawled onto the back of the black horse.

Corrie buried her face in the rose petals.

Rita Ann scurried back to the car and opened Haylee's suitcase.

Silas Paul Skinner pulled his blanket over his head.

And Dola tugged at O. T.'s alkali-dust-covered sleeve and called out above the noise, "Orion, I might never get over this bad back."

He slipped his arm gently across her shoulders. "I know it, darlin'. . . . I know it."

For a list of other
books by this author
write:
Stephen Bly
Winchester, Idaho 83555
or check out
www.blybooks.com

THE SKINNERS OF GOLDFIELD

Goldfield, Nevada, in 1905—with its unbearable weather, saloons on every block, and abundance of prospectors and gunfighters—is no place to settle a family. It's a hectic town where everyone would rather search for a quick fortune than seek lasting treasure. Everyone, that is, except the Skinner family. They have no intention of staying; they just need to earn a few dollars for supplies before continuing their journey to California. God, however, has a special plan for them. He's about to use this simple family and their simple faith to make a bigger difference among these people than all the gold in Goldfield.

BOOK 1: *Fool's Gold*
BOOK 2: *Hidden Treasure*
BOOK 3: *Picture Rock*

OLD CALIFORNIA

*They were women of courage in a land and time that would
test the strength of their faith.*

Though at nineteen Alena Tipton is a confident entrepreneur, her
heart is restless to fulfill its divine calling. But it could lead her away
from the place—and the man—she loves.

Martina Swan's marriage was supposed to be perfect. So why is
she fighting a devious bank and outlaws by herself, with the most
difficult battle—learning to forgive and love again—still ahead of
her?

Christina Swan is still seeking to find her place, her man, and
her calling. The answers will come in one incredibly surprising way
after another as she struggles to be obedient to God's leading.

BOOK 1: *The Red Dove of Monterey*
BOOK 2: *The Last Swan in Sacramento*
BOOK 3: *Proud Quail of the San Joaquin*

HEROINES OF THE GOLDEN WEST

They've come West for completely different reasons, but what Carolina Cantrell, Isabel Leon, and Oliole Fontenot are about to discover is that moving to Montana Territory will change their lives, their dreams—and their hearts—forever. With robberies and shootouts, love and romance, life in Montana is anything but dull for these Heroines of the Golden West.

BOOK 1: *Sweet Carolina*   BOOK 2: *The Marquesa*
BOOK 3: *Miss Fontenot*